PRAISE FOR

ONE WAS LOST

"Full of drama and suspicion."

—Kirkus Reviews

PRAISE FOR

SIX MONTHS LATER

"An intriguing story line… Readers will be drawn in to the mystery of what happened to Chloe and will never guess the ending."

—VOYA

"This romantic thriller will leave readers on the edge of their seats until the very last page."

—School Library Journal

"An intense psychological mystery. [This] novel has the feel of a high-stakes poker game in which every player has something to hide, and the cards are held until the very end."

—Publishers Weekly

WE ALL
FALL
DOWN

ALSO BY NATALIE D. RICHARDS

Six Months Later

Gone Too Far

My Secret to Tell

One Was Lost

WE ALL FALL DOWN

NATALIE D. RICHARDS

sourcebooks
fire

Copyright © 2017 by Natalie D. Richards
Cover and internal design © 2017 by Sourcebooks, Inc.
Cover design by Kerri Resnick
Cover image © Mike Dobel/Arcangel

Published by Sourcebooks Fire, an imprint of Sourcebooks, Inc.
P.O. Box 4410, Naperville, Illinois 60567-4410
(630) 961-3900
Fax: (630) 961-2168
www.sourcebooks.com

Library of Congress Cataloging-in-Publication data is on file with the
publisher.

Printed and bound in the United States of America.
WOZ 10 9 8 7 6 5 4 3 2 1

To all the kids the teachers call home about.

THEO

April 4

I stay in the car because I'm not welcome at the door.

Not today. I wouldn't say Paige's parents are ever *friendly*, but sometimes they're all right with me. They definitely like to offer plates of food and comment on how skinny I am. It's probably pity. Poor little ADHD boy, so *troubled*.

I'm not currently in the Pity Zone. Instead, I'm in the "We know your friendship with Theo is important to you, but we worry he isn't a good influence" zone.

They've got a point. Paige and I got wrapped up too long last Sunday, and she missed curfew, which, to her parents, rates about as dire as smoking heroin in a church pew.

I don't even know if I *have* a curfew. My parents don't aim high with me. I think they're happy any day I don't wrap a car around a tree—which, in my defense, I've only done once. The other wreck was a light pole, and the car wasn't technically totaled.

The light shifts on Paige's lawn. I lean forward in my seat, looking. She's on the porch, and that's all it takes. My heart does all the annoying flippy shit it's been doing for the past four weeks. How did that happen? Six years, she's Paige. Now? She's *Paige*, name encircled in hearts and floating in a fizzy bubble behind my ribs.

She's mostly hidden behind the giant shrub by her front porch, but I'm all caught up over half glances of strappy sandals and bare elbow. This is ridiculous. I need to man up. I have to tell her… Hell, what *am* I going to tell her? Hey, Paige, you know how we've been friends for like four hundred years or whatever? Yeah, well now I want to…what? Hook up with you in the front seat of my shitty Honda? Gross.

Paige is fiddling with the lock, which always sticks. Two years ago, I bet her I could go inside, up the stairs, and out through her bedroom window before she got it locked. I made it halfway down the front of the house before the trellis snapped. God, her mom was pissed.

I tap the steering wheel and check my phone. Then my zipper, then the neighbor's TV that I can see through their window. The car's front windows are cracked open because the cherry air freshener in here is new and strong, but the air outside smells like overripe lilacs, which isn't much better, and if she doesn't hurry up, I'm going to start honking.

2

Suddenly, I hear the soft patter of her feet against the walkway. The yard is dark, so I can't really see her until my car door snicks open and there she is. She's wearing a...sundress? Interesting. She also smells like lemon drops and something flowery.

"Took you long enough," I say.

"Patient as ever, I see."

"You know I like to put the *H* in ADHD."

Paige doesn't laugh, but her eyes crinkle up at the corners, and she doesn't get on me about the shit all over the floor, even though some of said shit is a packet of notes I failed to turn in with my World War I paper last week. Distinctly low-key for Paige.

I fling the crap into the backseat with a grin. "Oh, hey, I found my history notes."

"I see that." She fastens her seat belt. "Do you know how to get there?"

"I have party radar," I say, tapping my temple. "You know this."

"I know you'll end up taking a shortcut that adds ten minutes."

"Relax. We'll drive southeast until we hit the river. Then we'll look for the rickety-ass bridge hovering a million feet above the river."

"Fifty feet."

"A million feet, fifty feet...who cares? The question is, will you finally agree to walk across the stupid thing tonight?"

"Not likely," she says, but she's not pissy. She's checking her phone. Smiling.

"What is it about that bridge that bugs you so much? You used to be fine on there."

Paige turns up the music in response. It's my fault. I know better than to bring up her anxiety stuff, but as usual, I can't seem to help myself. For a second, I'm annoyed, but then the music snags my attention.

Four songs in, Paige flips down the passenger visor, a tube of something pinched between her thumb and forefinger. Is that makeup? I turn to her and laugh.

"Theo!"

Curb! I jerk the wheel to the left just before I clip it, swerving a little into the oncoming lane.

"Will you watch where you're going?" she asks.

"I *do* watch. At least half the time, anyway. Isn't this why you usually *don't* apply makeup in here?" I mean it as a joke, but she snaps the visor closed.

"That car behind you is getting annoyed," she says, glancing out the back window at whoever's behind us.

"He can bite me." I shrug. "And what's with the makeup? You don't need it."

"I'm serious. He's really riding your tail."

I glance up in time to see a shiny fender and a wide white

hood in the rearview before it swerves around us to pass, laying hard on the horn. I tense, pushing the accelerator to the floor.

"Asshole," I say, gunning it.

"Don't," she murmurs, but her voice is lost behind the lightning-fast roar of my anger. *Screw this guy. Who the hell does he think he is?*

He speeds forward, and I swerve, tires inching over the line into his space. Paige sucks in a hard breath. I should stop. Some small part of me knows this would scare her, that it *is* scaring her. But that voice is behind a wall of rage, and my foot mashes against the accelerator harder.

Doesn't matter, though. My ancient Civic—handed down through all three older brothers and the only car my parents will trust me with now—shudders. The Chevy sails past.

I pump the gas again, swearing at the asshole as he flicks me off in his rearview mirror. Then Paige's hand is on my arm, cool and soft. It's like a remote-control reaction, a pause button on my fury.

"Hey, it's okay." Her breath shakes, but her voice is steady. "We're okay."

My anger evaporates, water steaming off hot pavement. I ease off the gas and turn to look at her. Her hair is waving around her shoulders as she fiddles with the radio. Her hands are trembling, and she's pale. Not exactly how I wanted this night to go.

"I'm sorry," I say.

"I know," she says, her smile tight. "Not our first rodeo. It's gotten worse, though."

"Me being an asshole driver?"

"Pretty much." Her laugh almost makes it okay.

And hell, I don't know what to say. So I go quiet, and she plugs in her phone and finds a song she loves about everything changing. Paige is singing along when she leans closer to roll down our windows more. Her controls are broken, so she snakes her arm across to use mine. Her hand grazes my stomach, and I startle. She's *killing* me. And she has no idea.

The song is going on about a long drive. I need a longer drive, or I'm never going to talk to her about this. But Paige bobs her head and my shoulders relax, and ten minutes later, we're in Portsville. Paige checks the mirror again. I try another angle.

"You really don't need to fuss. You look great."

"Ugh, it's stupid," she says, closing the visor again. This time she's not mad; she's tense. We turn left on Turner, and she nods up ahead. "Isn't your uncle's house up there?"

"One street over."

"Are we parking there?"

"Less likely to attract a cop's attention. You know I always look like trouble to a cop."

"That's because you usually *are* trouble."

"Not when you're there to keep me in line."

She laughs, but checks her phone again, and this would be a whole lot easier if she'd stop texting for five minutes so I could attempt to flirt with her.

I park in front of Uncle Denny's house. There aren't any lights on, but it's a quick walk to the bridge, and Denny's cool enough not to mention us being here. We walk through streets of sagging, clapboard houses and kitschy antique shops in the Village. The Village is the south side of the river—artsy and crumbling and almost pretty if you don't look too close. The tourists love it, but those same tourists leave at five when the shops close. They've never seen it at night, when the people who live here roll home in work-stained clothes and rusting pickups.

We're still a couple minutes from the bridge when the first campus building comes into view on the north side of the river—a white cupola perched at the top of a brick tower.

"I wish I knew if I got in," Paige says, gazing in the same direction.

"Please. Your GPA is like 4.8."

She glances at her phone, smirking. "I'd need a lot more AP classes for that."

"I'm just saying, you'll get in. Though God knows why you'd want to."

"The summer program is for college credit," she says. "Plus, I get to spend four weeks in Chicago."

"And the other four you're trapped testing river water in Portsville, hellhole of the heartland."

"Every summer, this is where you end up."

"Maybe for now," I say, but I know better. Uncle Denny's been teaching me the contracting trade for years, and it's one of the few things I've managed not to quit.

It's a decent gig. There's no sitting still or long, dry-as-all-hell articles to read. It's loud music and constant movement, so not the worst job for someone like me.

Paige stops short when we turn onto Pearl Street. That's when we can see the bridge.

The Cheshire Walking Bridge is a mess, originally for trains that would carry goods north and south from the river. Then the trains dried up, and the town cobbled together a walking bridge on the west side, a ribbon of weather-stained planks moving joggers and antique shoppers across the water. Probably easier than tearing the bridge down.

From a few angles, with the right camera, it's gorgeous, but mostly the bridge is a sun-blackened relic of eons past, stretched precariously over the mouth of the Muskingum River.

On the far side, the college buildings rise, all bright brick and inviting warm lights. But we're not crossing the bridge. We're headed down the staircase to the left of the entrance to the docks below. Music drifts up from those docks, and

Paige's shoulders climb higher with every breath. I can see the faded canvas awnings of a few pontoon boats down there—the party—and I can also see Paige is nowhere near ready to deal with it.

I scuff my foot and pause. Not a lot of options. We're at the end of a dead-end road. We could go down to the party or back to all the closed-up shops and cafes. Or we could take a walk down the old railroad tracks.

Unless I could talk her into the bridge.

I nudge her shoulder. "Come on. We'll spit off the side."

"I hate this bridge. Also? Ew."

"You hate this bridge because you believe it's haunted." I waggle my fingers at her for effect. She stares at me like I'm an unimpressive homework assignment.

"I'm probably one of the few people who doesn't believe that. It's not haunted. It's structurally unstable."

I shrug and start up the ramp. "We won't go out too far. Come on, what's the deal? We used to run across this thing all the time."

"I didn't—" She stops abruptly, pressing her mouth closed like she's not sure how to explain. "The last time I was up here, it was a bad day."

"With me?"

"Yes."

9

"I don't remember," I say, but I don't have a hard time believing it. "Did I piss you off?"

"No, it wasn't… You know, forget it. Let's just go. It's fine."

"Are you sure?"

"I don't want to go out too far."

"Cross my heart," I say, and then we're up the ramp, at the mouth of the bridge. The party beckons below. Everyone's careful to stay under the boat canopies so they don't get busted, and the music is pretty low. Mostly, there's the creak of the ropes, the tinkle of wind chimes, and the occasional thin whine of laughter. Almost sounds like sobbing from up here.

Paige hesitates, staring first at the boats and then the bridge.

I point at the long-defunct tracks beside the wooden walkway. "*Trains* used this bridge, you realize."

Of course, there hasn't been a train for years, and the wood between the tracks looks rotten. Great hunks of missing timber reveal the dark streak of river below.

"All I can think about is falling," she says, but she walks out a few feet anyway.

I shrug because even if the wood planks are warped, I'm pretty sure the frame of black steel crisscrossing in arched beams over our heads extends underneath us too. Two summers ago, a paddleboat slammed into one of the cement supports below. They closed the bridge and checked it over for days, but in the end the old bastard held. But I'm not going to bring that up, because Paige is inching her way across it for the first time since…

"How long has it been since you've been up here?" I ask, still curious about that bad day. "What were we, thirteen?"

"Fourteen." Her tone makes it clear that's all I'm getting out of her on it, so I let it go and stroll on, dragging my hand along the railing.

Padlocks, every shape and size, hang from the rungs on the bridge's railing, some even hooked into holes along the support beams. It's a thing. Initials on locks. Locks on the bridge. It's supposed to mean eternal love or some bullshit. A little morbid since this bridge is also supposed to be Suicide Central.

I fiddle with them so I won't rush her, but I can tell my feet clunk too hard against the boards for her comfort. I'd fix it, but I don't know how to walk quietly. I don't know how to keep anything quiet. Except, apparently, the way I feel about her.

A third of the way across, she stops, moonlight casting a weird blue glow over her hair. For a second, I think she gets caught up in the view. She touches the railing, her face tipped toward the moon. Then she turns to me, eyes wide.

"I left my gel stuff in the car," she says.

"I have some."

She looks at me. "You have antibacterial gel. On you."

11

She doesn't believe me until I toss the bottle to her. "I come prepared."

"You've been known to forget your shoes," she says, but she takes it with a smile. "Did I leave this in your car?"

I shrug, because I can't bring myself to lie about it, and I can't spit the truth out either. I *bought* that stupid bottle, which makes it pretty damn clear how far gone I am.

"Every once in a while, I like having you around," she teases. It's the kind of thing she always says, and for six years I somehow missed how easy it is with her, how perfect it is.

This is stupid. I need to tell her how I feel.

I stop at the halfway point, looking out over the river and trying to think of a plan. She's texting, I think, but she's patient because she's Paige and never minds my wandering—and, shit, I have no idea how to do this with her. She knows all of my tricks, so how does this work?

I take a breath that sticks halfway in. "Come here for a minute."

She comes closer, tapping out the last bits of her message, her hair floating into her heart-shaped face. I wonder if some part of her is still kind of into me. I used to think she was, but now I'm not sure.

Screw it, maybe I'll try to kiss her—see what happens. I reach, but she turns at the last minute, and my hand lands clumsy and heavy on her shoulder. My stomach shrinks.

"Hey, is it true people are going to touch the flag tonight?"

I laugh. "Assholes, alcohol, and an urban legend. I think it's a given."

She squints up at the labyrinth of beams overhead, and I can tell she's wobbly in her high-heeled sandals. I force my eyes away from her legs to look up too, but I already know what she's talking about. A hand-painted American flag at the top support. One of the workers from way back painted it, Denny says. Kids get drunk and try to climb up and tag it for luck. Kind of a miracle no one's died doing it.

Yet.

"I don't know why they haven't painted over that thing." She chews her pinkie nail, and I stare at her mouth. I am *such* a creeper right now.

"Do you think *everyone* will do it?"

"I doubt it will be required for party entry." I tug at her sleeve and she ambles forward, distracted but not wary. Not the worst sign, right?

"I don't think I can do something like that, Theo."

"I'll be your safety net."

"Safety net? *How?*"

"I don't know, I'll distract everyone. Jump around at the top. Maybe fall off and break my leg."

She cocks a brow, looking cute as shit. "You'll probably do that anyway."

"Well, Paige, I think I owe it to the Portsville emergency-room nurses to keep up with my quarterly check-ins."

We both grin. In the water below, a fishing boat is coming in for the night, sliding under the bridge with a slow *putt-putt-putt*. Maybe this is as good a moment as any. I touch her face and she lets me, sighing. She makes it harder to breathe. And easier.

"You know I won't let anyone make fun of you, right?" I say.

She nods, cheeks pink. "You don't think Chase would make fun of me, do you?"

"Who?"

"Chase." Her blush intensifies, and I feel like I've swallowed a rock, a brick—something hard and heavy that is sinking through my middle. "Chase Moreland."

I drop my hand, and Paige fiddles with one of her dangly silver earrings.

"You worried about impressing Chase Moreland all of a sudden?" I toss it out like a joke, but she doesn't laugh.

"Sort of. Maybe. I don't know."

She does know. And now I do too. It's like a sucker punch to the throat.

"Color me surprised," I say, my grin so forced that I'm sure she'll see right through it.

But she's looking at her phone, and I suddenly know who

she's been texting. "It's not a big deal. I need to get out there more. You always say that."

The shit of it is, I *do* say that. I've said it for years, so all I can do is nod. My stomach is turning to stone, then to lead, and then it's melting out through my feet, but I'm nodding and nodding like a bobblehead.

She waves her hands, says it's no big thing. That he's nice to her, and the party sounded like fun and that's why she wanted to come—and I can't listen to this. I stumble against the railing, locks clattering against the metal. Paige is still babbling, but all I hear is the pinball machine in my brain, my thoughts whirring and banging off Chase-shaped bumpers.

Chase Moreland had the worst voice cracking of any of us back in the seventh grade. He used gel in his hair when the rest of us still weren't washing behind our ears. He rode a fluorescent green bike and played guitar, and he lives two streets over, so he's almost a friend.

He's also a bit of a dick, one who's too thin and too hawkish, but somehow still crazy irresistible to girls. Maybe it's the guitar.

Paige checks her phone and teeters in her pretty sandals, and my mind is popping and buzzing, but there's not a thing I can do. I've had all the time in the world. If she likes this guy, I need to suck it up and deal.

Hopefully Jolie and her crew will be there, because I'm going to need something to drink. A lot of something.

"We should get going," Paige says.

I push off the railing, and it groans so loudly that I jerk. It doesn't stop. There's an awful metal grinding that snakes down the railing like a chain reaction. Paige gasps, and the hair on the back of my arms pushes up in goose bumps. The noise is everywhere. Above us and below us. It's like the bridge is coming apart, and all I can think, all I can hear is—

You're going down.

Paige clamps her hands over her ears, and I grab her arm to run. The awful metal screaming fades. The quiet is sudden and strange, so I laugh, my insides liquid with relief.

"I thought this thing was going to fall," I say.

"Get me off this bridge," Paige says, her voice strangled.

No argument here. I know I've had enough of this bridge for one night. What I don't know is that the bridge hasn't had nearly enough of me.

PAIGE

I peel off from Theo at the docks, heading onto the largest, newest-looking boat. I'm looking for Chase. Somehow, Isabel finds me instead. I barely know her, but she links her arm with mine and walks me through cramped bodies lined up on plastic chairs.

There's a musty tarp at the center of the boat. Under that, a string of Christmas lights reveals a cluttered card table. Before I can say a thing, we're bellied up to that table. All I see are mayonnaise-based salads, casserole dishes, and half-empty chip bags. The back of my neck prickles. I can practically *hear* the bacteria crawling around.

"Half the soccer moms sent stuff from their banquet today. You know they're so chill about the party scene. Ooh, try the mac and cheese," Isabel says. She doesn't wait for me to respond. She takes a plastic spoon (also used for the baked beans) and shovels a glop of oozing noodles onto my plate. "Wait, you're not lactose intolerant, are you?"

"No." The plate goes warm on my hands. Is it leaking? Please don't let it be leaking. I try to hold the plate at the edges, but it folds in the middle, pasta sliding.

"Anyway," Isabel goes on, adding a spoonful of something else. "I'm glad you're here."

"Yeah?" I adjust my grip again. My palms feel sweaty. She's going for some congealed chicken wings. Why is she doing this? We're not even friends.

"I mean we don't talk much," she says.

"Not too much," I agree. I could say never, but we exchange the occasional *Excuse me* passing each other in classroom doorways.

"Well, we should. We should talk more."

"Sure," I say, smiling though I don't get it. Does she need a ride? A biology tutor?

I turn to her directly, hoping she'll get to it. Isabel seems nice enough, but not so nice that I want to spend my entire night making small talk next to the Botulism Buffet.

"There you are," Chase says, appearing at my elbow. He gives me that perfect wide, white grin and nods at my plate. "I see you got a little something to eat."

He and Isabel exchange a quick greeting. I mumble hello.

My cheeks feel hot. I know I'm blushing, and I can't help it. My plate's a reeking mess. I must look ridiculous.

"You look fantastic," Chase tells me.

"Oh." I think I smile too quickly, but I can't help that either. "Thank you."

The boat wobbles, and someone outside swears. Then Theo ducks under the awning, and Isabel perks up when he says hello. Her eyes follow Theo's every step. Suddenly, *We should talk more* takes on a whole new meaning. Isabel is a giggling, throat-touching mess, but too bad for her, Theo's oblivious. My heart squeezes in sympathy. I spent several years pining for Theo. I know when he's interested in a girl. I'm even better at knowing when he's not.

Theo reaches for Chase's hand, giving it a quick shake. "Hey, man, want a beer?"

Chase declines. Theo finishes his, and then takes my plate, offering me a small plastic bag of pretzels. Next, he wrestles a bottle of water out of his jacket pocket, proving exactly why I was so crazy about him for so long.

"Better?" Theo asks me softly.

"*So* much."

Theo grins and turns to Chase and Isabel. "So, what's going on?"

Chase says everything's cool, and Isabel mutters something small-talky. I don't say anything. I'm too busy watching Theo shovel one spoonful of macaroni salad after another into his mouth. Then the chicken wing. He even stops to make a face on that one.

"These are kinda nasty," he comments. He finishes it anyway and opens a second beer.

I clear my throat, and Theo hands me his keys…but two beers in ten minutes? Something's up. Is it his parents? Is it history? God, I hope he's not failing history. I also hope he doesn't throw up. Because that whole plate is a warning poster on food safety.

"Paige?" Chase smiles at me. "You want to take a walk?"

I pull my thoughts away from foodborne pathogens and academic failure. "Sure."

Theo looks like he wants to say something, but Isabel pushes his arm, laughing. She tells him he can't eat off the serving spoon. He tells her that John Baler is taking a leak off the bow, so he's a saint by comparison. Chase and I leave them, and the boat, behind.

Chase is nothing like Theo. Theo is noise and energy every second of every minute. Chase is confident. Relaxed. He's also almost a stranger, so there's a lot of small talk.

We walk up the stairs and behind the shops to a tiny, narrow park along the river. I can taste the start of spring in the air, damp grass and loamy dirt in the flowerbeds. It's getting chilly, though. I try to hold back a shiver, but Chase gives me his hooded sweatshirt.

We walk aimlessly along the riverbank. The grass is cold and wet against my sandaled feet, and a few late snowdrops peek up at the edges of flowerbeds. I walk as carefully as I can, but I'm sure my sandals will be a mess. The outfit is overkill, but I feel pretty. I wanted that tonight.

Our walk isn't perfect. Our elbows bump now and then, and the silence is awkward. Without our playful study banter, we run out of things to say.

When I finish my pretzels, we walk back, and Chase stops at the top of the stairs, hesitating. My hand clamps onto the cold metal rail, the one that curves right to the ramp up the bridge or left to the stairs to the docks. I think of the noise I heard earlier with Theo. The way the bridge shuddered. I want to go down those stairs right now.

Chase has other plans.

"Ready to head back?" I ask, hope lifting the last word to a whole new octave.

"Hold on, check it out."

Whatever response I want to make is strangled with the first squeal. Chase points, and I see them right away. People from the party are climbing the bridge.

I can hear them more than I can see them, the hollow clang of shoes against metal. The shrieks and laughs of people inching their way up. It's all dark shapes and occasional cell phone flashlights illuminating glimpses of beams, limbs, a swath of the flag.

They're still low enough not to kill themselves, but they're whooping and squealing, shoes scrabbling. Legs dangle where a few have given up and are sitting on a lower crossbeam, enjoying the view.

Even that's enough to give me the spins, so I look away, trying to focus on the soft trill of the wind chimes on one of the boats below.

"Come on." Chase catches my hand and tugs me to the ramp. I stumble after him in my ridiculous shoes. The bridge looms closer, and I can see myself up there earlier tonight. And the time before, when I was fourteen. I remember that too.

My trips to this bridge don't end well.

I hesitate, Chase's hand tightening on mine as he notices my resistance. "You okay?"

I let out a weird sound that's supposed to be a laugh. "Sure. Funny shoes."

"Want to try it?" he asks. "You could climb barefoot."

"Oh. No, not really my thing," I say, tugging my hand away from his and pulling them both inside his sweatshirt sleeves.

"Come on, it'll be fun."

"She won't do it," someone says. It's a group of girls. They are leaning against the railing with the locks. One of them is rooting through a rolling cooler. Another, the one who spoke, ruffles her hair in a way that lets me see the cascade of thin bangles up her wrist. Jolie.

"She's afraid of heights," she says, looking at Chase, not me. "She freaked out on the rope climb in gym last month."

"Be nice, Jolie," Chase says without much bite to his tone.

Jolie's girls snicker, and the wind chimes kick up in the breeze. Jolie sighs. "I'm not being a bitch. She's got anxiety issues or something. Don't you, Paige?"

I try to respond, but there's a fist-sized lump in my throat. I can't swallow it down.

"She doesn't have an anxiety thing." Chase touches my side. "We'll prove it."

My words finally come then, tumbling and breathy. "I don't want to prove it."

"We won't go high up." He says it close to my neck, and his breath is hot against my skin. I try not to squirm, but fear is crawling up my spine. The wooden planks that form the walkway curve up at the edges, warped. I wonder if it's a sign the wood is rotten, and my breath goes even tighter. I don't want to be out here.

"Come on, let's show her she's wrong," Chase says.

But she's *not* wrong.

Footsteps stomp up the ramp behind me. It's Theo. He moves right past me with a *Hey* and heads for Jolie. Or probably toward Jolie's blue plastic cooler.

"Come on, it'll be fun," Chase says again, tugging my arm so that I'm at the edge of the bridge. I'm right there with them. Me

23

and Chase, Jolie and her three little cronies, and Theo. He's got the cooler lid open and is elbow deep, sorting through ice.

"I need another beer," he says, sounding like he *really* doesn't.

"What the hell? This is your third!" Jolie's bracelets jangle. "Mooch off someone else."

"Need something to chase the shots I just did," he says, and then he looks at me. Drunk or not, he knows I'm scared.

He frowns. "What's going on?"

"Not much," Chase says, shoulders thrown back. "We're going to tag the flag."

Theo doesn't respond to Chase, because he was talking to me. But I'm speechless again.

"I'm game if you are," Theo says. "Wanna race?"

My insides flutter. I want to run. Hide. Theo just grins.

"That doesn't seem like a good idea, Theo." Chase is already moving us farther onto the bridge. I'm breathless and queasy as we pass Jolie. Theo stumbles after us.

Theo's laugh is brittle. "Don't get preachy with me, you little shit."

"Theo." I look at him, in case my tone isn't enough warning.

He shrugs me off. I stop before Chase can drag me to the train side, to the side he wants to climb.

"Chase, wait." My little purse slips off my shoulder. I'm cold all over. "Theo, I'm fine."

"Don't pull her," Theo says, ignoring me.

"Hold on, Paige," Chase says, then he turns to Theo. "Are you really going to do this?"

Theo's arms cross over his chest. "Define *this.*"

"Why won't you stop?" I ask.

Theo looks at me, eyes glittering. Too drunk to see his help *isn't* helpful. Someone shrieks, high and shrill—I hear the scrape of a rubber sole on steel. Something hits the wood and shatters, metal and plastic. A phone.

Someone above swears. More laughter. I take the chance to double back, scurrying past Jolie and the cooler until I'm safe on the ramp. Chase and Theo are right there with me.

"Maybe it's time for you to go," Chase says to him. But he takes my arm, his grip tight as he tries to steer me away.

I pull free of his grasp and tug off his sweatshirt. Something about this makes my belly twist. "Actually, I'm getting bored up here. I'm going to head down."

I rush down the stairs, Theo stumbling and laughing as he slip-trips behind me. It's hard in the sandals, but I move as fast as I can, grateful when I'm on the solid wood of the docks. The shadow of the bridge swallows us, but I feel better here. Safer.

Chase says my name as soon as he hits the dock, moving quickly toward me.

"Don't let him ruin this for us," Chase says. Then he takes my hand. A vague warning flares in my head. "Look, I know you're friends, but he's a total screwup. A wreck. Everyone knows it, and you deserve better."

"This has nothing to do with him," I say, pulling toward the boats. Chase doesn't let go. Whines my name.

Theo hits the deck, every step toward us louder than the last. "What are you planning here, man? Gonna *drag* her back up there?"

Chase turns, scowling. "Go to hell, Theo."

"You coming with me?"

Chase grabs Theo's shoulder. He pulls back so hard I flinch.

"Please don't do this," I say. My teeth suddenly chatter, but sweat rolls between my shoulder blades. They're going to fight. I can taste the certainty of it in the air.

"You need to back off," Chase says, stepping closer.

Theo lowers his head like a bull. "Do I look like the type to back off?"

"Just let it go!" I tell him.

Chase sneers at Theo. "What the hell is wrong with you?"

"You want the full psychiatric report? ADHD, ODD… Shit, Paige, help me out. I've got to be forgetting some letters here."

My face burns, eyes hot with tears. "I'm done with you."

Theo shrugs. "Who isn't done with me?"

I'm walking past them when Chase barrels into Theo, a hard

shove that bumps me sideways in my silly sandals. I suck in a sharp breath, and Theo looks at Chase like he'll kill him.

Or maybe like he's jealous.

Just like that, I get it. He touched my face on the bridge. My *face*.

This isn't happening. This *can't* be happening. But pieces are falling together, building a picture I can't miss. Theo reaching for me on the bridge tonight. His face when I talked about Chase. The way he's acting right now.

Chase tries to stroke my arm with an apology. And Theo explodes.

"No! *Please* no!" I say, but it's too late.

Time doesn't slow down. Everything's in fast-forward, the heel of my sandal sliding on slick wood. Chase reaching, Theo drawing back a fist. I move to pull someone away, to get between them. It's the wrong time, wrong angle, wrong everything.

Theo's aiming for Chase. But I shove my way between them in that last second.

The punch lands on my mouth. So hard I see a flash of white and hear the crack.

My head snaps back and then forward. And then I'm on the ground. Theo's screaming, cursing, *Shit, shit, shit, Paige! No!* My vision whirls, hands flying to my mouth.

The pain smears the world into a pounding blur as I struggle to sit up. Chase has Theo on the dock, calling him every awful name, slamming his face over and over, but Theo just looks at me, eyes wide with horror. A thin keening comes next, stretching long through the air. It's a terrible sound, and it's coming from me.

Chase screams to call 911. Footsteps are rushing. My mouth is full of copper and salt. Theo is crying, Chase's knee across his back. Chase is punching him, but Theo is still reaching for me, fingers clawing at the dock.

I open my mouth to say something, to stop the awful noise I'm making. Blood pours. Drips off my chin and hits my knees, my sandals. The pain keeps time with my heart, whiting out my vision one beat at a time.

There's a crowd now. A girl says she's going to be sick. The cops are coming. A plastic chair is pushed behind me, and it's cold when I sit down. Someone rips off a shirt and shoves it into my hands. I smell copper and salt and the river.

I don't know what he actually hit. My lips? My nose? Everything hurts. My jaw feels like it doesn't close right. My mouth is full of blood and pebbles. I don't know where they came from.

Theo's nose is bloody now too. Smeared with dirt. Chase tries to tell me it's okay, but I can tell he's grossed out by all the blood. He can't look at me. And Theo can't look away.

I open my mouth to say something, to breathe, and I can feel those two little rocks rolling along my tongue. I spit them into my hand and lean back to look at them.

They aren't rocks. They're teeth.

THEO

July 2

The heat in Denny's house is making me crazy. Well, crazier. I'm melting into the shitty pleather couch and leaving sweat smears on my phone screen. One window air conditioner is pumping cold, stale air in through the front window, but it's not enough. I'm sweating playing video games, for God's sake.

Ohio Valley heat wave. That's what the Weather Channel says. I've heard it eighteen thousand times today, because Denny apparently can't take a shower or a shit or make a trip to the fridge without a meteorological update. I tried to share the virtues of other channels my first couple of days here, but since then I've let it play, watching women with very white teeth and manicured hands trace the swirls of jet streams and cold fronts across the continental United States.

"Still looking like rain tonight?" he asks from the kitchen.

"Starting at ten," I tell him, though the time could have changed. I've actually had the channel muted since this morning.

Denny clucks. "It's going to wreck the fireworks Thursday."

"The front should move out by morning. Plenty of time to dry out." I can't believe we're talking about this.

"You know, I got a buddy with a boat."

I don't say anything, just bang my thumbs against my phone harder, trying to keep my pixelated guy on his pixelated platform so I can win absolutely nothing and waste an assload of time doing it.

"We can go out together," Denny says when I don't answer, aiming for casual and missing it. "Have a few beers."

I don't remind him that there won't be any beer for me. I don't think Denny really expects me to stick to that promise. I don't even think my parents expected it when I said it in the police station, cuffs still on, tears and snot running down to my damn chin. I guess words like *charged with assault* suck the wind right out of the parental trust sails.

Not that the sails ever had wind. I'm the youngest of four boys and the most messed-up to boot. They've never known what to do with me. Mostly, we tiptoe around each other. They don't kick me out, and I don't burn down the house. It's not the stuff of greeting cards, but whatever.

"You should get out of the house," Denny says.

My video game guy dies again, starting me over. "I'm on house arrest."

"Don't be a smart-ass. It's probation." He says it like it's a detention for skipping class. Maybe he sees it that way. I used to think Denny was cool—my uncle twin, the family always says. Now I want to pick at all that *high school trouble* he hints at. Was he as bad as me? Did he hurt someone too?

My phone character falls again, tumbling end over end to a concrete sidewalk. It's painless and bloodless. In other words, nothing like real life.

I toss my phone beside me on the couch, but it's too late. I'm already thinking of that night—Paige crying on a plastic chair, blood from her nose to the neckline of her sundress, her little glittery purse tangled under her feet. That's what real life looks like.

My fist and guts clench at the same time, and I scramble off the couch, spilling a soda and knocking over one of Denny's ashtrays. I pick it all up, the can, the cigarette butts, pushing a wadded-up paper towel around the clutter on the coffee table.

It's too dark to see what I'm cleaning. We keep the curtains drawn tight in this room, a sad effort to block the heat of the sun. Eventually, I pitch the paper towel and empty the ashtray and call it good enough.

"You all right out there?" Denny's voice floats out of the kitchen again.

I take a breath I can taste. Old smoke and soda syrup and somehow air conditioner too.

"I'm good." I'm not, though. There are ashes on my fingers, and my new meds are making me so jittery I can't eat, but it's not like I'm going to start skipping pills—

A sound cuts in from outside, a weak cry with a shudder at the end.

What was that?

I cock my head toward the window. I still hear it out there. An animal maybe. Like a cat? Are there any cats around here?

"Do you hear that?" I ask.

There's a scrape and bang of pans in the kitchen. Denny pokes his head into the living room, holding a half-burned sandwich. "Hear what?"

"I don't know. Like an animal?"

His face scrunches like he's trying to hear. "What kind of animal?"

A dying one, if I had to guess. The hair on the back of my neck pricks up as I move from window to window, listening. It's the same from all of them, faint and warbling, but definitely there. But what is it? A rooster? Maybe a kitten?

Oh, shit. Could it be a baby crying?

The sound fades abruptly, and I shake my head. "It stopped. Maybe I'm hearing things."

Denny looks at me, and I look down, noting my rumpled cargo shorts and the paint-stained Carhartt shirt I didn't bother to change out of after work. My fingers are cut up and shaking, and since I haven't shaved since last Sunday, I don't need to look in the mirror to know I look like shit. Sunburned shit.

The cry winds up again, and I point at the window that seems closest to the sound, cocking my head because I know Denny will hear that. He has to. Everything about his face says otherwise, though. *What the hell?*

"Maybe I was hearing the TV," I offer lamely. I even shrug for good measure.

Denny watches me for a minute longer, his jaw working like he's trying to chew through a bit of gristle. "Look, Theo. You've been through—"

I cough to cut him off, because wherever he's going with this, I can't follow. "You know, maybe you've got a point about me getting out of the house."

He nods slowly, still ruminating whatever armchair-therapist crap he was about to spit out. He must think better of it, because he adjusts his cap on his thinning hair and sighs. "Look, I know you need to stay out of trouble, but you're like a different person. You need to cut loose."

"The last thing I need to do is cut loose," I argue.

"I don't mean go out and rob a bank, but this new little

goody-two-shoes habit?" He sighs like it's a new little heroin habit. "I don't know. All those pills you take."

"I'm not on drugs, Denny. They're prescribed."

"I know, I know. But you're eighteen years old. You can't need that many pills at your age. Hell, I've never taken nothing in my life, and I'm almost forty."

"I've explained this. Things are different now."

"Yeah? Well, maybe different isn't good. You don't even leave the house, kid."

It's true. Other than following him from the house to our work site—and if we just got paid, Anita's for lunch—and back again, I haven't left. Not once in the two weeks I've been here.

Out of the corner of my eye, the TV flickers. The forecast loop starts over, and out of nowhere—or maybe everywhere—I'm about to come out of my skin being in this dark, closed-in room in this house that needs more work than any of the jobs Denny ever lands.

Whatever it is, it's enough to push me out the door without a single thought beyond a wave at Denny as I pass.

Outside, the sunlight hits me like a hard slap, and the heat is so lazy and sticky that I feel like I'm wading through soup. Maybe Anita's is open—I could go for a milk shake. There could be somebody playing baseball down at the park. I could watch that.

I pass Denny's truck, ladders strapped to the top and loose

screws and bolts in the bed. I'll probably drive something like this for the rest of my life. Used to think I wanted to be a paramedic or a fireman. Then this chick at a career day at school talked about all the records, from grades to social media, that a prospective employer might look at. It was probably a don't-text-nudes message, but still. I'm pretty sure they don't hire firemen with hefty mental health treatment portfolios, let alone arrest records.

The whining drifts around me again, and my feet stop. I'm halfway up the block, as I turn around and around, looking for the source of the noise. There's something pretty desperate about that thin cry. Something creepy too.

I follow it a little farther into the Village, over buckled slabs of sidewalk and past sagging front porches. Some houses hum with the efforts of hardworking air conditioners. Others are stuck with the buzz of box fans and shiny black carpenter bees instead.

I cut north, toward the river and Anita's Diner, the sound cutting in and out of different alleys, but it's moving toward the river—going to water. Maybe it's a power tool. An animal that sick wouldn't be moving. It'd probably be dead.

The little stretch of shops is quiet. Heat's got everybody slowed down, I guess. A waitress who wastes far too many flirty smiles on me is locking the front door of Anita's, across from the ramp up to the bridge.

I don't look at the ramp, and I sure the hell don't look at the stairs that lead down to the docks. But it's a small town, so options for a drink are slim. I cross the street, planning to con her out of a bottle of root beer, but she's on her phone, putting away her keys.

"Do you know how to get there?" she asks whoever's on the other end of the line.

I'm raising my hand to wave, so I don't scare her, and she turns to me, cocking a hip out as she smirks. She gives a little half wave, still talking on the phone.

"I know you'll probably take a shortcut that adds ten minutes."

I've heard that before. Paige said that to me.

My stomach twists, and I shake my head. No. It's coincidence, or maybe I heard her wrong. Because that night was four months ago. It's over now.

The waitress looks at me, lips curving up. My stomach slides sideways, and there it is again. The hurt-animal sound. Like something sobbing. Or maybe laughing. My insides go cold, and I give the waitress a two-fingered salute and walk right on by.

Back on the other side of the street—the bridge side—I swipe a sweat-slick palm across my forehead and try to breathe. To think.

I've been inside too long. I'm losing it.

I take a breath that is all river—water and fish and gasoline.

I'm at the bridge ramp, and I'm not sure how. Or why. But I'm still walking, boots scraping across the cement.

A soft, familiar beat with a whining guitar floats from the river. I can't hear the animal anymore, but I can hear this. That song she loved about everything changing.

Paige.

Even thinking her name rolls chills up my back. I close my eyes, and that night is unleashed. The song grows louder, and memories skip wildly through my mind. Us in the car, on the bridge, on the docks. There were other people there, but Paige is all I see.

Paige in her pretty sundress, smiling and smiling. Paige on a white plastic chair, bleeding and bleeding.

I open my eyes, and I'm halfway across. I can't be. I don't remember walking out here. It's all a blur of heat and memory, but here I am, perched fifty feet above the pumping vein of the Muskingum River.

The music—that song—it's *everywhere.*

I lick my lips and push my greasy hair off my face while the song cries on about slow rides on long nights and everything changing, changing, changing. Things did change. This is as close to Paige as I've been since they led me away in handcuffs. She's across the river, though, in the land of science programs, pretty brick buildings, and chemically treated lawns.

I take a step back, warped wood catching my foot and half throwing me at the rail. Locks rattle, and my gaze drifts to the redbrick college buildings with bright-white trim.

She's somewhere over there, doodling in a notebook or using a microscope or solving a world problem. Shit, I don't know. I only know she's healed and away from me. And thank God for that.

The song shifts to the chorus again, and I look up for speakers, look down too. Sound can be weird on the river—maybe there's a band on campus. The chorus rises, and I forget about the speaker, think of Paige instead. I wanted to kiss her that night. What if I *had*? The music tears at my ears, thumps in my veins. Man, I hate this song. I fiddle absently with one lock after the next. Small one, round one, big one—

My hand closes around hot metal, and the song cuts off.

Just like that.

It's so abrupt that I curse, my voice loud in the sudden quiet.

Someone shrieks behind me. I look back, spotting a trio of college girls. They're young. Freshmen. Maybe even high school juniors on a program like Paige. But they *aren't* like Paige. They don't have freckles or wavy hair that flips up at the ends. They're like every girl in every Ohio town, straight glossy hair, winged eyeliner and all.

They cut their eyes away from me, and I look at my unlaced

work boots. Try to shrink. They're afraid of me, and I get it. I look like the kind of guy that might hurt a girl.

Which is exactly what I am.

I turn back to the railing, still holding the padlock. The girls move a little easier now, hopefully convinced I'm mostly harmless. I want to ask them if they heard the music, but I don't. I listen to the retreat of their footsteps and the gurgle of the river instead.

The sun is fat and drifting west, and there are no dying kittens or strange songs. It's fine. I'll call the doctor. Tell him something in my ADHD cocktail is off, and he'll write a new list of prescriptions to make my hands shake and my brain settle.

I turn the big lock over in my hand and uncurl my fingers. Reading the initials. I pull back, cocking my head.

Because I can't be reading that right.

But I am.

The initials are TQ and PVY.

And I can't think of one other set of names that would stand for except *Theodore Quinn* and *Paige Vinton-Young*.

PAIGE

The sun is delicious, shimmering off tiny ripples in the water. We should be collecting samples, but Melanie is stretched out on one of the wooden picnic tables, phone in hand and lips moving silently.

It's French. She's been practicing some sort of speech she has to give to her online club all week. I don't know how she juggles it. She's in the Ecological Studies project with me, the French Intensive with a bunch of kids from back in Chicago, and she's always messaging her school news group about content ideas for senior year.

Melanie is twice as busy as I am, but done with everything in half the time. From her organizational skills to her perfect skin, I'm not sure if I should hate her or start a fan club.

She pockets her phone suddenly and squints down at the river.

"I miss the lake," she says.

"Hey, it's still freshwater," I say.

She laughs and stretches her brown arms overhead. "I didn't show you enough of the lake if you believe this mud strip is anything like it."

"True. Which is why we're doing all this testing, right?"

She wrinkles her nose. "I'm doing it to pad my college résumé. You can't tell me you're not missing Chi-town at this point."

"Definitely."

"Then my work as tour guide is complete," she says.

In a way, she *was* my tour guide. It's how we became friends. Chicago was totally overwhelming for me until she took charge. On our trip to Shedd Aquarium, I'd done nothing but gape at the seemingly endless stretch of tall, shiny buildings along Lake Michigan. Melanie squeezed in beside me on the charter bus. The whole drive, and every drive into the city after, she made it her mission to point out all the staples of her hometown. Buckingham Fountain, the new park along the lake with the climbing walls and the ice ribbon. The Bean.

I had no idea how big a city could be until Chicago. Or how small a town like Portsville can look in comparison.

"Sadly, not all your work is done," I say, waggling the plastic case full of water sample kits.

She nods, narrowing her eyes. "Right. We need to come up with an angle."

"How about we come up with more water first?"

I edge closer to the river, donning neoprene gloves and looking for an easy place to descend the bank. It's only thirty or forty feet high here, with walking paths that snake down for joggers and anglers.

I make my way down a narrow dirt path that leads to the walking path, and then down another path from that to the water's edge. I pop open the first of eight glass vials and start filling.

It's amazing how clear the water looks up close. It's different from a distance. The Muskingum is a brown ribbon that curls through miles and miles of the Ohio Valley. Every one of those miles looks muddy, but every vial I cap looks pure.

But we wouldn't be here if that was true.

"Did we schedule our next lab time yet?" Melanie asks.

"Yes. I grabbed Monday from two to six."

"Then we've got to collect the other three samples by tomorrow morning. Which is good. I have my French speech at two, so I have to get back by then."

"We should have plenty of time."

We've collected samples from twenty assigned segments, and now we're trying to determine four more sites on our own. This project culminates with a report justifying our independent site selection and evaluating our survey results.

I'm hoping it comes with a recommendation letter too. Because I want more than this program—I want to go to this college. I want to spend four years rushing across this campus, sleeping on flat mattresses in dorm rooms, and complaining about cold showers and communal bathrooms. I want it more than anything.

And my parents want me home just as badly.

When we're done here at the park—Melanie's pick, in the hopes that picnic litter and additional waste from pets might have an impact—we'll still have three to go.

"I still think that area with the high banks is smart," Melanie says, adjusting her sunglasses. "The chemical runoff could be significant."

It *is* smart. There's a lawn-care service perched on the south bank, so the chance of some sort of herbicide or pesticide by-product is really high. It's also tucked in a curve of the river with steep banks and virtually no easy access. Even thinking about trying to get down to that section of the river makes my stomach curl up tight.

"Think about it," Melanie says. "Since we have to take our samples from the shoreline, that's going to be the most challenging place to do it. Everyone else will avoid the work."

"Maybe. But that lawn-care service is practically a neon sign." I look around, wanting something else, something *easier*. The walking bridge is a possibility. The road bridge on the opposite side of town was on the assigned site list, but this one is older. There could be lead paint. Weird chemicals in the metal ballasts, maybe.

But can I handle being near that bridge again? Or will it remind me of my last night with Theo at the party? I've hated that bridge for years. Feared it too.

No. I'm done being the girl who runs from every scary thing.

I cap my last two samples and bump my chin toward the bend in the river that leads to the south side of town. "What about the bend near the elementary school? Or the walking bridge?"

Melanie wrinkles her nose. "The school is too accessible. It's also close to the water treatment plant, so it's probably been tested within an inch of its life. The walking bridge could be good." She pauses, biting her lip. "Except I heard bad things happen there. It's haunted."

She makes it as breathy as a ghost story, but I laugh, because she's right about bad things happening. She's just wrong about which ones. "It's not haunted."

Melanie shakes her head, dropping her voice low. "I'm serious. It's haunted by all these kids who've jumped and died. You know that suicide forest in Japan? This bridge is like that. People jump off and slam into all the debris under the water. Old sheets of metal and iron beams. Industrial leftovers."

I frown. "Have there actually been *any* suicides on that bridge?"

"That's what everyone around here says."

"Well, then it *must* be true."

"You didn't want to cross it. Remember the first day? We all wanted to eat at that diner?"

"Anita's," I say, dragged right back to that bright afternoon, surrounded by kids from the program with panic crawling up my throat. "And trust me, that was more about the food than the bridge."

It's a lie, but she grins, so I continue. "I don't live too far from here, and I've never heard of anyone jumping."

"Fine, I give. But rumors don't start for no reason. Something bad happened here."

Right again. But no one knows about the bad thing I'm thinking of. I've made sure of it.

"You've got a point about the water there, though," I say, looking a quarter of a mile downriver to where the bridge sits. "It's old. Could have toxic paint or construction compounds."

Melanie narrows her eyes, pushing her sleek, black ponytail behind her shoulder. "I didn't consider that. Most of the others are working at ecological imbalances due to the introduction of non-native species. If we go for chemicals—"

"Then we'll be doing something different." Our smiles widen at the same time. "We could discuss the long-term effects of out-of-date maintenance and poor industrial practices. We could include three other factory sites."

"It's a plan." Melanie stands up. "Come on, let's talk about tomorrow."

Fourth of July weekend. It's never been my favorite holiday, but it's a big deal for the Summer Experience program. After a day of festivities and fireworks on the water, family and friends are welcome to visit the campus the following day. Most of us are thrilled to see some familiar faces after five weeks away. I'm dreading it, because it's the beginning of the end.

Three weeks after Family Day, the term is over. I go home. And Mom and Dad will spend every moment of the next two months I'm back trying to convince me to commute from home for my first two years of college.

My hands ball up tight at my sides. There's no point in thinking about it now, so I keep walking. Ahead of me, the bridge stretches over the water. I see the glint of padlocks on the railing, and a single jogger making her way across to the Village. If she turns right off the bridge, she could go down the stairs like I did. She could stand on the docks where I lost my shoes. My teeth. Theo.

"Paige?"

I lurch and Melanie chuckles. "Wow, jumpy. Who are you bringing this weekend?"

"What?" I shake my head. "Oh, no one. But I know *Joseph* will be here."

47

Her eyes widen. "Oh God, have I been obnoxious? I have. I'm sorry."

"No, you're sweet. You miss him. I get it. You've been dating for two years."

Her grin goes wide. "Fine, I do miss him. So, spill already. Who do *you* miss?"

Theo. My tongue curls around his name, but I keep my mouth closed. Because I shouldn't miss him. I shouldn't wonder what movies he's watched, or if he's tried the new taco truck that visits campus on Fridays, or if he's wearing sunblock. I shouldn't think of him at all, unless I'm angry. And I *am* still angry.

For two months after he hit me, I almost hated him. It's easy to be hateful if you spend enough hours in doctors' waiting rooms. I didn't read or watch the TVs bolted above stacks of outdated magazines. I thought about Theo. Every time he made us late, or begged me to help him pull up a failing grade, or knocked over something at a restaurant on accident-purpose. I thought of dozens of reasons to hate him.

It almost worked.

"It's okay if you don't want to tell me," Melanie says, sounding a little hurt. We're at the bridge, the shadow falling over us to leave us in a blissfully cool breeze.

"It's not that I don't want to tell you. It's just hard."

"A breakup?" she guesses.

I shake my head. "No. My best friend. He…"

My jaw blooms with a phantom ache, but I hold in the words. Confessing the truth of that night erases all the other truth about Theo. My parents spent an entire weekend listing dozens of reasons why my friendship with Theo was damaging and, ultimately, had to end. I know they were right. But I know they don't see the truth about him either.

"You can talk to me," Melanie says. I know she means it, that we're friends in a way.

But what is there to say? How do I wrap words around what we were for someone like Melanie? It wouldn't matter if I did, because it's over. Theo-dectomy was the first of my surgeries. I removed the troubled boy. Then my broken teeth. Both were clinical procedures. Necessary.

I draw my shoulders back and remind myself that I won't miss him forever. It's all progress toward healthiness. Talking about it might be progress too, so I will. Just a little.

"My best friend and I aren't friends anymore." It feels both good and awful to say out loud.

"What's her name?"

I shake my head. "Theo. *His* name is Theo."

She smiles, happy enough with this morsel. I'm pretty happy myself. It wasn't a big deal, giving that small piece. I said his name, and I didn't burst into tears or flames or bleed at the mouth. It's nothing. And the soft ache in my chest is nothing too.

I grin, and Melanie drops the pack, setting her iPod on top and turning it up. She starts filling out the paperwork, and I agree to collect the samples. The water is murky and cool in the shadow of the bridge. Yesterday's storms stirred up the sediment, which might give us more interesting results.

The docks are on the far side of the river and the other side of the bridge. Seeing that glimpse of wood, the white gleam of boats docked for the summer—I thought it might take me back, but I'm wrong. It's like being able to say Theo's name, another bit of proof that I'm better now.

One by one I fill the vials, listening to the soft thump of people walking across the bridge. Melanie's talking about what to wear tomorrow when the music switches. Cold sinks through me at the first beats. I want a different song, one I didn't play for him that awful night.

But it's only a song. So, I slog my way through the rest of the vials and seal them with shaking fingers. I pack them in the kit and try to pretend it doesn't matter.

Everything's changing, changing, changing.

"Crap, I spilled one," she says. "I'm sorry."

Melanie meets me in the water, maybe for conversation or

maybe for the cool relief of the current under the shadow of the bridge. I've been in this shadow before. I've bled here. I close my eyes for a second, trying to pull myself together.

Something splashes in the water. I flinch.

"What was that?" Melanie asks.

My hand is at my chest, right over my pounding heart. "I don't know. A bird's nest?"

"It looked like a bag. It's right there! Did someone drop their purse?"

I can see it now, bobbing in one of the still pools off the current. It is a bag of some sort, close to the first support, so probably not too deep to reach. The song is still playing, and a strange feeling is building in my belly. I need to get that bag. It is meant for me.

Ridiculous.

I pull in a hard breath. It's probably trash. It doesn't matter. But I step into the water, one foot in front of the other in my program-issued rubber boots. The water is cool and deep. It sloshes over the edges of my boots. Melanie laughs, rushing past me until she's up to her thighs.

I try to laugh too, but it's a weird, hollow sound. She reaches for the bag, and everything in me goes still and tight. She scoops the bag from the water with a whoop and throws it.

I catch it on instinct, gut heavy with dread. My fingers test the brown plastic—a snack bag, one that makes my breath go tight.

Pain stabs through my jaw. Hard and fast. The song warbles on about everything changing, but it's not. It's all the same as that night. This song. That bridge. The fact that I'm holding a bag of pretzels exactly like the one Theo gave me.

It's a really awful coincidence, but it hurts like hell.

THEO

Denny and Bill are on their fourth beers, and I'm still nursing the piss-warm remnants of this morning's Mountain Dew. I don't know if it's the heat, the smell of fish and sweat, or the soft rocking of the boat, but I'm queasy as hell.

"You ready for a cold one yet?" Denny asks.

Not the first time he's asked. Probably the third time I've shaken my head and looked across the Muskingum. Crumbling mansions dot one side of the river, set back from the water's reach by long, well-tended lawns. Bill's house is on the other side, behind a cobbled-together wooden dock and discarded fishing bobbers. The houses behind the docks are cozied up to one another, narrow alleys of weeds and grass parting one property from the next.

Bill's got a pole in. Denny and I aren't even bothering. *Here for the holiday* is what Denny said, flicking his cigarette into the water. Maybe true for him, but I'm here because I'm going batshit crazy in the house, obsessing about that lock I found on the bridge.

Did Paige leave that lock for me to find?

Is it some messed-up way of trying to reach out to me?

And why was I even up there? Chasing a dead cat noise that no one else could hear and I haven't heard since? This place is making me crazy. Paige is making me crazy.

I slide my phone out of my pocket and pull up her number for the four-billionth time in the last forty-eight hours. I don't type anything, just stare at the string of three-month-old messages.

Me: They took me inpatient for a week. No phone. I'm sorry. So sorry.

Her: I know. I'm not mad. I know you didn't mean it. But I can't talk to you.

Me: I just need you to know… That night, I was going to talk to you.

Her: I know.

Me: You know? You haven't said anything.

Her: Because I can't say anything. Not anymore. Please understand.

I did understand. *Do* understand. But that text message sucked half of the oxygen out of the sky.

I close my phone and take a breath that tastes like rotting plants and beer.

"You are a moody little shit these days," Denny says with a laugh. "Need to cheer you up before you start getting everybody on the crew depressed."

"Ease up," Bill says with a knowing nod at my phone. "Girl trouble?"

"No trouble," I say. No girl either, but I don't mention that.

"Hey, you get the weather on that thing?" Denny asks.

It's going to be a long Fourth of July.

An hour later, Bill reels in his line and mutters something about heading downriver. Nothing's biting. Actually, plenty of shit is biting. My arms and legs are lined with little red welts to prove it, but I keep my mouth shut and lean back in the plastic seat.

Bill's boat moves at a decent clip, the engine whirring loud enough that nobody talks and the wind pushes my sticky hair off my forehead. It's only a few minutes, but it's perfect. I don't think or fidget. We move up the river toward town, watching the trees and houses slip past.

I expect Bill to take one of the bigger offshoots to the mouth of the river. There are a million inlets along them that make for good fishing, but he curves left instead. I chew my bottom lip as the boat slides to the west, right into town. The walking bridge stretches across the horizon, and my stomach goes heavy. The dock where I hurt Paige sits on the right.

For one electrifying second, I feel the boat drift that way. Before I can protest or freak out, Bill steers hard to the left, pulling the boat right up to the walking path on the college side.

"We need gas?" I guess when Bill cuts the engine. There's a boat rental station that offers gas just past the bridge on this side of the river.

"You need to walk the plank," Denny says, reaching into his back pocket. He hands me a twenty and winks. "Go find somebody to hang out with. Should be plenty of girls on campus."

My laugh feels sharp enough to cut my tongue. "I told you, I'm cool here."

"Maybe we need a little old-man time," Denny says, but I know what he's trying. My expression must show it because he sighs. Adjusts his ball cap. "Look, you've got to snap out of this. Where's the little hell-raiser who's been a pain in my ass since he was three years old?"

Currently? Dead and buried under a thick layer of stimulants and antidepressants. And he'll stay that way. I'll take every pill a doctor will give me to keep that part of me in check.

Theo!

Paige's voice is so clear and sudden that I bolt to my feet, sending the boat rocking wildly. Denny swears and I'm looking around, looking up. Is she on the bridge? We're too close, practically under the bridge, so I lean back, hoping to see the edge.

"Did you hear that?" I ask, but I know they didn't. I can tell by the way they're looking at me. I'm chilled by the sudden certainty that Paige didn't call my name. Not here and not now. I try to move back to center, but stumble left. Bill catches me.

"Will you watch where you're going?"

My face goes cold. Bill said it, I'm sure, but something's wrong. Something humming beneath his words. Paige said that in the car, *those* words. The boat's still rocking, Denny's arms stretched to steady it, his cheeks red from the sun and the beer. His expression is somewhere between concerned and amused, but four beers in, amused is winning.

"Sorry," I say, shaking my head.

Denny laughs, and I climb off the boat on rubber chicken legs. Blink down at them and try to look cool. Normal. Like I'm not panting and staring at the bridge, looking for a girl I know damn well isn't there.

"Look, go on campus. Or across the bridge to see that cute waitress. Take a break from all those…" Denny's voice trails off, but I know what he's getting at. The pills. He's been on me about my medications since I got down here.

I force a smile and tell him I will. Thank him for the idea as Bill pulls the boat back into the current. I even agree to call him before the fireworks. Lying has never been a problem for me.

I wouldn't step foot on that campus if someone offered me hard cash. So I turn toward the walking bridge as soon as they're out of sight.

The Cheshire Walking Bridge is always busy on holidays. Footsteps and voices rise around me as I head toward home, careful to stay in the center. Careful to keep my hands away from those damn locks.

Do no harm. It's what doctors say. My life has been the opposite of that motto. Do loads of harm, usually without even trying. I used to think about that when I wanted to be a paramedic. It sounded cool to be someone who made everything better. Now I clench my fists and give everyone a wide berth. Because all I want is to not break anything—*anyone*—else.

My throat goes dry, and I move faster. Need to get home. Close myself into that dark not-cool living room where there's a bottle of pills that will put me to sleep and the Weather Channel to pass the time until they kick in.

A chesty blond peels away from the blur of voices and faces. She's headed in the direction I'm running from, eyes bright and arm linked with a corn-fed boy in an Old Navy flag T-shirt. She smells like lemon candy and lilacs.

"I wish I knew if I got in," she sighs, and her voice is wrong, her mouth a fraction of a second off the timing of her words.

A chill runs down my spine as I pull my gaze away. Steady

my hand on the rail. I've heard that before. Just like I heard what Denny said. Why am I hearing what Paige said?

"It's for college credit." A mom says this, fluffy brown hair under a red-and-white-striped sun visor.

I stumble on, because I need a pill. A doctor. Help.

"Every summer this is where you end up."

A boy. Ten-ish with a wad of gum and a roll of his eyes that should not turn my bones to ice. But it does.

I stop, panting in the middle of the bridge. My hand looks for it, searching through plastic-coated combination locks and tiny suitcase locks. My fingers know the one I'm looking for. They steady the second I touch it.

I clutch the heavy lock, and my breathing stills. The world goes quiet, and the smell of lemon fades. Okay. It's over now, whatever it was. I drag in a breath and pull out my phone, because if I'm holding a phone, nobody will think I'm simply standing here. Paralyzed like a freak.

The foot traffic is thinning, and I hear the trill of a marching band in the distance. Parade must be starting. Maybe everything else is back to normal too.

I turn over the lock and check for initials. Still there. My laugh sounds like a sob.

"Wrecked," I whisper, squeezing the lock one more time, trying to sort out what the hell I'm going to do.

Go home. Take a pill and go to bed. If it gets bad, I can always call the psychiatrist. Or my therapist.

Like this isn't already bad.

I roll my shoulders and look up. I can't stand on this bridge all night; I need to move.

"Theo?"

My name sounds different. Crisp and less familiar, like she doesn't quite remember how to frame her lips around the two syllables. Like she's not sure she remembers me.

But I remember her. The sound of her voice, the way her hair goes red in the sun. Her bitten-to-the-beds nails and freckled shoulders. I don't even really have to look at her, because I remember everything.

And I'd know her anywhere.

"Hey, Paige."

PAIGE

He looks terrible. Every bone in my body is scrambling for a compliment to give. That's how I was raised. Even if you'd like to set a person on fire, you say something nice when you greet them. It's what you do.

Except I can't. He's sunburned. And gaunt. His shirt is so wrinkled and stained that I'm not sure he's changed it this week. And none of that is as bad as the hollowness of his eyes.

His lips quirk in a way that makes me think he's about to smile. It doesn't last. One flash of eye contact, and I'm dragged right back to him on the ground screaming my name, and me on a chair spitting out teeth.

Theo looks away, and I stare at the rusty metal railing, cluttered with locks that make me cringe. I hate those locks now. I wish I'd been smart enough to hate them all along.

Theo lifts one, letting it drop against the metal rail. I hear my heart beating—too fast—and Theo breathing one shaky breath after another. His hands are shaking too, and he's definitely thinner.

They upped his meds then. I shouldn't be surprised, and I shouldn't care, but my brow pinches anyway and my hands itch. I want to tell him to use sunscreen. Eat a sandwich. Get some sleep. I guess old habits die hard.

He breaks the spell of silence with a cough. "I didn't mean to…" Theo gestures absently at the other side of the bridge, the college side.

"Didn't mean to?"

"I wasn't trying to find you," he says. "I'm with Denny."

"Working for the summer?" I ask, but it's silly because I already know that.

"We're finishing up that strip mall."

"Up on Route 53? Yeah, I've seen it."

He pushes his hands in his pockets. Changes his mind and yanks them back out. "How's your class? Do you…do you like it up there at the college?"

"Yeah, it's great. I was coming across to get lunch." I don't tell him it's my first time across or that I'm only risking an almost-guaranteed panic attack because I don't want Melanie to think I'm weird.

"Great. So you feel…all right?"

I don't touch my jaw, but the memory of agony feels like a stain. "Oh yeah. Sure."

"Does it still hur—"

"No, no, it's all good."

We're talking around the flaming elephant in this room like it's a flea. Like he hit me with a rogue softball pitch instead of his fist. Maybe it's not that. Maybe we're just small-talking, like we used to do after we went a couple of weeks without hanging out.

It wasn't often, but sometimes there was a girlfriend. They never lasted. Some random girl would manage—for no comprehensible reason—to captivate every ounce of his attention for a few weeks. Just as inexplicably, she'd start boring him to death. It *crushed* me the first time. After that, it got easier. I'm never the girl he leaves behind.

No.

I *wasn't* a girl he *left* behind. That's how I have to say it. I have to use past-tense words, because that's what this is now. We aren't *am* and *is* and *are*. We are *used to be*.

"I miss you, Paige."

The words push bone-deep. All at once I'm the *used to be* me, the one who spent years wishing he'd see me the way I see him. *Saw* him. I'm still messing it up.

Someone bumps my shoulder and I tense, hand snagging the hot metal handrail. It's a family heading to the Village. A ponytailed mom and two little girls with red and blue beads in their braids. Theo steps forward and then back, looking twitchy as the family steers around him.

Another couple passes. A gull lands on a black ballast overhead. I need to go, but then Theo smiles. It's crooked and begs me to smile back. He touches another lock. It's different than the others.

I take a step back. "It's good to see you, Theo."

He winces. "That's not true."

Really time to go. I should have gone a while ago, but I wait. I know he's going to say things I'm not ready to hear. But maybe it doesn't matter if I'm ready. It's time I face it and move on.

"It's not *good* to see me," he says. "It can't be. After what I did—" His laugh is hard and sudden. "I'm sorry. For then and now. For everything."

My heart skips sideways. He means it. He meant it at the party, and he means it now. Too bad it isn't enough to fix the damage between us. I wished that changed the way things are, but it doesn't. I look down at my hand's death grip on the rail and the slick, brown water rushing below. Did people really jump from here like Melanie said? Bash in their heads on old slabs of concrete and steel beams under the water?

Wait—did Theo see us talking that day? Did he see me in the water collecting samples?

He could have dropped those pretzels. He could have seen me earlier too, on the pavilion with Melanie discussing lunch. He could have waited, knowing I'd come. Hoping to talk.

"Did you see me here, Theo?" I ask.

"What?"

"Up at the pavilion with my friend."

His face screws up. "Today? Here?" Then, "No."

He sounds honest, but good liars always do. "Theo, we can't go ba—"

"I know."

"We can't be friends," I say, because it needs to be said out loud.

For a second, it's like he can't figure out how to respond. And then he does.

"Not ever?"

I take a breath, and whatever I want to say—whatever I *should* say—won't come. I've practiced these words before in my therapist's office. I've written them in journals and said them to my mirror. In this moment, I feel a million miles away from the girl who could never be friends with Theo.

It's hard to say *never* to the boy who doesn't eat, but throws away my lunch trash. To the one who hates TV, but binge-watches anime with me. Theo once drove two hours to get me a Chipotle burrito when I freaked out over a B-minus on a final.

Road trips. Laughter. Love. Those are Theo memories. But

he is still the boy who hit me. Hairline fracture and two broken molars. Blood. Pain. Fear. Those are Theo memories too.

Theo's sigh tells me he understands my silence. He doesn't look at me, but his fingers wrap around that thick, bronze padlock again, and my stomach goes sour.

"Stupid." His laugh breaks my heart. "I thought this was a sign."

"I have to go."

The lock drops, clanging hard against the railing. "Okay."

"Theo, I'm…"

"It's okay," he says, trying to smile. His hands are shaking worse.

I could fix it. Everything in me wants to do it. I want to snatch him up in a hug and tell him I'm still mad, but I've gotten over mad before. I want to see the relief come over him when he agrees—because he *always* agrees when he's screwed up. Theo specializes in hindsight. He would apologize again and hug me so tight it'd be hard to breathe. And then he would tell me that I'm the only one who gets him. And I'd love it.

Because I love him, and in his own twisted way, he loves me back. Then. And now. Maybe always.

"Take care of yourself," I tell him.

Something in me rips in half when I turn away. I do it anyway, because it's the only choice that isn't wrong.

THEO

I'm on hold with Dr. Adams? Atwell? I check the smudged business card freshly pulled from my wallet. No, Atwood. Atwood was right. She's the fifth psychiatrist I've worked with in as many years, and frankly, they all ask the same questions.

How are things going? Have you been taking your medicines as prescribed? What kind of changes do you feel an hour after taking (and here's where you fill in the blank with whatever Focalin-Ritalin-Vyvanse-Adderall cocktail I'm presently on).

The hold music pauses, and an ultra-soothing voice reads a laundry list of doctors and counselors and mental health whoevers who are all uniquely qualified to handle any psychological horror a patient can deliver. She uses nicer words, but I feel like I'm listening to a recording asking me to stay calm and walk in an organized fashion when everything around me is on fire.

I switch ears and adjust myself on Denny's couch. Air conditioner is shot so I'm not only sticking to it; I'm leaving pools of sweat in every pleathery fold. Denny's outside with the worthless box now. Says he's wrenching on it, but I'm pretty sure he's chain-smoking, sucking down beers, and hoping to get a call on some big job in town he put a bid on. It's all he's talked about since the Fourth.

The line cuts in. "DoctorsFurthWilliamsAtwoodand-Sebatter." All of the names run together in a way that's not super soothing.

"Yes, Dr. Seb…Atwood. Dr. Atwood, please?"

"I'm sorry, Dr. Atwood is in session. May I take a message or direct you to her voicemail or is this an issue of an urgent nature?"

"Voicemail's fine," I say, though she and I both know Dr. Atwood is not in a session. She doesn't schedule Friday sessions, but saying she's in session is more of that soothing talk. Translation? Psychiatrists don't take incoming calls. They only return them personally in certain situations. Unless you have a razor poised over a vein, most doctors are confident it can wait until your next appointment.

At the beep, I leave my message. "Hey, it's Theo Quinn. I think I'm having a problem with one of my new meds. I'm experiencing some weird…" What is the doctorly way of saying this?

I'm hearing shit? Smelling things? "…uh, some weird symptoms and side effects."

I'm halfway through leaving my date of birth and callback numbers when Denny's head pops through the window, sweaty, red, and grinning. He thrusts his phone into the air.

"We got it! We got the job!"

I finish my message and hang up. "Got what job? You ready to give me details?"

"Get off that couch," he says, laughing. "Get your ass out here."

He ducks back outside, hitting his head on the window frame. I hear a trail of curse words, and then he's chuckling again. I pull myself off the nasty couch, my clothes clinging. Outside, a breeze is kicking up, flipping the leaves backward on the big hickory near the front porch. The temperature, however, seems determined to hold steady at a miserable ninety-six degrees.

Denny is already shuffling down the steps, adjusting his hat. "I want to get you down there right quick. You've got an eye for this kind of thing."

"What kind of thing?"

"Well, it's sure the hell not pulling wire in July."

I pulled wire through conduit for three straight days at the strip mall—and spent the next four days so sore I could barely move.

"All right, I'm game. Fill me in."

"No, no, you've got to see it. I want to see your face."

He walks me through town, three blocks past antique shops and little patches of grass with historical plaques. We turn on Pearl, and I tense. He can't be taking me to the bridge. Why the hell would he take me there? But he is.

He stops at the lip of the ramp, and the hair on the back of my neck prickles. It's a bridge. Not a ghost or a moral compass or whatever else.

But as soon as I turn away, I hear something whispering, and there aren't any leaves handy to blame.

My hands roll automatically into fists. "Are we sightseeing?"

"Got any guesses?"

"Not a one, so can you spit it out already?"

"We're lighting the bridge for the bicentennial in August."

I hate this thing, a voice whispers.

My shoulders hitch as I look for whoever that voice belongs to. Trees, river, Denny, bridge. There's no one here.

I try to step back again, but Denny stops me. Now there aren't words, but the voices surround me, a hive of bees buzzing everywhere. Up from the water and down from the arches of black metal overhead.

I don't want to go out too far.

I spin in a slow circle, heart slamming at my ribs. My throat.

"Did you hear me?" Denny asks. He grabs my shoulders hard. "Five thousand dollars. To dangle some Christmas lights and put down some fresh boards!"

I force out a laugh and choke on it.

All I can think about is falling.

I stumble back, throat tight. It's Paige—her voice again. That's what I've been hearing, things she said that night. But it's over, so I can't be hearing this.

"What the hell is wrong with you?" Denny asks, sounding pissed.

My grin is late, so I slap his arm, hoping that will cover my missed timing. "No, that's great. Five thousand dollars. So, who's on the job?" Because it can't be me. "Me and Phil, we could finish up the strip mall no problem. Then you and—"

"You'll be here. You're the one who could shimmy up a greased light pole, right?"

I shake my head before I can help it. I can't work out here, no chance.

"You're family, Theo," Denny says, his meaty hand clamping on my shoulder. "Expenses won't run more than six or seven hundred. I want you to keep two thousand. This is an opportunity for you. For your future."

My future. Funniest joke I've heard this week. Maybe I *could* do this, moving from one job to another, building shit. Fixing things. Hell, I don't know. Doesn't seem like the kind of future you plan for, though.

"Say something," he says, definitely annoyed now.

"Wow." It's all I can manage.

I breathe in hard through my nose and the sickly sweet taste of fruit blooms in the back of my mouth. Cherries, but not real ones. Cherries like that air freshener from my car. The car I had before my mom sold it to cover my bail.

Denny is pissed and his mouth is moving fast, but I can't hear what he's saying. It's not his voice humming in my ears, but fragments of that night all over again.

I thought this thing was going to fall.

Get me off this bridge.

"Paige!" That last one isn't in my head. From the look on Denny's face, I said it out loud.

I smear the sweat off my forehead before it drips in my eyes. I'm panting and shaking worse than normal, not just my hands, but a *knock, knock, knock* of my knees that is unlike anything I've ever felt.

"I'm sorry," I say, sounding strangled. "I'm not feeling great."

"Maybe you need to call that doctor of yours," he says, some of his anger having faded.

"I already have. Waiting for a call back. I need to adjust my meds, I think."

"You need less of those damn pills, if you ask me." Denny's brows pull together under the shadow of his cap. "Look, I can't have you like this, Theo. You've got to pull it together here. This is a job. It's important."

"I know." And I do. He's the only family I've got that hasn't written me off. And two thousand dollars—it's a lot of money. A hell of a nice gesture from a guy who's got a blue tarp covering a hole on the back slope of his roof. "Look, I know you don't like my meds, but I need them. They keep me in check."

"Hate to say it, but you don't look like you're in check."

"Give me a little time. A couple of days, and this will all be sorted out."

I say it like it's a guarantee, but in truth, I have no idea. I don't know if what's happening to me can be blamed on a drug, but what else can I say? I think the bridge might be haunted, and we should call an exorcist? Sounds ridiculous.

Too bad it also feels like the truth.

PAIGE

Mom knows me best. We all had lunch at Anita's—me and my parents, Melanie and her mother, and the beloved boyfriend, Joseph. Melanie's parents, who'd driven us, left after lunch, so Melanie suggested walking back across the bridge.

That part tripped my parents up. They stuttered over half sentences, well aware I wouldn't want to discuss our location or my incident in front of Melanie. So we didn't. We walked across without a hitch. If I had something to prove, I proved it. And if I felt like throwing up over the side of the bridge, I thought I hid it well. I was wrong. Mom's lips have gotten thinner by the hour. She knows something is up.

Now we're back in my room. Melanie's off with Joseph, so we're alone. Dad's flipping through my experiment book. I'm trying to direct my mom to my syllabus, but she's not biting. She's watching me.

I automatically start pulling my hair into a ponytail. My mother's eyes drift to my fingernails. Bitten raw. Scabbed. I know what she sees, but I also know I'm too late to hide them.

"Samuel, would you run down to the vending machine to get us something to drink?" My mom smiles, but the look doesn't reach her eyes. "It's hot up here."

Dad doesn't even ask what she wants. I'm not sure if it was a marital pact or what, but a long time ago they established roles in this sort of situation. Mom's job is to talk to me about the *anxiety*. Dad's job is to take me to the appointments. I guess you have to split up the work if you have a kid who's been having panic attacks since third grade.

"You're struggling," she says. "Can you tell me what's happening? Is it your schedule? Being away from home? Are you sleeping?"

I take a breath, deciding. Mom always lays out enough questions to give me options. I've often wondered if she picked that up in a parenting book. *How to trap your anxious wreck of a kid into giving you answers.*

"I'm sleeping," I say.

"You're not sleepwalking again, are you?"

"No, Mom, I'm not." She always stresses about my sleep. My trouble sleeping upset her so much when I was little that she delayed my start in kindergarten a year, hoping I'd grow into more normal patterns. Good thing she gave up on that or I'd still be learning my ABCs.

She takes a step closer, so I know she's not done. I should have come up with a story, maybe the workload. A bad grade to a test would work, but there isn't one to report.

"Did something happen?" she asks. This time there isn't much way around her question.

I shrug. "I ran into Theo."

"When? How?"

"On the bridge. It was nothing. He was polite."

My mom's sharp breath is followed by silence. It's like being back at the beginning again. Right after the party. I'm in our living room, Dad silently holding my hand. Mom sits on my other side, listing all the reasons to stay away from Theo. He's dangerous. Unstable. It's an unhealthy friendship. Probably codependent.

The bad part is that I knew she was right. Being away *would* probably be best.

Mom rests her hands on my shoulders, her eyes dark and soft. The pain unfurls in my middle, an old wound picked open. It's fear. I know that. Fear of not having Theo in my life? Or is it fear that I might let him back in?

"You have choices here, Paige."

"I know."

"You have options."

I nod, but I'm holding my breath. I know where she's going.

"We could take you home," she says. "There's no shame in it."

"No." I pull away from her. My smile might be too quick, but I have to try. "No, I want to stay."

"Paige, it's okay if it's too much. It's okay if you're too afraid."

Sure, *now* it's okay. Anxiety is handy if it'll keep your only daughter close to home.

Is that so they can make sure I stay away from Theo?

I keep my mouth shut and my breathing steady. I know better than to ask her any of that. She wants me home and I want a life on campus, and we're not going to see eye to eye on the subject.

As for the Theo stuff, I don't know what to think. I hate him a little. I love him a lot. I'm feeling plenty of emotions I probably shouldn't be, but I don't want to talk about them. Not with her.

Dad comes back in with two bottles of Dr Pepper, and Mom blurts it out.

"She ran into that boy."

"What? Here on campus?"

"I don't know much, because she hasn't filled me in." She gives me a pointed look. One that says *My patience with your silence will not last much longer.*

"Honey," Dad says. He comes close and hugs me until I feel suffocated.

"I'm fine," I say. "Really. He works here with his uncle every summer."

Mom's gasp is soft. "I can't believe I didn't think of that."

"There wasn't a reason to think of it." I cross my arms. "It doesn't matter. It was a totally chance encounter."

At least I think it was. There's still that awful, nagging question. What if it wasn't chance? What if he was waiting for me?

Dad sighs. Mom watches me, her gaze long and searching.

"I told her she could come home," she says, her eyes never leaving mine.

I cross my arms. "And I told her I can do this."

Dad frowns. "Of course you can. You've come a long way from Girl Scout camp."

Which would feel a whole lot better if he didn't mention that camp at every turn. I was terrified back then. Afraid of the bottom bunk. Afraid to walk through the cave. Afraid to climb the rope ladder. Afraid, afraid, afraid.

From third grade to eleventh, my fear was a war and my parents were generals. Counseling, group therapy, medicine, workbooks, aromatherapy—you name it, they tried it. Then Theo hit me. For the first time, my parents didn't mind that I was terrified.

Ironically, it was the first time I did.

I pull my shoulders back and force myself to make eye contact. "I *am* a long way from Girl Scout camp. I'm not afraid anymore."

"But you're upset," Mom argues.

"What that boy did to you would frighten anyone," my dad says, sitting down.

That's what they call Theo now. *That boy.* He lost his name when I lost my teeth.

"Theo didn't mean to hurt me," I say. "And please don't start, because I'm not trying to defend him. I'm only saying he's no one to be afraid of. Especially now."

Mom crosses her arms. "What do you mean?"

I close my eyes and see him, gaunt and sunburned, lips so chapped they're cracked. His hands shook terribly. "I think he's medicated better."

Better isn't the right word, but it's the one they'll like.

"Well, if you really think—" Dad cuts off midsentence, in the middle of crossing one leg over the other. He plucks at something glittery in the tread of his shoe, tugging it free. When he holds it up, I can see it. Silvery and looped and mangled.

"That's my earring," I say.

Dad frowns. "What earring? It looks like a wadded-up paper clip."

"It's not," I say, sounding breathless. "It's one of the earrings you brought me from Spain."

"It is?"

"Are you sure?" Mom squints, then waves it away. "Oh, I don't have my glasses. How on earth did you wind up with that in your shoe?"

"I must have picked it up on the floor," he says, looking around.

He didn't pick it up on the floor.

Mom and Dad are lightly arguing about the other earring, looking around the dressers, chattering about where the matching one could be. My ears hollow out, a steady ringing muffling my father's next words. And then my mother's reply. Mom checks the small jewelry box on the top of my dresser, and my palms go slick with sweat.

She won't find it there or anywhere else. Those earrings don't exist anymore. The first was lost somewhere at the party—or maybe in the back of the ambulance. I don't know exactly. I had two earrings when I arrived at the party. I had one when I reached the hospital.

While the nurse filled a pink, plastic tub with soapy water, I slid that single earring out of my ear and bent the thin silver in half. And in half again, pinching each delicate loop of metal until it was an ugly, wadded-up thing. A *mangled paper clip* that I swept onto my untouched lunch tray.

That earring can't be here unless it's the one I lost. And that's not possible. Not after all this time. I take a breath that gets stuck halfway in. How? How is it here?

Unless Theo found it. Would he do that? Just leave the earring on my floor? How would he even find my room?

It's ridiculous. He wouldn't.

"Paige, what is it?" Mom asks. "You look pale. Are you all right?"

I don't know what to say. I could tell them he might have returned it. But then they'll be terrified. They might call his parole officer or look into a restraining order again. Some part of me thinks it might be best. Another part thinks of Theo's hollow cheeks and shaky hands.

"Actually, I'm so hungry that I feel sick." I laugh. "Can we go down to the cafeteria before the assembly this afternoon?"

Mom closes the lid on my jewelry box and then touches my jaw. It's the side of my face that was such a mess. A mix of worry and fear feathers over her features. It's a look that tells me that she loves me, and that she still thinks I'm broken.

———

The rest of Family Day is a careful dance, and I know all the right steps. I smile broadly and keep my chin lifted. I talk about the Miriam Sutton Foundation that sponsors both the program and an amazing clean-water program in South America. I show them the taco truck and point out my favorite benches on campus. And

I do not think about that earring shut away in the back of my jewelry box.

In the parking lot, they are quiet. Mom cries a little and I laugh, telling her it's only three more weeks. Reminding her that next year she'll have to say good-bye to me for real.

She doesn't reply, and I square my shoulders. She won't challenge me here with Melanie—Joseph left with a friend before assembly—but at home it will be different. She'll push hard on me staying home for college. I'll have to be strong enough to fight for what I want.

For now, it can hold. I've got other things to do.

Mom and Dad tell Melanie it was nice to meet her. Two more hugs, and they're loaded into the car. I blow Mom a kiss from where I'm standing. My arm snakes around Melanie's waist. Because I want them to see me with a friend. Happy. I want them to drive away seeing nothing but success.

Melanie turns to me the minute their car is out of sight. "So, what gives with the super huggy, touchy stuff?"

"My parents don't want me to go away to college."

"Ah. Want you to live at home, huh?"

"Probably until I'm thirty."

"Huh." She frowns a little. "Well, they seem really nice. Some students love being at home for those first couple of years."

"Well, I'm not one of those students."

"Okay. So, are we headed to the park or what? Keaton has grilled brats."

"I don't think I'd trust Keaton to hand me a can of soda."

She nudges my shoulder, laughing. "Don't be fussy. C'mon, let's go."

My fingers press at my phone. "Go on. I'll meet you in a few minutes."

I watch her walk away, thinking somehow I'll change my mind about what I'm about to do. Because calling Theo is not a good plan. I should let it go, ignore the earring and the weird, maybe-not-accidental bridge meet-up. The only smart choice is radio silence. No contact.

But no matter how many times I say it in my head or run my tongue across the slick white implants that sit where my real teeth used to be, I can't forget the rest of it. Theo making me laugh and helping me breathe through a thousand anxious moments. Reckless as he is, he usually made me feel safe.

He isn't safe anymore. Nobody safe looks that hollowed-out and awful.

My fingers tug out my phone. He doesn't pick up the first time. No surprise. He probably lost his phone in a couch cushion. Or left it in bed. Or dropped it in the river.

I call again, and his voice croaks through on the second ring. "Hello?"

"Hey, it's me."

His next breath shudders against the speaker. An ache blooms in my chest as I picture him, clear as day, face open and hopeful. I can *feel* the way he misses me. It sits heavy in every beat of silence that passes.

"Hi," he finally says.

"Hi." The pause reminds me that this isn't normal for us anymore. We don't call each other at random. I need a reason.

"Um, I need to ask you something," I say.

"'Course."

"Have you been to my dorm?"

A sigh. He sounds tired, disappointed. "I wouldn't do that, Paige."

I feel a push and pull in my chest. Maybe finding the earring was coincidence. It could be. He could be lying to me too.

"I really need to know, okay? Did you come to my room?"

"Paige, I don't know where your room is."

"But you could find out."

There's a rustling noise. He's adjusting the phone. "Why would I do that and *not* talk to you?"

"I don't know," I admit.

"I wouldn't... I'm not—" He cuts off with a sound like a dresser drawer slamming closed. "I'm not here to make you uncomfortable. I'm working."

"I know."

"I'm on *probation*," he says. "I'm not looking to get into trouble."

"I know that too."

"Then why are you asking me this? Why do you think I was in your room?"

I bite my lip, trying to think about who else could have possibly found that earring. Trying to calculate the odds of another earring like it winding up stuck to my dad's shoe.

"I found something in my room. Something I lost at the party."

"Something you lost at the party." There's something about the way he says it that makes me grip the phone a little tighter. "Paige, about that night—"

"No." I exhale. "Theo, please don't. I don't want to talk about what happened. I …"

"I wouldn't do that to you. I'm not… I know what I did, but I didn't mean—" He cuts himself off with a sharp breath. "I'm not making sense. Look, I know what happened, and I don't think it's okay, but I would never intentionally hurt you."

"I know," I say, because suddenly I do. He wouldn't leave something like that, leave a possibly traumatizing piece of jewelry for me to bump into. Theo is a lot of things, and some of those things aren't great. He's not that guy, though.

But I can still see the metal gleam of that earring in my dad's fingers.

"It's weird," I say. "I know it's from the party. I'm sure it's mine."

"Have you seen anything else from that night?"

My eyes narrow on a corner of the science building where Noah and Keaton's partner are talking. "What do you mean?"

"I've…heard some stuff," he says. "On the bridge. From that night."

"What kind of things?" Worry prickles up the backs of my arms. "Are people talking about what happened?"

"No, no. It's not like that." He sighs. "Hell, I don't know what it's like."

"Then spit it out."

"It'll sound crazy, but I've literally heard conversations from the party. Almost like a recording. That song you played in the car, the one about changing."

"That song played every thirty minutes most of last year," I say.

"It's more than that. I've heard conversations. Your voice. My voice. It's confusing as hell. And the lock. Did you put a lock on the bridge, Paige?"

My jaw clenches. "You're not making sense, Theo."

"I know, I know. There's a lock on the bridge with our initials, Paige. TQ and PVY. That's us, right? I mean, who else could it be?"

He's talking faster. Working himself up. Nothing's ever different with Theo. And it has to be different. At least with me.

"You know, I probably shouldn't have called. I have to go."

"Wait. Listen, I think something might be wrong with me. Or wrong with—"

"Take care of yourself."

I hang up the phone and press the heel of my palm against my forehead. Theo's right about something being wrong with him. Something's wrong with both of us, and I don't know if we're the kind of broken that can be fixed.

THEO

There aren't many stimulant meds I haven't tried. Daytrana gave me tics. No appetite on Focalin. Evekeo and Adderall wear off too fast, and I didn't sleep for four straight days on my stint with Concerta. Antidepressants are the same. Paige and I once made up a song of all the different medicinal cocktails I've tested. It had three verses.

I've learned to dread med changes, but today I swallow an extra pill—white and small, a little added anxiety control that Dr. Atwood feels will take care of these auditory hallucinations— without hesitation. Whatever this is, it can't keep happening. I can't work on a bridge five days a week while hearing my ex–best friend's voice. Reliving the shittiest night of my life.

"So, that's the change?" Denny asks, his eyebrows lost under the rim of his cap.

"That's it."

"Seems like a little pill."

"I've taken pills half this size that have laid me out for a day."

"Must be the kind people pop." He cocks his head. "I'll stick to liquor. I lost six jobs in six months once. Can you imagine what I'd be like on a bunch of pills? Dangerous for people like us, Theo."

I clamp my mouth shut, because I can already feel my lips telling him that losing six jobs in as many months is a good indicator that some medicinal assistance might be a fine idea. But Denny doesn't want to hear that. He rolls around in his ADHD like a dog in shit. He loses jobs and forgets to pay bills and ends up in a bar fight at least twice a year, but I think he figures it's part of his charm. In his mind, maybe it's part of my charm too.

"We headed out?" I ask.

"We need to pull down the old lights. They haven't lit it since the last anniversary. Wires and shit are hanging all over that bridge. You got a harness?"

"Like a work harness? For climbing?"

Denny huffs around his cigarette, his face red. "Hell, boy, you think I can let you climb around that monster with nothing? Gotta be responsible."

"Sure."

He thumps my shoulder. "C'mon. We'll run by Reggie's and borrow his harness."

"Reggie? He's twice my size."

"Don't get your panties in a knot. It's adjustable."

"*How* adjustable?"

I follow Denny's laughter outside and climb into a Ranger with a cracked windshield and mismatched tires. It's got a broken strut, so the whole frame slopes down toward the driver's side. I spend most of every drive trying not to slide into Denny's lap. Which is good. It'll keep me from thinking about all that could go wrong today.

The twenty minutes to pick up the harness and then coffee from the Circle K pass a lot faster than I'd like. The sky is thick with a gray mess of clouds when we get to the bridge, and I sit in the truck as long as possible before dragging myself outside.

I don't trust any new pill to kick in that fast, especially when I don't feel any different. After Paige's call—after her finding something—I'm less convinced a pill can fix my life.

My boots crunch-hiss on the ramp leading up to the bridge. Fifty feet to the water, according to Paige, but I don't care. I've never worried much about falling when I'm up high. Now, though? Every time I'm on this bridge I wind up on some sort of acid-worthy freak-out, so I'm not exactly thrilled to be climbing around up there today.

But what am I going to do? My parents are probably counting the days until they can boot me out legally. I need some way to make a living.

I look up at the metal arching overhead and take a sharp breath. The bridge seems quiet today. No music or faint smells of cherry air freshener or lilacs. I shrug and move a little closer, trying to focus on the struts. Stringing up Christmas lights won't be that bad. Probably be easier if we planned it out, but Denny and I aren't known for our preparation skills.

Denny joins me and hands over Reggie's harness. "Looks like some sort of weird sex contraption, don't it?" he asks.

"How do we anchor it?"

"What's that?"

"I mean, if we don't anchor it to something, the harness is basically worthless, right?"

Denny swears and adjusts his cap. "Maybe I'd better get Reggie down here to take a look. Have to pay him."

Which means sitting around waiting for him to get here. "Screw it. We'll figure it out later. Kids climb this damn thing all the time." I point at some of the larger bolts joining the beams together. "You think we can just loop the strands of lights over those? If I wrap them twice, it might look like buttons in between the strands of light. And we'd know the spacing will look right."

He cranes his head back, squinting. "You think? How will you keep them on?"

"Wire clamps? In the back. They're cheap, right?"

Denny's smile is a flash of teeth under his hat. "Told you this was right up your alley."

"Let me check them out." I touch the dark metal, finding a good grip. We're going to have to work early because it's not quite nine and the metal's already getting hot in the sun. Still, it's got the right slope for easy climbing and plenty of toeholds thanks to all the seams and bolts. Above me, a gull squawks and takes flight, raining a couple of white feathers down from its nest.

I'm going to eat a lot of bird shit up here.

But the view is unbelievable.

I find a good spot halfway up, where some old light strands are broken off and dangling. I yank one free and drop it, spotting an old twist tie on one of the wires.

"They used twist ties before," I say.

"That won't cost us nothing! Can you do it?"

I test the bolts with my fingers and then the ridges. I think it could work. I could follow the last guy's design, looping the lights and clamping them. The twist ties won't be easy, but cheap is good, and if I can make Denny happy—

Theo.

Denny's voice sounds strange under the wind. Soft and close, like he's climbed up behind me. I turn to look, but he's still on the ground, harness in one hand and cell phone to his ear. Chills roll up my back.

That wasn't Denny.

A mourning dove coos softly, shifting along the steel beam overhead. It's nothing. My damn imagination is running wild because of everything that went down up here.

Theo, I'm fine.

My heart double thuds, and goose bumps rise in angry rows on my arms. Another dove lands—*right* next to me. She cocks her head, watches me with a tiny, beady eye. The scent of lilacs curls through the air. Lemons.

Why won't you stop?

The wind pushes up from below, and I move my foot one toehold lower. My knees go rubbery, so I grip tight and breathe. *I got up here. I can get back down.*

I think.

The voices whisper-buzz around me. Snippets of Paige laughing. Screaming. My sobs.

My hands shake, and my head spins. One steadying breath. *I can do this.* I glance down to find my next spot and see a boat gliding under the bridge. It looks like a toy from up here, plastic and surreal.

If I fall, I'll look like a toy down there too. A broken one.

The fear of it gets me moving. I use the adrenaline, hauling myself down fast. One foot, one hand. Over and over I go, stomach cramped and heart flying.

A gull swoops ahead, white wings dancing at the corner of my vision. Whispers I don't want to hear lurking behind each wingbeat. I don't look; I just move.

The toe of my sneaker slips.

My lungs bottom out. I grip harder, my left foot scraping at the rough metal. I find a lip of metal with the side of my shoe. *I've got it. I'm fine.*

I can't say it out loud, because I don't have enough air in my lungs. Something's taking it from me, something that's staining the breeze with rotting lilacs and dredging up voices that should be long gone.

Maybe you should go.

It's Chase this time, but still from that damn party—and what the hell is this? Why is this night playing over and over in my head? Is this happening to Paige? Is that why she found whatever she found in her dorm?

"You all right?" Denny is caught somewhere between a laugh and real worry.

I take a slow breath through my nose and nod. "Yeah. Yeah, I'm good."

"Get on down here then. We're going to pick up Reggie. See how this works so we can get you up there tomorrow for real."

I find the rest of the way down without trouble, but the whispers don't stop. I can hear them in the distance, echoes of the worst night of my life. This doesn't have a damn thing to do with medication. This is something else.

I roll my shoulders and follow Denny to the edge of the stairs. "Hey, what do you know about this bridge?"

"You mean all the legends?"

"It's a little creepy, yeah?"

Denny snorts. "If by creepy you mean haunted as shit."

"Wait a minute, you don't really believe that crap."

"You can look it up. They do a piece in the paper every Halloween."

"So, were there really a bunch of suicides up here?"

"Not a bunch," he says, then his brow furrows. "Are we going to chitchat all day or get this harness situated?"

I stop, looking back across the bridge to the brick towers and green lawns of the college. I can just make out the white stripes of clean sidewalks between the buildings. I have to talk to Paige.

"Hey, do you need me at Reggie's?" I ask. "I was going to run and check on a friend."

"Good." Denny doesn't even stop walking. "You're like a bad rash anymore, always turning up and driving me crazy."

Yeah, I am. And this time, I'm going to turn up exactly where I'm wanted least.

PAIGE

I wake up to pain. It's a pulsing deep in my jaw, keeping time with my heart. Every beat electrifies my gums and teeth with a white-hot burst of agony.

I sit up, tenderly testing my skin with the pads of my fingers. Not swollen. But I haven't hurt like this since the surgery. Maybe since the party.

"You didn't sleep well."

I blink to clear my vision. The room is still dim, but Melanie is on her bed across the room. She is very still, hands on her knees and hair neatly brushed.

"What time is it?" I ask, my voice rasping with sleep.

"Almost nine. I tried to wake you." Her voice sounds tinny and strange.

"My alarm didn't ring?"

"It did," she says. "For twenty minutes. I finally shut it off. Are you sick?"

She's still not moving. I wonder why she's chewing the corner of her lip like that. Her eyes flick once to the three orange prescription bottles on my dresser. My stomach flips over, landing in a knot. It's me. She's biting her lip about something I did.

"What is it? What's wrong?" I ask.

"I'm...*worried* about you."

The word isn't one she uses. Neither is the feeling. Melanie doesn't worry—she's cool and collected. But I know who *does* worry, and that someone met Melanie very recently. Maybe I'm imagining things, but the way she's looking at me reminds me of my mom. It turns the knot in my stomach hard and small.

"I know you've got a lot on your plate," she says.

I'm not imagining anything. That one's straight from my mom's phrase book.

"Did my parents talk to you?" I ask her.

She shrugs a shoulder, obviously feeling guilty. "It wasn't like that. They said they were concerned because you've had a hard year. They asked me if you seemed anxious and if you'd been having panic attacks. Have you?"

I throw back my covers, heat rushing up my face. I can't believe them. I can't *believe* they'd do this. "No, I haven't."

Melanie shoots another glance at the bottles. "I thought you said you had a *little* anxiety."

"I do," I say, rubbing my jaw. The pain is intense. Thrumming. "Along with millions of other Americans. Did my mom ask you to talk to me?"

"No, I swear. You were talking in your sleep last night. Talking about it hurting and so much blood. You even sat up like you were going somewhere. It scared me."

My rage-heated face frosts over in an instant. I was talking in my sleep about pain and blood. That's why she's looking at me like this.

Because she doesn't know what happened with Theo.

"I had an accident," I say. It's a lie, but it's close enough.

"An accident?"

"This past spring. My jaw was broken. I lost two teeth. Sometimes I remember it." I shrug as if that gesture and all of my very passive words will make it less of a deal.

Her shoulders relax. "So, you still don't have the teeth?"

I nudge my chin against my chest, touch my jaw, then pull my fingers away. Pain is shooting up to my temple. Getting sharper. That can't be normal after all this time.

I stand, needing ice or ibuprofen, or simply to move. Melanie is still looking at me. Which is when I realize I hadn't answered her. "They fixed my teeth. I'm okay, but I have bad dreams sometimes."

"But your parents—"

"My parents are overprotective. I'm an only child."

"Okay." Her posture loosens further, and she tries on her standard goofy smile. It looks like it doesn't quite fit. "Won't be many breakfast options if we don't get down there soon."

"You go ahead. I'm going to clean up. Will you grab me a banana?"

"Of course."

In the bathroom, I hope getting dressed and washing my face will help the pain. It doesn't. My eyes are tearing by the time I squeeze a mint-green stripe onto my toothbrush. I brush my teeth quickly, figuring I'll take a few ibuprofens when I get back to my room. I just need to get out of this dorm and I'll be okay. The pain is no worse brushing, so I get on with it and spit. And pull back with a cry.

It's blood.

Some toothpaste but more blood. I spit again, red streaking the sink. It's on my toothbrush too, not a touch of pink from a place I didn't floss—this is vibrant red.

Like I've been hit again.

My heart feels wrong. All the beats land a half a second off where they should. I rinse my mouth, but the blood won't stop. The faucet hisses out a steady stream of water, and I spit over and over, reach into my mouth feeling my teeth, my tongue. I can't find a wound. I can't find anything.

Blood is dripping off my chin, off my fingers. What is happening to me? What is this?

My head goes lighter, vision graying at the edges. I grip the cold lip of the sink.

The bathroom door bangs open, and I plunge my hands under the rushing water, catching my reflection in the mirror. I feel a strange, urgent need not to let anyone see. To hide. I splash water onto my face and rinse my mouth, but suddenly the basin is white and clean.

When I spit, it's clear. I don't even think; I turn and smile, hands shaking so hard they rattle at my thighs.

"Hi!" I say before I can even fully see who it is.

"Hey," Melanie says, that same not-quite-comfortable grin on her face. "No bananas left. Nothing but gruel and this muffin."

"Oh, no big deal. I'll eat a big lunch." I wipe at my chin, checking my fingers over and over. They're perfectly clean. "Let me finish up here."

I turn back to the sink and rinse my toothbrush, which isn't even pink. I rinse it again, but there's no trace of what just happened. No blood.

Maybe I already rinsed it. Maybe I cleaned everything up.

Or maybe you're going crazy.

I push my toothbrush and paste into my bag and zip it shut

with shaking fingers. There's no pain now. Nothing. What the hell is happening to me?

"Are you sure you don't want half of this muffin?" Melanie asks.

"No, I'll be fine."

"Then let's get moving," she says. "We're running late already."

I spot it as she's walking out, a tiny speck of red on the back side of the sink. My thumb smears it across the smooth white porcelain. Blood. I didn't imagine it. I'm not crazy. I'm—

But if I didn't imagine the blood, then why did it happen like that? Out of nowhere? And what made it stop?

We drop my toiletries in our room and jog down the three flights of stairs. We should still make it to class by quarter till ten, but we need to hustle. Late isn't in my DNA.

Outside, it's muggy and gray. Thank God we collected our samples already. The river will be stinky, hot, and miserable today. The overly enthusiastic air conditioners in the lab will probably chill us to the bone, but it will be better than sweating.

"Okay, so evaluating the first set of results and then the library for records?" she asks.

"That's the plan. We should probably start on the presentation structure."

"Ugh, I hate that medium. We need something more than statistics and slides if we're going to stand out. What about a video?"

"For water research?" I wrinkle my nose. "Seems a little tedious for video."

"Which means it will be twice as tedious if we don't find a way to make it interesting. I can find some videos of the river, the treatment plant…maybe some of the old factories. We can do voice-over with some of the historical information and statistics. Think of it… It will look like a news segment *and* a science project."

I pause, resisting a cringe. I don't know anything about video work. That kind of technology has never been my strong suit. But how do I say that to a girl who speaks three languages and has earned awards in a variety of academic clubs back in Chicago?

Melanie touches my arm, giving me a smile that I'm sure is meant to make me feel better. "I can totally take on this portion! I've got a great multimedia team on my school website. We do stuff like this all the time."

"I guess I can focus on the labs and statistics then."

"See?" She links her arm with mine, her slim gold bracelet cool against my wrist. "We're a perfect team."

We are a good team. Melanie is the star of the show, and I'm usually more than happy to stay behind the scenes. And we're friends—or something like it, at least. Sometimes when I'm around her, I think I could be as successful as she is.

Melanie sighs. "I was hoping for better cutting-edge lab

equipment. Maybe I should have gone with the urban sustainability program at Duke."

Then, there are times like this. When it's crystal clear that Melanie and I come from very different worlds and have very different futures.

"I'll start on the chemical tests today," I say, eager to bring the topic back to what we have in common.

"I doubt we'll find much on a chemical level. They'd already find most of that at the water plant where the water is filtered. Anything alarming would probably have made news."

That catches my attention. "Water company executives would be the most likely people to hide that kind of information. Look at what happened in Flint, Michigan."

"True..."

Her voice trails off, and I think it's because she's working out a response, but her gaze moves right past me, and the vague appreciation in her eyes tells me that someone is behind me. And the someone is both male and attractive.

"Paige?"

I turn as I hear his voice, my fingers uncurling from the fists I hadn't known I'd been holding. He's cleaned up from the last time I saw him, freshly showered and sporting a new scrape down one of his shins. It should feel terrible and scary seeing him here.

Mostly, it feels like coming home.

THEO

Six years. That's what I'm thinking while we stand here on the sidewalk—me, Paige, and the girl I don't know. I'm not introducing myself because I'm still caught up in the fact that I was joined at the hip with Paige for six freaking years, and I somehow never noticed how perfect her face is, freckles and pointy chin and soft lips and—

I punched that face. I aimed at an asshole and somehow hit the only person on the planet I really give a damn about. What the hell is wrong with me?

"What are you doing here?" Paige asks. Probably because I'm not saying anything. I'm standing here, hands in my pockets, staring like an idiot. Her friend—cute girl with an expensive-looking smile—nudges her shoulder, singsonging her name.

"Oh, sorry," Paige says, gesturing at me. "Melanie, this is Theo. Theo, this is Melanie."

"Hey, nice to meet you," I say, and then, because we're all standing around awkward as can be... "I'm sorry. Do you have a second?"

"I'm on my way to the lab," Paige says.

"Ah, I had something I wanted to ask you about."

"You couldn't have called?" she asks.

She probably wouldn't have answered, and I give her a look that says as much. Her face washes pink under her freckles. Melanie waves her hands at us.

"Don't worry. I can get our experiment started. I'll tell Dr. Lutmer you ran back for notes. We'll meet up after?"

"I'll only be a minute."

When we're alone, Paige's guard slams up, her arms crossing over her chest. "You probably shouldn't be here."

"I know. I know. And I'm sorry. I should've called, but I didn't think you'd answer."

"I probably wouldn't have," she admits. She looks tired.

"Are you sleeping all right?"

She laughs harshly. "Why is everyone obsessed with my sleeping?" Then she sighs. "Sorry. Things are... My mom found out I ran into you."

"I bet that went super well."

She smirks. "Definitely not super well. And if Melanie gets chatty about meeting you, it could get a lot worse."

I cringe. "Melanie knows about me?"

She shakes her head. "No. Mom wouldn't—she tries not to talk about it. Because she still thinks I'm a mess. She wants me to go home. To *recover*."

She doesn't have to use air quotes, because we both already know her mom's deal. Nice enough lady, but cut the apron strings already. I cock my head. "How the hell is she going to handle it when you get in at NYU or something?"

Paige laughs. "At some point, are you going to loop back to your original question?"

My whole chest goes warm. She used to say that to me, whenever I'd be prattling on and on, totally forgetting whatever I was getting to in the first place. Squirreling around is what she called it.

She fights back the smile, but I can still see it in her eyes. And I see more than that. I see the shadow of how she looked at me when I didn't bother to notice, or care. But I care now—now that it's too late to matter.

"You shouldn't be here," she whispers, and I can't help but step closer.

"I know."

I'm itching to touch her. Reaching. I shove my hands into my pockets. Because I can't. The last time my hands were on her, I ruined everything.

"Why did you come?" she asks.

I shake myself. "You mentioned finding something from the party. Was it on the bridge?"

"The walking bridge?"

I nod and lick my lips. "I think something weird is going on. On the bridge. Remember how I told you about that lock with our initials?"

She tenses, and I get it. It's certifiably nuts. But screw it.

"The lock is weird, right? I mean, it shouldn't be there, and—" I stop because I can't tell her the lock with our initials is some kind of lucky magic charm that makes the weird voices go quiet. I mean, all of this is crazy, and that makes me sound like a creeper.

I glance around, making sure no one's close. "Thing is, Paige, I think something's wrong with that bridge. Something supernatural. I know you don't believe in stuff like that, but ever since that night...I've heard voices. Even smelled things. All from the party."

"You've smelled things."

"Yes. I know it sounds crazy."

She exhales, and I can tell she doesn't know what to make of this. Hell, *I* don't know what to make of it, so I wait her out.

"Theo, what I found was nowhere near the bridge. My dad found it on his shoe in my dorm room."

Huh. Didn't see that coming. I palm the back of my neck. "Did he walk on the bridge?"

She looks down. "I really need to go."

"Okay, I just wanted to check. It's weird and…" I don't want to use the word *scary*, but it's the only one that fits. So I shift gears. "I'm working on the bridge for Denny. Christmas light duty, if you can believe that."

"What about the strip mall?"

"Denny assigned the other guys to finish it up. He won a bid to hang lights and do some walkway improvements before the bicentennial. You always said the bridge needed work, right?"

She grimaces. "You're climbing around that thing?"

"Well, with a safety harness," I say, which is actually a lie at this point, but intentions and all. "I'll be good."

She glances over her shoulder, at the direction Melanie headed, but she looks reluctant. Like maybe she doesn't want to leave. Or maybe I'm desperate for her company and deluding myself. Probably that.

"I'll let you go," I force myself to say. "I guess I wanted you to know about the bridge. I thought maybe whatever you found—"

"An earring," she says. "I found an earring I lost at the party."

I feel sick so fast it makes my stomach cramp. I can see her clear as day on that plastic chair, one silvery earring tangled in her hair. The other gone, because of me.

"I'm sorry I came," I say, my voice breaking. "I should have called."

"It's okay. I should get to the lab."

"Yeah, of course." I turn to leave and hear her feet scuff on the sidewalk.

"Theo?"

"Yeah?"

Her face is all screwed up like she's chewing on whatever she wants to say. Trying to hold in the words maybe, but she finally blurts out a sigh. "Eat something, will you? You're too thin. Whatever meds you're on…"

I laugh like an idiot. I can't help it. I don't even *want* to help it. I want to stand here forever watching her worry about me.

⸻

Three hard knocks on the bedroom wall wake me up. I flop off the half-deflated air mattress and hit the wooden floor. There's a slant of light in an open doorway, and Denny's long, dark shadow spills across it.

"Gonna hit eighty-nine today," he says.

I scrub a hand over my face. "And I need to know this right now?"

"If you want to get in any work before the metal on the bridge turns into a skillet you do."

I sigh up at the dark ceiling. I don't give a crap about the bridge. It's oh-dark-thirty, and the mattress is still inflated enough that my hip bone wasn't jabbing into the floor yet. Plus, I was actually sleeping, which is pretty unusual at this point.

His toe nudges my shoulder, none too gently. "Get your ass out of bed, Sleeping Beauty."

"I'm up."

I'm not actually up for ten more minutes, but that's all spite. It wouldn't matter if I stayed here all day; I'm not going back to sleep.

By ten till five I'm sitting in the passenger seat of Denny's truck, looking baleful, I'm sure. I hook one hand through the armrest so I don't slide into him and pop a handful of pills into my mouth with the other. I swallow them with a drink of coffee so hot it scalds my throat all the way down. That's when I really start to wake up. That's also when it hits me that I don't want to be on this bridge in the dark.

I squirm on the seat and stare out the passenger window as Denny smokes his morning cigarette and steers us past dark houses and shops that look like skeletal remains in the strange light before dawn. He takes the same road I took with Paige, and I squeeze my eyes shut until he parks against the curb.

"Denny, you know the bridge crap? Have you ever felt anything creepy up there?"

"What, like a ghost?" He turns to me, the vinyl seat croaking in protest. "Did you take one of those damn tours? I don't need you to start spooking over every scary story."

I wrench the door handle open, shaking my head. "Forget it, man."

"Theo," he says gruffly, and then he takes a long drag off his cigarette without looking at me. Makes me wonder if I imagined him saying it. "People only see strange things when they are looking for trouble. So don't look for it."

I turn back, and Denny's face is a dark smear under a green hat. My mind fills in strange features, eyes that aren't right, a mouth of sharpened teeth. The hair on the back of my neck stands up, and I shake my head. I'm being stupid. A kid seeing monsters in the closet.

Denny loosens his grip on the steering wheel, and the spell is broken.

"But people *do* see strange stuff. What do you think is behind it? You think it's a ghost?" I ask.

"I don't know about ghosts. I think it's something to do with all those damn locks. Forever love bullshit." He scoffs. "I know half a dozen guys who've got a lock on that bridge, and we're all single. Half the guys I know think those locks are a curse. Probably crazy, but if you put too much stock in those kind of superstitions, it can mess with you. Still, we're going to piss off a lot of people who think otherwise."

"Why's that?"

"We're cutting off the locks. The ones on the rails at least."

He gets out of the truck and I follow suit, closing my door with my shoulder. We're cutting the locks off. Maybe it's not the worst idea. If the superstition in those locks is causing all the haunting problems, getting rid of them might be a solution.

Except that the lock with my initials has been useful. If anything, it holds the worst of this bad stuff down.

At the top of the ramp, Denny is at a dead stop.

I dodge left, barely missing a collision with his back. "What is it?"

"You tell me." He turns to me, the red cherry of his cigarette glowing. "Because I'm pretty sure she isn't out here to visit me."

He nods at the bridge. I see her immediately, dressed in a ratty T-shirt and shorts—sleeping clothes. She's not moving.

Chills climb up my sides, rib by rib.

She shouldn't be here dressed like this, standing so still. Wouldn't be here at all in any normal situation. I can't even think of an *abnormal* situation that would find Paige standing on the bridge at five-thirty in the morning, but whatever it is, it can't be good.

PAIGE

Everything is soft and blurry when Theo touches my shoulder. I don't know exactly where we are or what we're doing, but it's all right. I can't make out what he's saying though. He's speaking so softly. Like maybe I'm upset. Am I?

I wake up like I've been doused with cold water, gasping. My eyes water in the sudden, glaring details of consciousness. My surroundings come into focus. I'm cold. I'm outside. Someone's touching me.

Theo.

He's here, hands on my shoulders. The smell of fish and rot. I close my mouth and taste blood.

And then I scream.

"Paige," he says softly.

It quiets me, my scream gurgling into nothing. No more blood on my tongue, but I can smell it, sharp and coppery.

My hip bumps the rail, and I look down, down, down. Shiny tar-colored water gushes fifty feet below. I can't breathe. Can't. Breathe.

Theo's fingers brush my elbow. "How about one slow breath. Just one. Nice and slow."

He says it like always. It's been months since he's pulled me out of a panic attack. It feels like no time at all. Because he still knows how. I close my eyes.

"One slow one," he says again so softly. "Nice and easy."

His fingers are rough and warm. It grounds me to this strange world where I am outside and barefoot and with Theo. Nothing here makes sense, except the part where I'm with him and he's calming me. He's been my safety net many times.

"One more breath maybe?" His voice is an anchor. I shouldn't cling, but I do, edging closer to him. Closer to his warmth.

"You're okay, Paige," he says. His words break a dam I've spent four months creating to hold us apart.

I nudge my shoulder against his, and my emotions spill over. I feel his forehead drop to the crown of my head. Another shaky breath. His or mine, I don't know. But I feel so much better.

His hands shake on my arms, but I soak in the touch. I've craved this. His jittering and twitching and talking and...*him*. I missed him. He is Theo and I am Paige and this is us. And it wasn't always bad.

I scoot a baby step closer. My bare feet scrape against the rough wood, and my stomach shrinks. Reality rolls me under again.

I'm barefoot on the bridge in the middle of the night. *How am I here?*

"I don't know," Theo says, so I must have asked it out loud.

"I was in bed. I wasn't here," I say. And then, "How did you find me?"

"Working here, remember? Have you been sleepwalking again?" He says it right into my hair, our shoulders angled together like two walls meeting in the corner of a room.

I want to say no, but I start crying instead. It's humiliating, because I know he must be right. Sleepwalking is a stress symptom for me. Since I was little. If my mother knew, if she had any idea, she'd rip me out of this summer program so quickly. But I'm doing better. I'm better now.

I don't want to go back to being that terrified girl anymore.

I push away from Theo, and he looks as gaunt as I remember from earlier. His hand is still hovering midair, where I'd pulled out of his embrace. I feel even colder now. More frightened.

"I wouldn't have walked this far," I say randomly, only I don't know if it's true. My father found me in the backseat of the car once when I was nine years old. Three in the morning, and they woke up when they heard the front door open and close. Found me sitting there, staring dead ahead. I don't remember, but I remember them talking about it in therapy.

"You sure?" Theo asks.

I'm not, so I don't answer. I cross my arms over my chest, shivering. Theo tugs off his sweatshirt and hands it over. I feel like I should argue, but I don't. I pull it on and breathe in the smell of bacon grease and construction and old cigarettes. Denny's house.

"Come on," he says. "I'll walk you back."

There's a second where I hesitate. There's no logical reason for me to need an escort. It's sleepwalking. I've done this before. Not this far and never over a bridge, but it's nothing I shouldn't be able to handle. When I'm on campus alone, I'll have to handle it, right?

Theo slides his work boot across a warped plank and gently nudges the side of my foot. I nod and we fall into step. It's almost like nothing ever changed.

"I know this is wacko," I finally say when we've made it to the other side of the bridge.

"You wandering the Portsville streets at five in the morning? Pretty average Thursday, if you ask me."

I laugh, but catch myself. "You don't have to do this. I don't want things between us to be weird."

"I'm not sure how things could be any weirder than they already are."

We hit the campus lawn and shuffle toward the bleached sidewalk. Theo's dirty boots look strange against the pristine grass. He looks right at me, but I don't feel watched.

It makes me think of Melanie. Sitting across from me with wide, worried eyes after the dream. "You might be right about the sleepwalking. Melanie said I was talking in my sleep."

"You said they go hand in hand, right?" Off my nod, he plunges his hands in his pockets. "Are you on anything? New sleeping pills can aggravate that kind of thing. Mine have warning labels."

I've already considered that, but it's nice to have someone else say it out loud. Med talk isn't something you bring up in the cafeteria. "I don't know. I've been on it a while."

We're close to the center of the lawn, where I'll take a walkway to my building, when Theo stops. "Look, I don't want to beat a dead horse or sound like a crazy person."

"You always sound like a crazy person," I say with a smile.

"Well, in that case I won't worry."

My throat tightens at the familiarity of it all. It's hard to hold on to the reasons we can't be *us* when he's *right* here, grinning and bouncing on the soles of his feet.

"Okay, I'm lying," he says. "I *am* worried. I know it sounded weird, but I really have been hearing voices from the party. It's like the party is haunting the bridge."

I scoff. "Haunting?"

"Yes." He doesn't brush it off or acknowledge that I don't believe in ghosts or boogeymen or things that go bump in the night. He's serious, and he's afraid.

Cold air dances up my spine. "How much bad TV have you been watching?"

The attempt at a joke falls flat.

"You remember when we walked over the bridge before the party, that noise we heard?"

"I remember," I say, thinking of that terrible metal groaning. My certainty we would fall. I guess we did fall that night. Just not in the way I expected.

"I didn't think about it—figured it was settling like an old house does, you know?" He shakes his head. "Now, I don't know. I've been drawn to that stupid bridge. Hell, I'm even working there. What if we woke something up that night? Something bad."

Goose bumps shrink the flesh on my arms, but I force a smirk. "Like what? A ghost?"

"I know. You think I'm crazy for even thinking it."

"No," I say, because I'm not thinking that at all. I'm thinking about spitting blood in the bathroom sink and waking up on the bridge.

"I'm not saying it's a ghost," he says. "I don't know what it is, but I think it has something to do with that night. And with me hurting you."

Old me would break eye contact, but I don't want to do that this time. New me is brave. And maybe this conversation is way overdue.

"Look, I know you didn't mean to hurt me," I say. "I know that you were…jealous."

"I was." He swallows hard, takes a moment. "You know for years I thought you were into me."

"I was."

It's the first time that's been said aloud. All those secret feelings I hid are out in the open, and it's not awkward or uncomfortable. It just is.

He finally shakes his head. "It doesn't matter. None of that matters. Me being sorry or not meaning it will never change what I did to you. Hell, maybe that's what this stuff on the bridge is. My sins come back to haunt me."

My throat feels thick and tight. "Theo…"

"You don't have to say anything."

Except I do. I close my eyes and steady myself with a breath. "It's not only happening to you. The earring my dad found… We *did* walk across the bridge earlier that day. I found a bag of pretzels under the bridge too. You got me pretzels that night."

"I remember."

"Anyway, I figured it was coincidence, but then I showed up there today. And there was also a weird problem with my jaw."

119

"Your jaw?"

"The other morning I had all this pain, even bleeding. It wasn't normal. It's healed now, and this was out of nowhere."

He scrubs a hand into his hair, hard enough to leave scratches. "I'm still hurting you. I'm still freaking making you bleed."

He hauls back and kicks the curb. Another kick.

"Stop!" I grab his sleeve. "What are you talking about? You weren't even there."

"But all of this leads back to me. That night, I was so wrapped up in—you know what I was wrapped up in. And I lost it, and now we're haunted because of it."

"You're haunting yourself with weird music and voices and making me bleed from the other side of the river? Come on, Theo. Why would *you* have anything to do with that? How?"

He doesn't have any answers, and neither do I. The silence stretches between us, the pink sky a reminder that I've got a life here waiting. I've got to go inside and get ready for class. I may need to convince my roommate I'm not doing a walk of shame. Or losing my mind.

"You should go in, right?" He takes a step back and nods. "Look, I don't want to make this worse. I just want you to know I'm sorry. And I'm going to fix this. I'm going to find a way."

He takes half a step back, ready to go. I don't want him to leave.

My parents would tell me it's a good thing. They'd remind me that our relationship isn't healthy, and we should never have talked at all. Maybe not, but I'm glad he's with me.

Theo is already walking away when I feel the last bit of my resistance crumble.

"Theo?" He looks surprised when he turns. "Text me if you find something?"

The hope on his face is palpable. I smile, because even after everything, that look still gets to me. *He* still gets to me. And I don't feel weak when I smile at him. I feel brave.

Brave enough to change my mind on the friends thing?

"I'm not going to read anything into this," he says, but he's grinning. It's infectious.

"Yeah, you are."

"Yeah, I am."

He walks away with shoulders higher than I've seen them in forever. I tell myself that it doesn't matter. We still aren't friends. We couldn't possibly be friends. Not after everything.

I tell myself a lot of things. I'm not sure who I'm trying to fool.

THEO

The thing about construction? There's always a thing. After dropping off Paige, Denny and I spent our day measuring and arguing and placing signs that indicated intermittent bridge closures due to walkway repairs. Then we drove up to a wholesaler to pick up the lights. Denny didn't say a word about running into Paige, but then he didn't say much at all.

I didn't bring it up either, because I didn't want to go there. Denny would tell me again that he's pissed with her parents for pressing charges. He's my uncle, and I get it. But he's wrong too.

Her parents probably saw this coming a long time ago. Paige and I were two peas in a pod for years, and if I'd figured out how she felt about me, they probably had too. They were smart to warn her. And who could blame them for losing it after what I did? I wouldn't have been top pick on any parent's list, especially not after that.

But if there's a chance for Paige and me now? What then? Her parents aren't wrong about her deserving better. But am I a good enough person to let that stop me? Doubt it.

Dawn hasn't broken when we find our way to the bridge. I want to cut the locks, but Denny had to order special cutters and nothing's ready. So, I'll be stringing lights instead.

A cool mist clings to the river as I snap into my safety harness, grateful it was secured in the light of midafternoon. The climb creeps me out, every bird coo warning of the voices that might follow, every truck that rumbles or bangs in the Village sounds like a ticking clock.

When is it going to happen again? When is whatever this thing is going to show itself?

It's quiet for longer than I'd expected. A steady breeze hisses through the trees clustered at the edges of the river. Denny measures boards on the walkway. A pair of early joggers make their way across, legs pumping in rhythm. It's all too normal to fit with what I've heard up here.

I'm stringing lights along the frame, messing with a plastic bag of cheap twist ties. I have to use two for each section, and my fingers are raw already from folding and pinching. I press them together, and the steady breeze turns to a murmur.

Dread pulls, low in my gut. The murmur is indistinct, and then it's not. First I pick out syllables, soft consonants and lost vowels I can't quite understand.

He's a total screwup.

I jerk so hard that the line on my safety harness goes taut. That's Chase's voice. So clear, he could have been sitting beside me, saying it again like he did that night to Paige.

Everyone knows it.

I press my back to the steel beam and breathe in and out. It's just words.

A row of doves watches me from the darkness, cooing their long, sad calls. They are pale smudges of life beneath the black lip of the top beam. I feel them watching me with their cocked heads and shiny black eyes.

They know he's right. I am a screwup.

My sneaker tread slips. Catches on the next ledge down. I press my head to the metal and close my eyes. This is bullshit. Birds are not judging me, and voices, past or present, can't hurt me.

I wrestle my headphones out of my pocket. Push them in and crank up the volume until the music is banging hard at my ears, and my hands are busy again. The music does nothing to fight the smell of lemon candy or the strange electric heat skimming the surface of my veins.

But it gets the job done.

In the hours before the sun heats the metal, I string lights along the top and sides of the first two trusses. There are a few things to fix—an extension cord issue and a strand that doesn't light—but I get those trusses fully lit.

I climb down, exhausted, and turn off my music. Silence rushes at the hum in my ears. I swallow hard, twisting my earphone cord over and over, winding up the tiny speakers until they're shoved deep in my pockets.

My neck prickles, and I'm sure—absolutely sure—something is coming. Something bigger than music or phantom whispers or whatever else I've been through. I feel like I'm about to bear witness.

Nothing happens, but I pull out my phone just in case. A strange heaviness lingers in the air, a stretch to the shadows that feels all wrong. My hands shake, so I hold the phone in both of them and hit the record button. I don't know what I'm waiting for—what I'm expecting—so I swing the phone left and then right, even down at the slats underneath my feet.

The air is hot, reeking of river and rot and the sickly sweet scent of overripe lilacs. But the lilacs are long out of season.

You deserve better.

The wood beneath my feet thrums, and I feel more than heat rolling off the trusses. Where? Where is this coming from?

I turn to the locks, and my ears pop. A presence moves behind me. A person—I can hear them breathing in hitches and starts—but when I turn, there's no one. It's as if I am feeling someone's pain. The push of someone moving closer. Reaching.

"Theo!"

I smack into the rail, the locks rattling. I spin, fists up. Denny crosses his arms and chuckles at me, pointing.

"You look like you're about to shit yourself," he says.

I'm still breathing hard, and my attempt to laugh stutters into a sad excuse for a grin. My hands drop, worthless, to my sides.

"Yeah, sorry."

"It's quitting time," Denny says, adjusting his pants. "Want to grab some early lunch? Maybe a beer?"

"Actually, I need to head into town."

I wasn't alone up here today. I didn't imagine the presence I felt any more than imagining the voices I've heard. It's time to find out what happened on this bridge, and what might be left behind.

I pause on the library steps, frowning at the heavy wooden door. I got kicked out of this library once when I was twelve. And then again when I was fourteen. So, if that old librarian with her unnaturally dark lip liner is still in charge, this might not go well.

I haul open the door anyway, stepping into a room with bad carpet and a vaguely floral, powdery scent. It's strong enough to stick in the back of my throat when I walk to the desk. I don't see the lip-liner lady, not standing at the high wooden desk that flanks the left side of the room or in any of the visible rows of bookshelves in front of me.

There is a balding man at one of the tables to the right and a mom pushing a stroller through the children's section. Otherwise, the place is a tomb.

"Hello?" I ask the empty counter.

A dark head pops up fast enough to send me jumping back. The kid—definitely not the old lady—props two thin hands on the counter and looks at me like I've interrupted something fascinating.

"Hey," I say, smiling.

He doesn't respond and doesn't smile. He also looks way too young to be a librarian, or even a college student, so I look around again, hoping to see someone more…I don't know, official. Someone who might remove a kid who decided to wander behind the desk and play librarian.

"Well?" he asks out of nowhere, his voice croaky and strange in that way I remember from my sophomore year of high school. "Can I help you?"

I glance at his ratty cartoon T-shirt, and I must look skeptical because I get a glare in return. I shake my head. "Uh, sorry. I'm wondering if you have any information about the history of the town bridge."

"Which bridge?"

"The Cheshire Walking Bridge."

He stares at me, so I stare back. He's got dark hair, a narrow face, and skin just a shade darker than mine. He'd look like any kid alive, except that he's way too still. Almost motionless. It's kinda freaking me out.

Suddenly, he thrusts his chin to the left and walks off, tossing over his shoulder. "I'll show you the reference section."

I scramble to keep up as he darts around the guy at the table, behind the ancient copy machine, and then left down one of the aisles with rows of matching black books that might be encyclopedias. I'm moving too fast to know for sure.

He stops at a section where the shelves are half full, and there's a faded label: Local History. Maybe fifteen books are leaned on the middle shelf, and the kid goes for two of the least-interesting-looking ones.

"There's a chapter on engineering in this one," he says. "Probably mentions the bridge."

He hefts a thick volume into my hands and then pulls out a thin book with what looks like a bridge blueprint on the cover.

"This one might have a sentence or two," he says. "But if

you're doing a research paper, you're going to have better luck with the campus library. You won't get credit if you try to pull all your sources online, so—"

"I'm not in the college," I say absently. "Is that really the only information?"

He shrugs. "I suppose you could look up old building permits or blueprints at the Department of Engineering or maybe with the city planner. You know the city planner?"

I don't, but I nod.

He wrinkles his nose. "I wouldn't expect to find much, though. There are a lot of bridges along the Ohio River Valley. Nothing special about that one."

I snort. "So bridges covered in padlocks and rumored to be suicide hot spots aren't special?"

"There was only one suicide in recent history off that bridge, and the guy was mentally ill. Not the kind of tragedy people write books about." The boy studies me now, lifting his thin nose into the air. "What exactly are you researching?"

"Forget it," I say, turning away. "I'll check these."

I do check them. And the kid watches me like a little creeper the whole time, nothing but those weird eyes and a mop of hair visible above the top of the librarian desk. It's unnerving, and the books are worthless.

In one, there's a chapter that mostly talks about the bidding for the bridge, which was originally constructed in 1849 but is now on its third incarnation. It's also maybe the most boring story I've ever read, including the shit Paige had me read about Valley Forge for American history last year. It's also worthless, unless there was a section on a violent mass murder on the bridge that I somehow skimmed right over.

I close that book and push it aside.

The second one doesn't even mention the bridge, unless I'm missing something. Which is likely, knowing me, so I start back at the beginning and flip through more carefully. I have to do it a third time before I finally find it. Three sentences that give me the basic engineering components of the current structure, along with some notes about repairs made after a hurricane-related flood.

Terrific. I push the book across the table and stand. The boy appears across from me, so I swear and startle, knocking my chair over backward.

"Didn't find what you're looking for?" he asks.

I pick up the chair, glowering. "Okay, are you actually a librarian? Because librarians don't creep. They aren't usually twelve years old either."

"Fifteen," he says, nonplussed. "And no. My grandfather is the librarian, but he's in the back working on fall book orders."

"It's July."

"Exactly."

I take a breath and push in my chair. "Thanks for the help with the books."

"It doesn't seem like they were helpful. The books, you know?"

This kid is super weird. He doesn't move enough. Or sometimes at all. He's got an almost plastic stiffness to his features when he's not speaking.

"You don't read very often, do you?" he asks.

I laugh. "What gave it away?"

"You've been mouthing the words since you started," he says. Then he leans forward, looking at my mouth. "Also, your hands are shaking and you're really fidgety. Are you on meth?"

"Are you shitting me?" A woman two tables down looks up, alarmed, so I school my voice to a whisper. "No, I'm not on meth. I'm—"

Actually, what I'm on is methylamphetamine, which is definitely in the meth family but also prescribed and completely different, and I don't need to go into *any* of this with a fifteen-year-old stranger.

"Forget it," I say. "I appreciate you trying."

"I've seen you on the bridge, you know. You work up there, right?"

I pause, my mouth half open. Have I seen a kid walking back and forth? I spot a hooded sweatshirt on the back of his chair, pricking a vague memory of someone small trekking across toward the Village.

"I like the Greek place next to Anita's," he says to explain.

"That place is awful," I say, but it's not the point. "But yeah, I work on the bridge."

"Then you're here to get information about the hauntings, right? That's why you were so freaked out when you got here. You saw something."

"Excuse me?"

"You won't find it in these books, but I know someone." He's very still again, motionless and narrow and suddenly looking much smarter than his ripped T-shirt would indicate.

A cough and a thump come from the office across from the desk, and the boy tenses. "Come back tomorrow, and we'll talk."

He's gone before I can ask, and I don't really have room to argue. He's right. I'm shit at research, so I'm going to need all the help I can get.

PAIGE

I think I'll be good at college. It's a lot of independent work. Research papers and organization of thoughts and ideas. The science and math courses will challenge me with all their hard rules and specific answers. But I'm good at that. Melanie is even better than me. She's brilliant at the hazy-rule, vague-answer things too. Sometimes I think it would be easier to hate her.

I didn't see it at first. I blame it on the way she missed so much class the first week and seemed obsessed with her phone. Pretty as she is, I assumed her conversation was all shallow—about boyfriends or trips to the mall. Doesn't say good things about me, but that's where I went.

Turns out, she was finishing up another summer program before this started. And the phone? Clubs, special interest projects, and culture exploration groups—stuff I've never even heard of. I have no idea how she does it all.

I'm in the top 10 percent in my school. I've always been one of the smart kids. But here, I'm nothing special. And next to Melanie? It's hard to know what I am at all.

"You're staring," she singsongs, looking up from her row of tap-water samples. Already done with half of the video addition to our project, she's here helping me with my piece.

"I'm marveling at your time-management skills," I say.

"You should be marveling at the fact that thirty-year-old technology is still managing to keep this water clean."

I nod and check another testing strip. Another normal range. Funny that we never think about water. We turn on the faucet and watch it fill our pots and pans and bathtubs. We don't stop to consider what's hidden inside.

Some of the testing makes perfect sense. Microscopes will reveal tiny wriggling things. Impurities will settle in gray clumps at the bottom of spinning test tubes. But colors on a strip changing? Chemical reactions that show us what a microscope can't? That part feels like magic.

"Are you going to fill me in on the guy?" She doesn't look up, but pushes another slide under her microscope.

"I'm sorry?"

"The one who came to see you," she says, glancing up with a quick wink. "Cute smile and incredible arms."

I feel myself grimace. "Yeah?"

She laughs. "Yeah? You took off in the middle of the night! I was hoping you'd have some scandal to dish. Seemed like there was a history."

My heart double beats. I dip another test strip, watching the colors change. Invisible chemicals creeping up the waterline. Pure or tainted?

"I...had to use the restroom last night," I say. "The pizza didn't settle well."

"Oh. I guess I figured you were out with him." She frowns. "Paige, you'd tell me if you were sleepwalking, right?"

The hairs on the back of my neck rise. "Why would you think that?"

Melanie goes uncharacteristically quiet, leaning in to study her microscope. Jotting down a few notes. Finally, she sighs. "Your mom mentioned it."

"In your conference about my mental health?" I wince, wishing I'd watched my tone.

"She's just worried about you. She cares."

"Has it ever occurred to you that maybe she's too worried? Overprotective?"

"It might," Melanie says. "If you'd ever talked to me about any of this."

"About what?"

"About life, or your parents, or the things you're dealing with.

Or even about that guy."

"*Theo*. My former best friend. Which I'm sure my mom already told you."

Melanie's shoulders straighten, her mouth tightening. "No, she didn't."

I sigh, part regret, part relief. "I'm sorry. Mom is… It's hard. I don't like her having my friends check in on me."

"I swear it wasn't like that. She told me you were anxious, and that you had a history of sleepwalking. That's it."

I don't think Melanie is telling the truth, and I'm not sure why. I'm good at knowing when something's off, even if I can't put my finger on what it is. Maybe that's magic too. Maybe there's a little magic in lots of things. Laboratories. Lies. Lost earrings that wind up stuck in my dad's shoe.

I don't look at her when I speak. "I know they want the best for me. But they hover."

"Because they care about you." Her tone makes me wary. Whatever they said, they convinced her. But she hasn't mentioned Theo, so from what I can tell, they gave me that bit of dignity. So, what *did* they say? Did they want to know about my social life? Did they ask her to keep an eye on me? I have a sudden mental image of her counting my pills while I'm sleeping. I hold back a shudder.

This is paranoid and absurd. My parents are overprotective. They aren't stalkers.

"I know they care about me," I say evenly. "But they're having a hard time letting go."

"Ohh." She draws out the word, her eyes going wide like she's talking to a kid. "That totally makes sense."

I want to ask her what my parents want from her. What they talked about. To keep an eye on me? To report back? None of it can be good, and asking too many questions will make me look paranoid.

"I think it's hard for them when I do well without them. They want me to succeed, but they don't want to let me go."

"Sometimes parents can be like that. But it comes from a good place."

I force a stiff nod. I have the sticky-palmed feel of being asked to stay behind after class. Or like I'm sitting in a guidance counselor's office, letting her awkwardly discuss one of the issues in the brochures decorating her office walls. Well, if Melanie wants to armchair psychoanalyze, I can play that game.

"I worry about how they'll cope when I move out. Her whole life revolves around me, which is sweet but a little concerning. Sometimes I feel like graduation is going to be more about how they'll cope than how I will. My mom has her own struggles with anxiety. I get it honestly."

"Oh," Melanie says, looking genuinely surprised.

I smile brightly, pleased that she's taken the bait. "But she's doing *great*. I just want her to continue to take care of herself, and not to get too caught up in taking care of me."

Melanie blinks, as if she's not sure what to do with that new information. I'm not surprised when she flips her ponytail and grins, sliding back into friend mode. "And what about Theo? Were you really just friends?"

Alarms flare in my mind. I shouldn't have said his name. Shouldn't have talked about him at all. What if she says something to my parents when they pick me up?

"No, I was sick. Like I said. Took a walk to try to settle my stomach." My next grin is a calculated move. "You're so caught up on Theo, but he's not the only cute guy around."

She mock-gasps. "Are you hiding a crush from me? Who is it? Is it Noah? Keaton. Oh my God, it's Keaton, isn't it?"

I'm not sure I've spoken directly to Keaton since this program started, but I smirk. "Let's say I'm keeping my options open."

"I'll get it out of you sooner or later."

I turn back to my test strips, hiding my shaking hands. I dip another, and the little pale spots turn green, then blue, then red. You wouldn't know what's in this water at first glance. Maybe that's how I have to be around Melanie now. Perfectly transparent, so that no one will question my insides at all.

THEO

The next morning, I move fast and keep my headphones blaring. There's something about the sky I don't like, something about the heat that's suffocating even before the sun pushes a bit of light into all this darkness.

One song pounds through my speakers as I haul myself up, my arms brown and wiry thanks to all the breakfasts I've skipped. Dinners too. The meds keep me moving quickly, focused on moving lights from one bolt to the next. And then the next.

The song switches and I freeze, one foot wedged in the hole where two beams join, another braced against a beam. It's the song Paige loves and the one I hate.

And I do not have this song on my phone.

Images and sensations slam into me machine-gun fast.

Headlights from that white Chevy. Paige's hand grazing my stomach. The smack of my fist colliding with her face.

It kicks the breath out of me.

I rip my headphones free. My legs tense, feet gripping the beam through my sneakers. I perch there, breathing hard. Tinny remnants of a song I've never owned dribble out of my earphones.

Maybe it's time for you to go.

I tap in my code. Press Record.

No more words now. It's still as hell. Creepy quiet. A girl with a backpack slung over one shoulder moves across the bridge below me. She's got shiny hair and clean sneakers and probably a bright future to match. A future that's nothing like mine.

You ruined a girl like that.

I stop recording. How much of this is really happening, and how much am I imagining? Because the only paranormal manifestation I'm encountering is my supernatural talent for destroying everything I touch.

I force myself to keep working. Keep my hands busy and my mind moving. I finish the lights on the first truss of the day, marking the halfway point. By then, the sun's come up enough to see. Denny has made reinforcements to the handrail at the start of the ramp. Looks like we've both had a productive morning, but where the hell is he? Coffee run, maybe?

A clattering at the far end of the bridge startles me. A group of guys are tearing across the bridge, moving from the Village into Portsville proper. They're shoving into each other, sucking down energy drinks, and swearing often enough for me to peg them at thirteen, maybe fourteen years old.

I switch my safety harness down to the next truss while they walk beneath me, a parade of heavy footsteps and voices.

"Check it! That poor dick's up there stringing lights!"

"That's a shit job, man."

"I'm not busting my balls like that. You seen those big buildings in Columbus? That's where I'll be working."

"You're full of shit, Aiden!"

"Shut up, you dick."

The boys howl and jostle, and I hear the clang of a body slamming into the railing. I grip the beam tighter and look down. They're fine, all laughing and shoving, but my head feels foggy and thick. I've been up here too long.

I watch my feet, carefully finding every toehold and double-checking it. My head and stomach are a washer on spin cycle. My ears catch bits and pieces of their conversation.

Don't let him ruin this for us.

Look I know you're friends, but he's a total screwup.

A wreck!

It's not three boys, and it's not three voices. It's all Chase, all from that night. Always that damn night.

My throat tightens. I plant my toe on the nub of a bolt and hook my arm around the nearest crossbeam. Then I pull out my phone, stabbing the record button with my thumb.

The boys are almost directly beneath me. I hear them, but I also hear something else, like two radio stations cutting in and out, their songs overlapping.

What are you planning, man? Gonna drag her up there?

Go to hell, Theo.

You coming with me?

I go cold all over as that night replays, my voice and Chase's voice coming out of kids I've never seen before.

I check my phone, still recording, the steady red counter ticking up, up, up. My hand is shaking, but I hold the phone, pointing the tiny in-phone mic right at them.

Don't do this.

You need to back off.

Do I look like the type to back off?

I don't know if I sit down on the crossbeam so much as my legs give out, but that's where I end up, panting hard and my vision going gray. The boys jostle and bump their way off the other side of the bridge. I stop the recording and check my files. It's there. Fifty-one seconds.

I move fast now, sneakers slipping on the bolts as I descend. I hit the walkway with a thud that rattles the planks and move into the shadow of the frame, away from the foot traffic. I hit Play, still catching my breath.

There's a brief rustling, and then a shot of beams and blue sky. Chase's voice is crisp and clear when it comes. Mine is slurred and drunk. I sound like someone wrecking everything. I sound like me.

The back of my neck goes hot, and the recording stops. The bridge sits empty and quiet, not a single jogger, not one filthy bird cooing in its nest.

I'm alone, with nothing but my own shame and the smell of lilacs gone to rot.

PAIGE

I review the results three times, but it's not going to change. There's arsenic in the water. Most of our samples are fine. We found a trace of lead near the picnic tables, but Reagan and Matt found the same levels near the old plastic factory south of town, and it's all well within the acceptable range.

But arsenic?

That's not supposed to be here. Not at these levels. Of course, I don't have a definitive result. Six samples were fine. The seventh is off the chart.

"It's an outlier," Melanie says with a shrug. "An aberration." She's been using that word a lot this week. She's also used *contravene* and *aggrandize*. Maybe this is the way people talk at private school?

I roll my stool back from the lab table and look around the room. Keaton and Noah are gone. The two Laurens—who paired up immediately based on their shared name and nearly matching OSU sweatshirts—are in the corner, but I don't know them well. I turn to Melanie.

"Do you think the results are wrong?"

She shrugs. "Like I said: aberration."

I frown. "Still, it's a significant amount of arsenic. I think we should check with Dr. Lutmer to see how to handle it."

Her mouth goes a little tight. "Can you not?"

I give her a look, and she rolls closer in her chair. "Look, I'm all for robust data."

"Robust?" I chuckle. "Are you studying SAT words in your spare time?"

"Yep, started last week. And I'm trying to keep up with my French club and prepare for a calculus intensive that starts the day after I get home." She slouches a little. "I know this is important to you. I just don't want to wind up with more work than we can handle."

More than *she* can handle is what she means. I don't have French club or calculus whatever, so I have time. Plus, this isn't college résumé padding for me. This is all I really have.

Which is why I stand up and give her an apologetic smile. "I'll do the retesting. Promise."

Melanie is agreeable enough about it, back to formatting her tables before I even walk away.

Dr. Lutmer's office is attached to the lab. He's big on independence, so other than an after-lunch lecture and weekly partner check-ins, we're on our own. A big change from the four classes a day and mandatory field trips for the first half of the program.

The door to his office is open. I knock, and he looks up. Gray hair fringes the shiny dome of his skull, and his eyes are small and pale behind his wire-rimmed glasses. He'd be the perfect picture of a seasoned professor, if not for his plaid flannel shirt and jeans.

"Paige, good to see you. What can I do for you?"

"Thanks, Dr. Lutmer. I noticed an unusual test result for one of our samples."

I slide the printout across the desk. "On all of the other vials from this sample, the arsenic is nonexistent or in trace amounts. The level on this result seems exceptionally high."

Dr. Lutmer puts on a pair of reading glasses and studies the information with a furrowed brow. "I agree. Where was this water taken?"

"By the Cheshire Walking Bridge."

He leans back, his office chair groaning. I have the unshakable feeling that I'm being evaluated. "What do you make of it?"

Sweat blooms under both of my arms. It's definitely a test. He wants to know what I know. It hits me that until now, Melanie has done all the talking. She moved smoothly into the limelight with wide smiles and SAT vocabulary words and…I don't know if I can compare.

"Well…" My throat is dry, and my heart's going too fast. I can barely think about the results. I feel pinned to the carpet.

This is when I hate anxiety the most. When I can feel it, like a big hand pushing me down. Making it hard to breathe and speak.

If I don't answer correctly, he could think I'm dead weight. That Melanie did all the work for our project. Maybe I'm not her, but I'm not in this program for nothing either.

I square my shoulders. "My partner thinks it's an aberration, but I felt it warranted more research."

"Oh?"

"I recognize that only one vial yielded this result. Something could have happened in the test process, creating a false positive."

"Possible," he agrees, his face giving nothing away. All I want is to ask him what he thinks, but that's exactly why I can't.

My shirt is clinging between my shoulder blades now, but the words come easier. "If the implications of a result like that weren't so serious, I might be able to write it off, but I looked it up. That reading is three times the acceptable max."

"What's your instinct?"

"To run another seven samples from the same source."

"I agree. Good plan." He takes his reading glasses off and

leans back even further in his chair. I can't see the legs from here, but I bet the front two aren't touching the floor.

"We haven't had much opportunity to talk, Paige," he says. "Are you enjoying the program?"

It's probably more mature not to smile, but I grin anyway. "I love it."

He smiles back. "I understand you're hoping to pursue a career in chemistry. Do you have a specialty?"

I shrug, because I don't have a clue. Most of the kids in my school are interested in pretty basic careers. Business. Nursing. A few of the ambitious kids—the ones vying for valedictorian—are aiming for prelaw or premed tracks. My biology teacher told me I'm the first kid in our school for years who's been interested in a chemistry degree.

Until I started looking at college brochures, I had no idea how many directions I could go in the field.

"I'm still considering several programs," I say, because every one of those programs is a complete blank for me in this moment.

He smiles, and I have that same feeling. Like I'm still being tested. "The lab work and the independent study? You feel comfortable with those aspects?"

The right answer is easy. "Yes, completely."

"Not too stressed out?"

My smile wavers. Why would he ask that? "No. No, I'm good."

"Good. You're doing terrific, but it's not just grades we care about here. We want you to come out of this program feeling confident about your experience and your college plans. We try to provide an opportunity that will highlight your strengths and personal challenges. Everyone's college experience is unique."

"Of course," I say, swallowing the painful lump in my throat. He knows. It's ridiculous, but somehow, I'm sure he knows about my *challenges*. My jaw aches with remembered pain, and I think of my orange prescription bottles. The ones I *don't* keep on my dresser anymore.

Who talked to him? My parents? Melanie?

"I'm really grateful to be a part of this program," I say. "It's been wonderful."

"Good," he says. "But if at any time the pressure is too much…"

I smile again, and it feels stuck on the wrong way. "Of course."

I excuse myself from his office. My heart is pounding, and I feel hot all over. Melanie is still at the table, hunched over, but I think about her in our room. The questions she asked.

Would she have spoken to Dr. Lutmer?

I'm being paranoid. My parents haven't talked to everyone at the school. That would be ridiculous. Almost as ridiculous as them discussing my mental health with Melanie.

Or Dr. Lutmer asking about my stress level for no reason whatsoever.

My face burns. I tug my phone from my shorts and look at it. My thumb hovers over the speed dial for my mom. I try to picture the conversation. Me furiously demanding the details. Who did she call? What did she ask? How many people are going to be checking on me?

She'll tell me, because she probably doesn't think it's a big deal. Mom's a big believer in open, honest communication. I'm not sure what's worse—spending the next three weeks wondering if people are keeping an eye on me, or calling my mom and verifying it beyond a shadow of a doubt.

One point feels crystal clear. If she finds out I'm worried about her saying too much to my friends, she'll use it. It will be another piece of ammunition to justify her belief that my stress levels would be better managed at home.

I take two slow breaths to center myself and pocket my phone. Melanie is calling one of her website friends about musical backgrounds for our final presentation. When I tell her I'm off for more samples, she's all too happy to wave me away.

I grab a pair of rubber boots and a collection kit from the supply room and head out.

The walk to the river is short, and I wish it wasn't. I'm knotted up inside, so I could use a long stroll to unwind. At the crest of the hill above the bridge, I stop. I miss Theo so much in that moment that I feel a little sick with it.

Normally, he's the first person I'd call. I could count on him for a burst of righteous indignation on my behalf. Then he'd make me laugh. And then he'd talk me down.

I know this can't be healthy, the way it is with us. He's a walking contradiction. Theo is good for me. And Theo is terrible for me. Those statements are both completely true and impossibly opposite at the same time. How do I make sense of that?

He's not on the bridge. Denny's there, working on the railing, but Theo's nowhere in sight. Odd, since it's only two o'clock. I think about calling or texting, but decide against it.

I head down the banks, my ballet flats nearly silent in the grass. I pass Melanie's favorite picnic table and head straight to the walking paths that switchback down to the water. There's a shallow section near the bridge support where we collected the first time. I tug on my boots and head out.

The water is moving fast, so I'm careful. Even with cleanup programs in place, I could run into a million unsavory things on the bottom of this river, and I'd rather not.

I make my way closer to the supports. The wind is whipping tiny waves across the river. Water sloshes over the tops of my rubber boots, little rivulets of filthy water soaking my feet. On the bridge overhead, two bikes *bump-bump* onto the wooden walkway and roll their way to the Village.

I shudder. It's weirdly cold down here—maybe it's the wind.

I just want to be done. I push a few feet closer to the original collection site, near the first support pillar.

The current drags cold and fast at my feet, and my fingers fumble with the first vial. I plunge it into the muddy water and pull it out. Once the cap is on, I fill the second. The third.

The wind whips my hair into my face. My teeth chatter.

Come on, finish already.

I cap the fourth, and the air goes still. Utterly motionless, as if someone switched off the weather.

My hands shake as I push my hair out of my face. I can hear my own heart. A *thump-thump* that's growing faster. My body can tell something is different. Wrong.

I cap my final sample and shove it in my bag. Something brushes my boot in the water. A fish? I kick my heel free of the silt in the riverbed. The thing I can't see wraps around my ankle.

I kick hard, thrashing. My other ankle twists... I'll trip. I'll fall!

I recover with a step to the right, hands wide, samples rattling in the case.

Stop. Stop freaking out!

I pull in a deep breath and test a step, feeling the drag of whatever's caught on my boot. A tangle of weeds or maybe fishing line. I'll be fine.

The samples are my first priority, so I settle them back into the slots in the case and snap it shut. Once it's tucked safely under my arm, I reach into the water. I feel my way down carefully. A wad of fishing line could have hooks. But it's not fishing line, it's cloth—maybe old rope or a cotton strap.

See? Nothing.

It untangles easily enough. I pull my foot free and fish the rope out of the water. There's something dangling off it, caked and dripping in mud. It's a little purse.

I turn it over, hearing heavy footsteps start over the bridge, rusty-red sludge dripping off my hands.

Like blood.

It's *not* blood. It can't be. But blood is what I think of when my throat goes dry and my heart squeezes out two beats together. My finger drags across a smooth metal clasp, and I'm struck with immediate familiarity. I know this purse. I remember the crisp little *snap* it makes when I pinch it closed.

This is my purse.

I turn the muddy hunk over in my hands, wondering if my lipstick is still inside. Or the single tampon I had hidden in the zippered compartment because I was going to get my period soon. My hands shake and pull at the bag. Liquid weeps from the seams, dark red, black, brown, and it's on my hands. It's all over me.

I can't breathe. I can't—

Above me, the clomping tread goes silent. I freeze. Someone's up there. Chills slither up my spine as I look up, water lapping at my boots. Light peeks between each slat of wood. And two dark smudges appear at the edge. Feet.

Who is that?

My teeth clack painfully. I stare up at the underside of the bridge, blood roaring behind my ears. I can't see who it is. Are they watching me?

One of the planks groans. Like that person is leaning. I gasp. Are they going to jump? The feet are planted. Unmoving. I feel a strange weight in my chest.

I look down at the purse, at the putrid liquid running down my arms. Dripping on my legs. It's like my blood from that night. It *is* blood, isn't it?

I recoil, flinging the purse into the river. The current takes it fast. The shoulder strap trails behind, a coiling snake dancing in the water. My heart pounds as I watch the purse disappear. Then I plunge my hands into the river. When I pull my arms out, they look clean.

Was there ever any blood?

My hands shake as I swipe them down my shorts. I slosh toward the bank, panting. It's like running through honey. Or sand. I can't move fast enough. My lungs are burning by the time I reach the shore ten feet away.

I climb the walking path quickly, boots slipping on the gravel. I go down on my knees in the grass at the top, folding into an awkward heap as I look at the bridge.

There's no one there. No one on the ramp leading into the Village or even on the street beyond.

What did I see up there? What did I fish out of that water?

Not what I thought—that much is sure. Now with my breath steady, I know that bag couldn't have been my purse. My purse is at home, hanging on a hook in the back of my closet. It was in my bag from the hospital, and I watched my mom pull it out and put it away.

Which means I dreamed some random purse into something personal and terrifying. Why would I do that? Unless, of course, I'm a completely anxious wreck who flies to the worst possible conclusion at every turn.

I look up, squinting into the blotch of bright white in the overcast sky. So, what do I do? Can I call my doctor for a dosage increase? I turned eighteen in April, so technically it's my business now. My parents shouldn't have access.

But I think of all the forms I blindly signed after the party, forms at the hospital, at the dentist, at the therapist's office too. My mother filled out those forms. She would have taken steps to be the decision maker, and it's not like I paid attention to what I was signing.

What if I told her? Not the craziest parts of what happened—but that I need a bump in my meds. Because it's true, and I know my parents want to help me. But I also know they want me home.

What if they're right about that?

I close my eyes against the thought. If it's true, then I'm exactly where I've always been, the little girl afraid to go through the cave at camp. The one who won't climb the rope in gym. The me who's afraid of every new story because she doesn't know how it will end.

I don't know if I can live with being that girl for one more minute.

But I can't ignore this paranoia either. I need help. I stand up, knees wobbly, and start toward the bridge.

THEO

I'm officially blowing off work to talk ghosts with a fifteen-year-old librarian named Gabriel. Denny didn't seem pissed, but pissed is difficult to interpret when you're dealing with monosyllabic responses. Through text, no less.

Screw it, though. It's too hot to work on the beams now, and he messed up his bolt cutter order, so we can't do the locks.

It's too hot to be inside, so we're out on Denny's porch. No furniture, and I'm too lazy to drag out one of the kitchen chairs, so I'm sitting on the floor, and Gabriel's sitting on the dead air conditioner.

"Let start at the beginning," he says, sounding really serious for someone with an untied shoe and a can of orange soda beside him. "Tell me about your paranormal encounters."

I push my legs out in front of me, my socks catching on the splintered porch. "Who talks like that? Also, sorry to be an ass here, but how much experience does someone your age have with paranormal encounters?"

"I used to live in the Village," he says. "We live in one of those apartments by the library now. Back then I lived on Maple Street, and I'd run across the bridge a lot. Getting ice cream and stuff. You know the ice cream shop?"

"Okay."

"I lived with my uncle for a while, and he used to let me walk over there. I'd buy a vanilla ice cream cone, dipped in that butterscotch topping that gets kinda hard. You know that topping?"

I do. I just can't understand why a dipped cone is relevant to a conversation about seriously messed-up haunting shit. But I nod to get him to go on.

"I liked to walk there every day, even if I didn't have the money for the ice cream, because there was always this nice lady saying my name over and over. She said it like a song."

"So, you were haunted by a creepy lady on the bridge?"

"No lady. Just her voice."

"Just her voice?"

"Yes. I was too young to realize how scary that was. I thought it was cool, like the bridge knew I was coming and liked me, I guess."

He bursts into a flurry of motion for a moment, adjusting his notebook and shifting around on the air conditioner.

"So, who do you think the lady was?"

"I have no idea. But it went on until I moved in with my grandfather."

"In the library apartment."

"Right."

"And you never heard it again?"

"When I moved in with my grandfather, he didn't want me on the bridge. Didn't go for years."

"Okay, fine. Not sure what it has to do with me."

"It doesn't, but it's how I know about the voices people hear. The things they see. People come in sometimes too. To the library, you know? They want to know about ghosts and stuff. Some people see things. Some people hear things. One girl smelled things."

"I've smelled things," I say. "So, what is it? What's behind it?"

"I don't know," he says. "But it doesn't happen to everyone. There were enough rumors that the ghost tours tried to add the bridge for a while. But it never caught on. Too far from the hotel and old school that really creep out customers. Plus, most people think the bridge and locks are romantic."

"So, what's your theory? If you want to help me, you obviously have one, right?"

"Yes, but I want to hear your story first."

I fill him in on the basics and flip my phone over and over in my hands. I know that's what I need to get to—the recording.

That's the point of all of this, but it's the start of my worst night. I don't know if I want him to hear me like that, especially since I'm going to have to explain the rest.

But hell, it's not like he didn't peg me as a screwup already.

I put the phone on the porch between us and turn up the volume before pressing Play. There's the soft static hiss of recorded wind. Rustling like I'm adjusting the phone. I glance down, because I thought the audio would have started several seconds ago. We're at ten seconds, then fifteen, then twenty, and my stomach wads up because this isn't right. There were voices on this recording, mine and Chase's. I heard them on the bridge.

"Something's screwed up," I say, grabbing the phone and checking my videos. I play it again, but it's the same. Fifty-one seconds of me rustling and breathing. One or two distant whoops that sound like the kids who crossed over. There is no Chase and no Paige and no former drunk me blundering into the worst mistake of my life.

"What the hell? I heard an entire conversation, one that happened with me at a party a few months ago, but I was hearing it *today* on that bridge."

"Maybe you just remembered it really clearly in that moment. You know, those memories that are so real you think they're happening again?"

"No, this is not some sort of memory-lane bullshit. I heard

myself talking. Word for word, I heard a whole conversation, and it should be…"

It should be what? A clear recording taken *today* of an event that happened four months earlier? A minute of rustling and breathing makes way more sense, but I'm disappointed.

Not that I was dying to relive it, but somehow the conversation not being there is worse. Makes me feel crazier, like I made the whole thing up.

"I don't know what happened," I say. "I listened to this on the bridge. It was all there."

Gabriel shrugs. "Or you thought it was. Just like I thought I heard a lady calling my name."

"You think the bridge is haunted by some sort of voice-mixing ghost deejay?"

"My theory is it's an amplifier," he says, looking completely serious. "A spirit that finds emotions in us and turns up the volume."

"Then why wouldn't it amplify everyone's drama? I mean, it was strong enough to drive one guy to suicide."

"No, it didn't. I looked into that guy, figuring maybe he was the reason. But he was a really sad guy, a tragedy waiting for a place to happen. You know people like that?"

I cock my head. "The bridge might have pushed him over the edge."

"I think he was always on the edge. He didn't have a great life, but he didn't have some crazy experience on the bridge either."

He stands up suddenly, snapping his notebook shut. "Look, I have to go. I'll pick up some notes from the historical society, and I have a contact I want to talk to."

"A contact?" I laugh, but he doesn't flinch—simply watches me in that strange motionless way. "Sorry. I can't tomorrow. I have to work, or I'll piss off my uncle."

Gabriel cocks his head. "Maybe you should try to talk to the voices."

I narrow my eyes at him? "Really? Would *you* want to talk to the voices?"

"I don't need to talk to them."

"Why not?"

"They've never tried to scare me." Then he stops suddenly, looking down the sidewalk with a frown on his face. "Are you expecting company?"

"No." I say it half a second before I hear the soft pat of footsteps. Paige's wavy hair and freckled shoulder slide into view as she turns for our porch stairs.

Gabriel waves as he passes her, then disappears from my mind completely because I really don't care where he went. Paige is here. She's right here, standing on the busted steps of my uncle's porch, looking like the cure to everything that's ever ailed me.

I notice she's upset about the same time I see the ridiculous rubber boots she's wearing. I edge to the steps, having no clue how to approach this.

"Going fishing?" I ask, trying a smile. She doesn't bite. But she keeps looking at me, like she's fighting some battle in her head. I can't tell if she's winning or losing.

I climb down until only two or three feet separate us. It's close enough that I can hear the way her breath is shaking in and out. In and out.

"I found the purse I carried to the party in the river today," she says matter-of-factly. "It was in the water. I was under the bridge."

"Why were you in the water?"

"I had to collect new samples. We encountered an arsenic outlier." She's talking too fast, words mashing together. "Melanie thinks it's an aberration, but the test was conclusive."

"Those are all seventy-five-cent words, and I'm going to need you to bring it down to normal-people speak. What are you talking about?"

"We found something bad in one of our water samples," she says, and now the emotion hits, wobbling some of her vowels. She looks up at me, her eyes gleaming with the warning of tears. "I think something is happening to me. I saw someone, Theo. Someone was standing on the bridge when I found my purse."

"When you found it in the water, this guy was on the bridge? Did he drop it?"

"No, it was in the current," she says. "But he showed up too. I could see his feet from underneath. I had this weird feeling that he might jump. And that he was watching me."

I want to touch her so badly that I can feel my fingers flexing, but I can't. I shove them into my pockets, and pull them right back out. There's nothing that feels right so I push them into my hair. "All right. You're all right. Could it have been a jogger? Sometimes if you're already freaked out, it could—"

"*No.* He wasn't moving. He just stood there for the longest time. Watching."

"Then what happened? Where's the purse?"

"I threw it. I couldn't… It was leaking all this stuff… It was… Look, I don't know what I was thinking. I was freaked, okay?"

"Okay."

She pushes her hair back, and I can see traces of mud on her hands and all down her shorts and her legs. She's a mess.

"What happened next?" I ask.

"When I got to the bank, there was no one on the bridge."

"Okay. And you're sure the purse was yours? It wasn't just… I mean, I know I've been talking about it, so I could have freaked you out."

She nods. "I know. I know how I am."

But everything about her face tells me she's having a hard time buying that it was only anxiety. And since I heard ghostly voices rehashing the five minutes where I destroyed her jaw and our lives, I'm having a hard time arguing with her.

"I didn't know where to go," she says softly, looking at her feet. "My parents are worried about me. They talked to my roommate. Maybe my teachers."

"What the hell? Is it your grades or something?"

"No, my grades are good. They're worried because I ran into you, but Melanie might have told them I had a nightmare. I don't know… They want me to go home."

"Do you want to go home?" I ask, terrified that maybe that's why she's here. Maybe she really is that messed up that she doesn't want this program anymore. Maybe I made her too afraid. The idea of it makes my chest hurt.

"No, I don't want to go home." She huffs, her eyes bright. "You didn't break me, Theo."

My chest constricts until it's hard to breathe. It's all I can do to not break down crying.

Suddenly, a new light comes into her eyes, and she looks around and glances in the direction Gabriel walked, like she's figuring out a piece of the puzzle she hadn't before. "You were busy. You had company. I'm sorry to drop by like this. I'm—"

"Paige." I want to hold her, but I wouldn't dare do that. I push my toes at her foot instead, my dirty socks against her rubber boots. "I'm not busy. I'm glad you're here. Thrilled."

"Oh," she says, and then for the first time in four months, Paige is looking right at me when she smiles.

PAIGE

We walk to a school playground on a hill. It's not much. Some apple trees and a playground with a dented slide and mostly broken swings. I know Theo picked it based on location. We're far from the dilapidation of the Village. Far too from the austere buildings of the university. Most of all, we're far from the river with its stink and its terrors. Here, it's only us.

I sink into one of the two rubber-bottomed swings left. Theo takes the other. I sway back and forth and Theo spins, twisting in his seat until the chains wrap over and over. I point my toes out and whoosh forward. Theo pulls up his feet and unwinds in a shiver of noise and motion.

We could do this for hours, and he won't ask why. He'll let it be and roll along. Maybe that's why it's always easy to talk to him.

"Who was that kid on your porch?" I ask.

"Gabriel. I met him at the library. He's kind of weird."

I smile. "You're kind of weird."

"True enough." He starts twisting his swing around again, boots clomping against gray remnants of mulch. "He knows about the stuff on the bridge. He works at the library."

"Does he think there could be a way to stop it?"

"He's fifteen. God knows what he thinks."

"Then why are you talking to him?"

He scuffs over closer to me on his twisted-up swing. "Because I'm desperate?"

"Generally speaking, or now?"

Theo laughs and lets his swing unfurl again. I still love the way he looks—wiry and lean, with a smile that curls a little higher on one side and eyes that are too pale to label any one color. Even his brows arch in a way that promises mischief.

He doesn't look like a guy who would hold open doors or buy me antibacterial gel. Or bring me pretzels because he knows I'd rather starve than eat lukewarm potluck food. Then again, he doesn't look like a guy who'd hit me either. Not even by accident.

Funny that he's the one staring at me this time. All those years, I was hoping he'd look at me. Then he did, and everything fell apart.

"Our timing is terrible." I don't even realize I'm talking until the words are out.

Theo's mouth opens a little, like he wants to say something, but he wants to pick and choose each word. Very unlike Theo. "I know. I'm trying not to talk about it, because I don't want to mess this up."

"Mess what up?"

"You being here." The way he looks at me would have leveled me a year ago.

"Me being here?"

"Yeah. You're here, breathing my air and generally making my life less shitty. Except for the whole haunted-out-of-my-mind part."

My hands suddenly itch with the memory of the purse. I can feel the weight of it on my boot and in my fingers. The image tenses my shoulders.

"I can't handle much more of that," I admit. "What are we going to do?"

"We're going to walk you home the long way," he says, getting up. "And I'm going to keep working with Gabriel. World's youngest paranormal investigator."

I stand up too, letting the swing drop away with a rattle of chains. "It's not just at the bridge for me. It's happened in my room."

"The earring you found, you mean? You said you found that in your room."

"Yeah, but there's been other stuff. My jaw hurting and

bleeding." I breathe in sharply, remembering the coppery taste on the back of my tongue.

"Did any of it start before you were on the bridge?"

"No. Not really."

We walk a little farther before he stops, tugging my arm. "Have you told your parents?"

"About the haunting? God, no. My mom would lose it. She'd admit me somewhere."

"We could avoid the bridge. See if that works."

"Even if I could, you can't. And I don't know if that would fix it. It keeps reminding us, looping us back to what happened."

"Replaying that night. I know." He sighs. "I don't know what the hell we're supposed to do with any of this. What we should learn. It's not like we can go back and change the past."

He's right about that, and it leaves us both quiet as we walk. Traffic zips by on the State Street Bridge. It adds half a mile to our trip, but it's nice. The heat is easing its grip. The sun hangs lower over the university rooftops. A reminder that I should have gone back a while ago. I don't really care. I feel peaceful with his boots clomping beside me. I'm content.

He stops at the edge of campus. "Will you call if you need me?"

"Yes. And you? If you find something?"

He nods, I nod. Everything between us feels the same, except *this*. He's hesitating. And Theo never hesitates. He also never looks at me like this, his expression so open and hungry that I can feel it under my skin.

I think of those same words again. Terrible timing.

Is it, though?

We can't be together. I know that can't happen, but I want it to. It's scary stupid. We've brought out the worst in each other before. Enabled all the wrong behaviors. We could slip right back into all of that so easily.

I clear my throat and my head. "We still need to talk. We're still not…"

He winces. "I know. I do."

He shuffles back with an awkward wave, but it's not what either of us wants. I grab the front of his shirt before I can think. There's the barest hint of heat through his shirt. He crushes me to his chest before I can feel anything else.

It's exactly what it's always been to hug Theo. Even like this, he fidgets and jitters like burning energy is his life's mission. I feel that energy now in the hard arms that flex around me, in the sigh that shakes the hair at the crown of my head. In the way his fingers trail, just through the tips of my hair.

I pull back far enough to see his eyes dart to my mouth. I'm smart enough to know why he's looking. Something sparks deep in my chest. And burns.

What if it could be different with us? What if I found a way to live this normal, healthy college life and be with Theo too? Is that possible? Can you go to the darkest imaginable places with a person and still walk with them in the light?

My therapist wouldn't tell me no. She'd ask me if being with Theo is a *best choice*. And I would know the answer, no matter how much I hated it.

Theo pulls his hands away from me, and I feel my insides split open. I love him. Then. Now. Always. In a movie, it would be enough to undo every bad thing. Out here in the real world, though, love isn't enough.

THEO

I've strung lights across the rest of the bridge by eight o'clock the next morning, and not one disembodied voice has come calling. I blame Gabriel. He's been here since six, sitting on the bridge twenty feet below while I'm working. He's wearing headphones, eating corn chips, and generally driving Denny out of his mind with his lurking.

Denny and I closed the bridge with cones this morning, since he's replacing planks. He wanted Gabriel gone as soon as the poor kid showed up, said he didn't need some punk kid breaking his neck on his watch. I convinced him Gabriel was a friend, and Denny let it drop. Guess he's more worried about my social life than I thought.

Not sure I can blame him. Last night, I almost kissed a girl I sent to the hospital less than six months ago, so clearly I need to brush up my social skills.

I hook another strand of lights and clamp it into place. Then squat on one of the crossbeams. It's time to take down my harness anchor, and everything about that process is a pain in the ass. I push my back against the steel. Heat's already climbing, but I'm finished and Denny's got ten or twelve fresh planks on the walkway. Decent progress for both of us.

"You got something else for me to do?" I holler down.

Denny looks up, pulling his cap low on his eyes to block the sun. "Done with the lights?"

"Probably. After we check them lit, I might need to make some adjustments, but I'm sick of climbing around like a monkey."

"Suit yourself. You can see if you have any luck getting the damn locks off. Broke two sets of bolt cutters working on it yesterday, but the good ones came in."

"I'll give it a whirl." I start climbing down and Gabriel watches, mildly interested as Denny moves for something behind his toolbox.

It looks like a giant pair of wire cutters, complete with red padded handles and a wicked-looking set of blades sandwiched together. A pinch strong enough to sever steel. I'm intrigued.

The cutters are heavy in my hands, and the silver head looks dangerously effective. I'm careful not to get twitchy when Gabriel moves closer. He lifts a finger to the closed blades, and an image blooms in my mind. The blades open and then snap shut. Severing his finger at the first knuckle.

That doesn't seem like a good idea, Theo.

I jerk back, revolted by the disturbing turn of my thoughts and the words—this time with no buzz, no telltale smell to warn me. I look left and right, but there's nothing.

Gabriel is watching me, his slim dark brows pulled together. Did he hear it too?

Or does he somehow know what ran through my mind?

"Well, are you going to gawk all day or try to get the job done?" Denny asks. I head for the first stretch of fencing and Gabriel follows, watching as I inspect the locks. I want to start with an easy one, so I'm checking the girth of the bars.

"Wait," Gabriel says suddenly. "You're cutting off the locks?"

Denny snorts. "Why, you and your true love have one up here?"

"No." Gabriel sounds affronted. "But they're a piece of history, you know?"

"Asshole kids carving their names on shoplifted padlocks is hardly what I'd call history."

A few colored ones pop out from the rest, flashes of confetti in a sea of faded silver and brass. They look cheap enough. This is where I'll start.

Gabriel reaches for the tool again and I pull the blade back, not trusting myself.

I cough out a laugh. "Watch your digits, man."

Gabriel nods and shifts to the left so I can get to the rail. I tap the tool on a few locks, and my stomach rolls. I try to ignore it. It doesn't matter. Even if it starts—the voices, the music, the smells—I have to remember it can't hurt me. The hurting is already done.

I open the blade with a *shink*. Gabriel's eyes go wide. He walks away without another word, past the rail, past Denny, all the way to the ramp that leads into town. I want to call after him, but Denny's watching. And there's something buzzing in my ears. A speaker turned up too loud. A bee's nest in a wall. I feel the sound in my mouth and throat until my teeth shudder.

Denny points at a pink lock that looks both new and cheap. My vision tunnels out until all I can see is the fleshy tip of his finger.

Then the curve of the cutter's blade.

And his finger again.

"Try that one," Denny says.

"Sure," I say, my throat sandpaper dry.

I position the blade carefully around the arm of the lock. My hands are slick with sweat as I push the handles together.

It's a cheap thing, bubbly seventh-grade writing and dollar store written all over it. It should give, but it doesn't. I push harder, ears ringing. Lean into it because this is stupid. It should have cut the metal with the first push, and it isn't… It won't—

I ease the handles open, and slam them shut fast and hard. The lock drops, and a scream erupts in the air. So shrill, so loud that I'm sure I have cut off a finger. I drop the bolt cutters, hands clamping over my ears as the scream grows into a hundred...a thousand. All I hear—all I *feel*—is this noise, a terrible shriek that electrifies my teeth.

It goes on and on and on.

And then when my mouth is stretching around my own scream, it stops.

It should be quiet now, but my ears are wrecked, ringing and throbbing like I've been standing too close to a fire alarm. Or a bomb.

Denny grabs my arm, and I can see he's concerned. Checking my hands. His lips are moving, pressing together, opening and shutting. He's saying something I can't hear, because my ears don't work. His voice is a low, underwater hum beneath a high-pitched whine.

Denny's lips move again, and I hear him.

You said it meant something.

That's not Paige, not us.

I thought it meant something!

Someone else's voice. Someone else's words.

A glimpse of shiny pink catches my eye. The lock—broken—sits on the decking. My foot shoots out, kicking it off the bridge.

My ears right themselves in an instant. No ringing. No humming. No strange girlish voices floating out of Denny's mouth and into my ears.

I can hear him now, the real Denny, shaking my arm hard. "—into the damn railing, and what the hell is going on with you?"

"Nothing," I say automatically. My voice rattles out with a wheeze. I clear my throat. "Sorry, I hit my funny bone."

It's bullshit, and he knows it. He watches me for a long minute. Lights a cigarette and picks up the bolt cutters.

"Sorry," I say again.

"I can't babysit you, Theo."

"I know."

"This is a job. It needs to get done. If you're too… If you can't do this…"

A stab of worry hits my middle. "I can. I'm sorry."

"I don't have time for this shit up here, kid. I've got to earn a living."

"I know. I do. I think…" I reach, searching the bridge, the river. I need an explanation that is less batshit crazy than the truth. "I think I need to stay hydrated up there. I'm achy all over. Every little thing is setting off my nerves."

"You're not drinking?" Denny asks, but he's already nodding. He wants to believe it, because it makes sense. Hell, I want to believe it too. Except I know better.

"All right," Denny says. "Run up to Anita's and fill you up a jug."

Gabriel catches up with me at the end of the ramp. He looks sallow and frightened, like a sickly kid.

"Where'd you run off to?"

He doesn't answer, but falls into step beside me. I don't have any money, so I grab my thermos from the truck, a dented mess with a broken handle. There's still water from yesterday, and even though I'm not particularly thirsty, I drink several long swallows.

"Did you hear something up there?" Gabriel asks, his voice small.

I wipe the lukewarm water off my chin. "Yeah."

"I thought I heard something too," he admits.

"From all the way down here on the street."

I'm teasing, but he flushes hard. "I got scared. It was a whisper, real far away. You know how that is…when you're sure you can hear something, but it's too far away to make out?"

"Yeah, I know about that," I say. "But that's not what I heard. I heard a scream like someone was getting their spine ripped out an inch away from my ear. And then a girl's voice saying something about it meaning something… Hell, I don't know."

"Was it Paige?"

"No. Not Paige."

Gabriel looks at me gravely. "You shouldn't cut those locks, Theo."

"Because some ghostly *woo-woo* voice is going to scream at me when I do?" I shake my head, feeling a familiar rush of anger. "Screw that. Screw all of this shit."

"No, because it's not helping. You're making whatever this is angrier."

Heat flares in my chest, and my hands roll into fists. "*Good.* Maybe I'm doing something right. Maybe cutting these locks is exactly how we break…whatever the hell this is."

"Your uncle. He didn't hear anything." It seems like Gabriel is talking to himself. He's gone very still again, leaned against the truck. "I'm going to talk to one of the ghost hunters."

"Ghost hunters? What the hell are they going to do?"

"Hopefully they'll help us figure out how to stop this. Cutting that lock could have started some sort of downward spiral. We need to talk to someone who knows what to do."

My laugh sounds mean. "The only thing they know how to do is to con drunk tourists into handing over hard-earned cash."

"They're as close to experts as we're going to find."

"Fine," I snap. "Tell you what. You go talk to your ghost hunters."

"And what are you going to do?"

"I'm pretty sure you can make a solid guess."

He swallows hard, looking terrified. "You're going to cut off more of them."

"Yes, I'm going to cut those locks. First, because it's my damn job, and I need to not get fired. And second, because I want to do it. I'll do whatever it takes to end this, and if that means cutting off a thousand screaming locks, I'll do it."

I storm back up the steps, not bothering to look back. My head is pounding and my vision is smeary, and I don't give a shit. ODD is generally nothing but hell, but today it's exactly what I need. I don't say a word to Denny when I jam in my headphones and crank my music.

I pick up the bolt cutters and move to the first lock. My music blares loud enough to make my headache throb, but when I cut off the next bolt, it's not loud enough. The scream cuts right through the chorus. It tunnels past the headphones, deep into my ears until it's clawing at the inside of my bones.

I move as fast as I can, throwing my whole weight into every cut. Ignoring the waves of agony and nausea that follow. None of the locks come loose easy, and the voices—God, the voices are a nightmare. No amount of thumping bass or shrill guitar drowns them out. Young and old, male and female. They whisper and cry and moan, interrupting each other, tripping over each other's sentences.

Never ever—how could you do this—you never meant a

word—I love you—you're always—forever—don't touch me—my everything—this is special—what we have—I should kill you for this—I love you—you never—I always—it's over.

Then there's no music, no screaming, no sound at all. I stumble to the railing and spot the glint of our lock—Paige's and mine—down the line.

The whole world whirls harder and faster. Something gray closes in at the edges of my vision. I realize too late what's happening, that I'm passing out. But I don't feel myself hit the wooden walkway. I don't feel anything at all.

PAIGE

After lecture, the entire day is a blur of rewrites and independent work. It's what I love most about this program. In high school, class ends and you go home. The learning stops. Here, it's endless. Melanie and I sit on our beds, fingers flying across phones and laptops alike. Music plays softly, and we take breaks to sing and to raid the vending machines on the third floor. I can almost forget about her strange questions.

I feel so normal, so completely *right* in this place.

Melanie orders pizza late at night and still doesn't ask about my anxiety. With notes strewn across the foot of her bed and her hair in a messy ponytail, it's hard to imagine her spying on me. But *is* it spying? A healthy friendship might include that kind of concern.

I wouldn't know much about healthy friendships.

I try not to think about Theo. I'm mostly successful, until we turn off the lights. Then I can't think of anyone else.

I hugged him today. I felt his arms around me and the heat coming off his body. What does a hug like that mean? What does it change? Our feelings for each other are out and open, and somehow it's muddier than ever.

What are we supposed to be now?

Because Theo is different, and Theo is the same. I am broken, and I am a survivor. We are good and bad together. I don't know how to make sense of it.

Hours pass, and my sleeping pills sit, untouched, on my end table. I clench my sheet to my chin and listen to Melanie breathing. I'm sure I won't sleep. Absolutely sure of it. And then Melanie's phone alarm jangles me awake.

I bolt upright, blinking in the jarring brightness of morning. My heart pounds as I smooth my hair and force myself to my feet. I don't want her to think I was dreaming, to have anything to report to my parents.

I dress quickly and brush my hair and teeth in record time, and this time there is no blood. There's also no pain. My universe is one hundred percent normal. Except that there's an awful feeling swelling in my chest and sinking in my middle. A feeling that something is wrong—even if I'm not sure what.

That part is normal for me too. It's the feeling I've lived with most of my life. Maybe I'm not the healed, fully functional girl I thought I was.

Back in the room, I slide my bag over my shoulder and force myself to smile at Melanie. I even suggest picking up coffee at the decent shop just off campus, putting all the perk I can manage into my tone.

After lecture, we're last in line for the equipment, and some of the water tests take six hours to develop. After a quick check-in with Dr. Lutmer, Melanie and I take off for the day to practice our project presentation. We're two days out, and we seem to have it together.

Melanie starts us out with the video. It looks so good that I feel a little sick watching. She's covered everything—testing sites, methods, data validation. My palms sweat on my phone as I flip through my notes for the conclusion.

That was my piece. I slaved every night over it, and the research is solid. But after Melanie's multimedia piece, it feels small and plain. I have note cards on a phone app. Melanie produced a motion picture.

Also? She doesn't require note cards. She didn't even glance at her phone while speaking, and she still sounded smart and polished. A total natural. In contrast, I'm stilted and unconvincing. I stop a few cards from the end, feeling my cheeks go hot.

"I need more practice."

"You're doing great!"

"Not really. I need to make a few tweaks."

"Don't give up! You've got this!"

My stomach twists. Her tone makes me feel like I'm back in gym class, trying to climb that rope. Jolie and her crew are snickering on the bleachers. And Melanie is the gym teacher brightly cheering me on—and secretly knowing I'll never be the girl who will get this right.

I close my phone, sure I won't be able to string together two sentences now. "I'll get it. Your part was pretty mind-blowing. I'm just nervous."

I leave off the part about me possibly also being inept, but it's in there. My nerves are in knots. How am I going to keep up with her? She's got to *hate* that she did this project with me.

"Look, it's only a video," she says. Because apparently she's a mind reader too.

I try to play it off. "What do you mean?"

"Making a video is great and we've got good information, but the arsenic you found is the ticket. That's *interesting*."

"I'm not even sure it matters. Like you said, it's all filtered out."

"Still, you're the reason we know it's there to begin with. Your instincts are good. If you hadn't asked the right questions, we wouldn't have this angle in our report."

One that my conclusion doesn't reflect yet. I nod and close my phone. "I'm going to edit it a little. Could we look at it later?"

"Don't worry, okay? We'll think of something together." My shoulders tense. I feel like she just patted me on the head.

I'm not being fair. She's probably being nice. Unless she's not.

I don't know how to read her anymore. Does she see me as a good partner, or some kind of charity case? Someone who's exceptional at research, or a girl who'll never be strong enough to handle real college on her own? Who knows what she thinks of me.

Who knows what *anyone* would think of me. I've got medicine on the dresser, but a stack of academic recommendations. Bitten-down nails, but a neat and tidy wardrobe. A friend like Melanie and a friend like Theo. Maybe we're all contradictions in the end.

"Okay. Twenty-five minutes till our lab time," she says. "Break ideas?"

"Enough time for more coffee?"

"Definitely. But I'm going to postulate that when you say coffee, you actually mean the milk shakes with a vague coffee aftertaste that I prefer."

"Postulate? Really?"

She frowns. "I know. There are way too many *p*-words this week."

We hit the lab by ten, with half-empty drinks and a serious caffeine buzz cranking. We have the place to ourselves so far, so Melanie starts the music, and I check the samples we left to process last night. This time *two* are positive for arsenic.

"That can't be right."

"What?" Melanie asks.

"Two of the samples are positive now."

"Positive?" She turns down the music and looks, frowning. "You were right."

"It was just a hunch."

"No, it was smart thinking." She presses closer to the screen.

"Should we call someone?" I ask, eyeing the results. "This water is the source of the city's drinking supply. Arsenic builds in the system."

"The filtration system still would eliminate it," she says. "They check the water and equipment around the clock. Remember the tour?"

I do. Pipes and machines and pumps...and I don't know what I expected, but it wasn't that. I thought it would feel more—sanitized.

"It's a fascinating angle for the report, though."

"What do you mean?"

"The way history affects us. That angle will give your conclusion some real spark."

I close my mouth so I won't say what I'm thinking. I didn't know my conclusion needed a *spark*. But now, it's all I can think of. Her video with tasteful font overlays and background music. And my note cards. Of course it needs more.

"Oh, yeah, this is totally it," she says, nodding at her phone. "The factories that sprouted up along this river have been rising and falling for more than a century. Failing businesses aren't concerned with what they toss out or leave behind, but garbage tells a story. History stains everything. I think you should use that."

My thumb is in my mouth, teeth worrying at the nail before I have the sense to pull it free. I press my hands to the table, noting her glossy manicure and perfect skin. What stains did her history leave? In that moment, I think I hate her. For being better. For having more. Maybe because I feel so small beside her.

"Okay, where do you think it would leak from? We found it near the bridge," she says. "Runoff from old trains is my suspicion."

I force my tense shoulders to unclench. There isn't time to change any of this. I need to do my best and finish the job.

"It's not the trains." The steadiness of my voice surprises both of us, I think. "It's been decades since trains used the bridge. Anything that dripped out would be long gone. I think it's leaking out of the bridge itself."

"From underwater?" she asks. Then her eyes go wide. "Like those supports."

"My friend told me about a boat crash a few years back. It hit one of the underwater supports. They did repairs, but maybe they missed something."

"It also means that someone in the water near there could be really exposed, right? You said arsenic can build up in the system, causing all kinds of medical issues."

I pull it up on my phone then, a list that churns my stomach. I recite some of the heavy hitters out loud. "Headaches, dizziness, respiratory failure. Psychosis."

She laughs. "Maybe that's why I've been nuts this week. We were *in* that water!"

My body goes cold. Could I have missed a detail like this? Is it possible that all this stuff I'm experiencing isn't what I thought? Because tainted water feels a lot more likely than some spooky ghost out to haunt me.

"Either way, it needs to go into the report," she says. "I say we check the supports. If we can find any existing damage from that wreck, we could totally propose that. Nothing better to end a project on than a little bit of conspiracy, right?"

I try to answer, but my voice won't come. I nod instead, and Melanie frowns.

"If it scares you, you don't have to." Her expression is gentle. "I don't want to force you to do something that's difficult."

Goose bumps push up on my arms, and I struggle to find a neutral expression. She's watching me, waiting for an answer. Maybe still waiting to report back to my parents on how I cope with a change in plans.

"Difficult?" The sound I make is a terrible imitation of a laugh. "No, it sounds fascinating. I knew my conclusion needed to be stronger."

She leans in again, and her little arm touch feels the slightest bit forced. God, maybe it's not. Maybe it's all in my head, and she's completely concerned.

"I didn't mean anything by that, Paige. Your conclusion was incredibly well researched."

"Oh, I know. But it did need a little punch." I'm saying it now like it's my idea, and it's not. This is one more lie to add to all the others. I smile again, and I feel like I'm wearing someone else's skin. But this is who I want to be, right? Fearless and competent. More like Melanie. I can get there if I keep trying.

"Okay, just remember, I'm here for you. If it's too much or whatever."

"Sure." My voice is a small, choked thing. "Want to go first thing in the morning? Before it's too hot?"

The door to the lab swings open before she can answer. Three of our classmates push in. Jenna is in front, looking flushed with excitement. Elise and Keaton—I can feel Melanie's eyes on me and remember she thinks I have a thing for him—are behind.

"You have to come quick!" Jenna says.

Melanie frowns. "What is it?"

"Someone died on the bridge!" Jenna punctuates her statement with a grin.

"Shut up, Jenna!" Elise sighs theatrically. "No one's dead."

"Well, he could be." Keaton shrugs. "They've got a squad there working on him."

Squad working on him. *Theo.* Theo is on the bridge.

"What are you even talking about?" Melanie asks.

"I don't know… One of the guys working on the walking bridge. He fell or something."

I stand up, and my stomach falls away.

"They say the bridge is totally cursed."

Melanie takes my wrist. "Paige, are you okay?"

No. Not even close. Everyone is watching me. Everyone is waiting for me to say something. My ribs crank tighter with each breath.

"I'm so sorry." I yank my phone out of my pocket and stare at the blank screen. "I have to take this."

I press the phone to my ear and mimic the start of a fake conversation with a mother who didn't call. It takes all the strength I have to keep myself at a brisk walk past the lab and the campus buildings. At the end of the grass, I drop the act and pocket my phone.

But the bridge is empty.

Well, not empty.

I can see people strolling back and forth. A pair of bikes, riding single file, zip past the walker. I see Denny too, at the far end of the bridge. He's sitting near the railing on the opposite side of the bridge. Smoking and checking out a tool with red handles.

What I don't see is Theo. The conversation about an ambulance and an injury feel surreal. If something happened, why would Denny still be here? Did I mishear that whole conversation? Did they mean the State Street bridge?

I don't know. The only thing I'm sure of is that Theo's absence has me terrified.

THEO

The text comes through just like the last six.

Get your ass back in bed. Stop texting.

I throw my phone and smear my hands over my sweaty face.

"Sure, Denny. Can't sleep at night, but why not at two in the afternoon when it's eight hundred degrees in this shithole?"

I drop my fists to the mostly deflated air mattress and crawl out. It's a little early for my evening meds, but I swallow the two pills dry anyway. A fast-acting, short-duration stimulant and that antianxiety pill that's supposed to help with the auditory hallucinations so I can sleep. Of course, I'm not going to sleep anytime soon, and unless I'm planning on having Paige and Gabriel pop the pills too, I think the so-called hallucinations are here to stay.

Whatever. If the pills take off any kind of edge, I'm not keen on trying life without them.

Standing up doesn't help. I feel like shit that's been hammered flat and laid out in the sun to dry. My head is killing me. They might have been right about that concussion. The squad wanted to take me in *for observation*, but Denny and I both refused. I still remember my mom bellowing about the sixteen-hundred-dollar bill that came in the last time I took a little ride in an ambulance for eight stitches in my hairline.

I don't need six hours in a hospital hooked up to machines. I need to get out of this sweatbox. And I need a shower and some fresh clothes because I smell like I've been wrestling a dead yak.

I tug a pair of dirty jeans off the floor, but my shirts are rank. There's a basket in the hall, everything a wadded, wrinkled mess, but God love Denny because it smells like soap so he must have thrown some of my stuff in with his wash.

I move through the shower fast, and there isn't much improvement in the mirror when I'm done. There's a long bruise on my cheekbone, plum purple and trailing up toward my eye. Must have hit the railing on my way down.

Maybe Gabriel was right about the locks being bad news. They broke the cutters I was using. That seemingly indestructible blade was chewed up and twisted. Denny found that out while the paramedics were asking me to count to ten and spell my name.

Denny was pissed, but I'm grateful. I don't want any more locks cut today. Every time I think about the scrape of my blade down the arms of those locks—and the screams and voices that came after—it's worse than fingernails on a chalkboard. It was more electric shock than noise, and I can still feel it, buzzing and sparking deep in the marrow of my bones.

Downstairs, it's all of four degrees cooler, and I'm already starting to sweat. I close my eyes and brace my hand on the wall by the couch, and my mind stretches long fingers back to those awful moments before I fell.

All those voices. What the hell are they trying to tell me?

I hold my phone and consider a call to Dr. Atwood. Fat lot of good it would do me, though. My brain is a twenty-four-seven shit show, but I don't think any of this can be filed under a diagnosis.

I need to talk to Gabriel and find out about those experts. There has to be a way to stop whatever spirit or power is behind this. An exorcism or whatever. We have to stop it before something worse happens. Denny firing me for turning into a lunatic, or hell, Paige sleepwalking right into the river. God knows what could happen, but I doubt anything good.

Outside, the sun is blinding, so I stay inside the door to text Gabriel.

What's up today? You at the library?

Yeah, and I found something interesting online. Did you cut off any more locks?

Yeah.

Did anything happen?

I smirk. You could say that. I'll come over.

It'll have to be later. I'm shelving.

I open the door and jump. Paige is here—on the broken air conditioner in pale shorts and a gauzy white tank. She's chewing whatever's left of her thumbnail.

"Hey," she says.

I roll my shoulders. "Hey. Did you knock?"

"No. I wasn't sure…" She stops and sighs. "I heard there was an accident on the bridge."

"Oh. Yeah. Sorry, I'm fine. Did you talk to Denny?"

She shakes her head. "Just a lucky guess. I figured he wouldn't still be there…"

"If I was in real trouble."

Paige gets up slowly, and I can feel the bruise on my face burning when she crosses the porch. She frowns a little, and then she reaches like she's going to touch me. I hold my breath, and some part of me can already feel it—her fingers cool and soft and small against my cheekbone. She changes her mind and drops her hand.

"I'm all right," I say automatically, nudging the coffee can that serves as Denny's ashtray.

Paige doesn't respond, and I'm not sure what else to say. I

don't want to tell her what happened, even though I probably should. I don't want to ask her why she's here, because I don't want her to think about it. I want her to stay.

"Tell me what happened," she says.

"You won't like it."

"Do I ever?"

I laugh. "Fair point. I cut off some of the locks on the bridge, and it didn't go well. The paranormal activity went into overdrive. And by overdrive, I mean the voices knocked me out cold."

"Was it more voices from the party?"

"No. This was weird. I heard voices again, but not us, and not from that night. It was other people, conversations I'd never heard. Like every bad night any couple on those locks had. And I had to hear them all."

She's thinking about that. I can see it in the crease between her brows.

"You sure it was the couples from the locks?"

"No idea." I sigh. "It's my best guess, though. The whole situation doesn't make any sense."

"Maybe it does," she says, sounding distracted. Then her eyes are clear, and she's studying me. "Do you usually hear me, Theo?"

I drop my gaze to her shoes, pretty beige slip-ons that make me think of dancer's shoes. Paige is like those shoes: sensible and beautiful. And I put her in a plastic chair with broken teeth and blood dripping off her chin. That's what I'm like. "Yes. You and me and Chase. Always from that night."

"I don't hear us talking, but I see things," she says. "The earring and the purse—they were both at the party. But maybe that's not a supernatural haunting, Theo. Maybe it's just our memories, or maybe it's baggage from that party. Maybe we *are* haunted, but not in the way you think."

"I don't know," I say.

She looks at the door. "Can we sit inside?"

"It's miserably hot in there."

"But no one's home, right?"

"No, why?"

"Because I think we need to talk about that night, Theo. It might help."

She's right and I know it, but my stomach swings low and hangs there. I don't know if I want to play true confessions in that hot, dark coffin of a living room. I don't know if I want to revisit everything that led us to that nightmare. But then somehow, I'm unlocking the door and holding it open.

PAIGE

I've only been here twice. Denny's house is small and dark. They usually have an air conditioner humming in the living room window. Theo explains that it's broken. I already know because I was sitting on it on the porch. I tell him it's okay anyway.

My shoulders tense at the cluttered coffee table. He's automatically moving, clearing me a space. I don't sit down, but he heads to the kitchen for a rag. Wipes down my place because he knows me. And because I matter to him.

That last part is easy to forget when he knocks out your teeth, but it's impossible to miss when he's standing in front of me, doing what I need without asking. He turns on an ancient oscillating fan and sits down.

I finally sit too, while the fan whirs slowly back and forth. The air moving over us is still warm, but better.

"You drank that night," I say, to start. "More than usual. You'd been cutting way back."

He smiles at his lap. "Someone told me I probably didn't need another substance to depend on."

"*Someone* thought you weren't listening."

"I was," he says. I hear him swallow hard. "Paige, you know why I was drinking."

He's right, and we don't need to play these games. I sigh. "When did it start?"

"My feelings for you? Probably the day I locked my keys in the car in the rain."

I shake my head, because I remember it. I also can't fathom what it has to do with anything. "That was February."

"I hid the way I felt at first. It sucked."

"So did locking the keys in the car."

"Yeah, it did." His voice goes low, and his fingers fiddle at the edge of his pockets. But he holds my eyes, so I know this matters. "I was such an annoying shit that night. Laughing about locking them in there. I rode that shopping cart over to the car, while you were trying to figure out a plan. I even threatened to smash it into the window."

"Yes, and then we went in and bought a wire hanger, and how is that the moment when things changed for us?"

"It's not the moment they changed for us. It's the moment

they changed for me." He swallows. "You knew to buy the hanger, and when that didn't work, you knew to ask security, because they might be able to help, and they did. That little bar tool they had popped the lock right open. And you were so quiet and calm, even in the freezing-ass rain, and that's the first time I realized."

"Realized what?"

"How amazing you are," he says.

His voice is reverent, and I know this is no throwaway compliment. This isn't a crush for him, and I knew that. I *knew*. But it is different to hear it.

"I thought it was just me being me," he says. "It's not like I never noticed you, and for a while, I know you noticed me." The fan clicks and hums its way back to the left side of the room. My hair sways, and my heart pounds.

Theo scoots the tiniest bit closer to me. "I don't even know if this makes sense. Do you even understand what I'm saying?"

I do, but I can't force a single word past my lips. I feel untethered.

"I thought it was one of those things," he says. "Hormones and me being me, but this isn't some hot girl I met at the pool, this is *you*. You aren't other girls. That night, I wanted to tell you. Hell, I almost kissed you at one point on the bridge, which is crazy—even for me."

He shakes his head. "You were there for *Chase*. You grew up and wanted something better, and you should. But it was *Chase*, and he was being such an ass to you at that party, and somehow all that shit ran together. Add in the world's greatest fuckup and..." His voice catches, and it splits me open.

"I threw a punch," he says. "I *hit* you. *Hurt you.*"

He's close to crying. I can hear it. "I hoped... I thought that maybe the voices on the bridge were trying to teach me a lesson. Make me better. But I can't dig out whatever broken thing is lodged in my head and turn into a role model. Eighteen years of being me has taught me that much. But *you* could, Paige. Maybe that's what this is about. Reminding us that you're not too screwed up to get past all this."

"Don't say that," I say. "I'm not better than you."

"Really? When's the last time you were suspended? Or arrested? This isn't self-pity, Paige. It's truth."

I suck one gulping breath after another, but the air feels thin. He's wrong, and he's right. My crazy has always been easier to hide.

We're both tainted water, but Theo's bubbles up on the surface like an oil spill. Mine is invisible. Arsenic hiding in plain sight.

I'll never get fired. I'll never get in a fistfight. When you stand me next to Theo, I'm the picture of mental health and stability. I'm not better than him, but I know I look like I am.

Theo's hands shake on his lap. The fan moves his hair, and

he watches me like I am all he's ever wanted in this world. I feel so strong and loved that it's hard to think about what the world might think. It's even harder to imagine why I'd care.

He closes his eyes, his voice barely more than breath. "Say something?"

I'm breathing hard, and I can't look at him. I drop my eyes to his hands. His palms are turned up on the awful couch, fingers curved a little. He holds his hands out to me so I inch my fingers forward. I graze my index finger along the side of his thumb. The tiniest brush, but it's electric.

I don't know who's trembling more when I slide my palm over his. His fingers curl into my wrist. The sigh he lets out hooks behind my ribs. And pulls hard.

I lean in until our foreheads touch. He's breathing fast, and my pulse is flying. It's all we can do to hold ourselves there. To not close that final gap.

"God, I wanted that lock to be telling me something," he says.

I shiver, feeling each word against my lips.

"Maybe it is," I say, moving my hands to his face, thumbs feathering against his lower lip. "I thought it was stupid, but maybe…"

"Paige?"

My name is a strangled question. He's pleading for a confession I waited years to give him. And now it's time.

I shift until our mouths are close, and then I find my voice. "I put that lock on the bridge."

THEO

She put our lock on the bridge. Touching that lock kept the ghosts away—it kept me sane. That's *her* lock, and I've never been one for patience or for knowing the right thing to say at the right time. So I kiss her.

I never really thought about kissing her, but I should have, because we kiss just like we do everything else. There's no fumbling nonsense. Her hands are on my face, and I'm stroking her neck, and it is easy and right. We fit together like we're meant to be.

She pushes closer and I help her, pulling her knees over mine and bumping the coffee table with my elbow. It doesn't matter. Her body is warm and her hands are cool, and she tastes like every good thing I've ever known. Because she *is* every good thing.

And I'm not.

I wrench myself from her mouth, wincing at the reluctant

sound she makes. Hating myself for tangling her up with me again. This is exactly what I swore not to do. All of it.

"No." I have to pant it out, because I can barely talk. Her hands are on my shoulders, and she smells so good this close. It's like tearing apart magnets. I groan and force myself back another inch.

Across from me she is red-cheeked and breathing hard. Her eyes glitter with sudden tears. "What's wrong?"

"We can't do this. This is crazy."

Her face falls. "Kissing me is crazy?"

Leave it to me to screw even this up. I take her hands in both of mine, and she lets me. "No, not like that. After what I did, this feels—"

"Unhealthy." She supplies the word easily.

It's not the one I would have picked, but it works well enough.

She pulls her hands away and goes on. "My therapist talked to me about this."

"About us?"

She flushes. "About the way I felt about you, at least. Mom suspected too. She worried about it because she and Dad think we're codependent."

She rolls her eyes, but my stomach drops. I've heard that word in my own therapist's office when discussing our friendship. I told him I preferred the term *symbiotic*. But I get it.

Paige is like the bumpers on a bowling alley for me. Without her, I wind up knocking random pins out of twelve different lanes before landing on a plate of fries. I guess I help Paige when she falls apart, but that doesn't feel the same.

"I always believed we were helping each other." She sighs. "But neither of us was getting any better, Theo. I was still an anxious mess, and you were still…"

"Me. I was still me." I sigh. "I swear I didn't mean for this to happen. I was going to leave you alone…let you live on or whatever."

"I know. Me too."

I scrape my fingers at the sides of her knees because letting her go is impossible. The idea of it swells up high in my throat, colder than fear. I push it out with a breath.

"Look, Paige, I know we can't be like we were. I don't know where we could go from here, but whatever's happening to us on that bridge, I think we have a better shot of ending it if we're together."

"You can't know that," she says, but she's tracing a finger over my hand.

"Maybe not," I relent, "but I know I feel steadier around you. Even when I touch your lock, the haunting crap stops."

She laughs, and it's almost sad. "Theo, that lock isn't magic. I put it there when I was fourteen. It was no different than wishing on a star."

I look up, remembering. "That was the last time you were on the bridge, wasn't it?"

"Yes." She shakes her head. "And I felt incredibly stupid afterward. Trust me, Theo. That lock didn't bring us together. It isn't magic. The answer to this so-called haunting is probably more logical than we think."

"Paige, come on. I'm hearing voices. You found an earring you wore three months ago. It isn't logical."

She goes very still, as if she's thinking that over. "But it could be. Coincidences do happen. And with me being anxious—"

"Anxious? You can't *anxious* a purse into the water. That bridge is *haunted*."

"What if it isn't? I found impurities in that water. We're both on medication and fresh out of a pretty serious trauma. There could be another explanation."

I relent, pushing my hands into my messy hair. "Okay, I get it. Ghosts are well outside your comfort zone, but you can't seriously sit here trying to tell me it's all in our heads."

She scoots back on the couch, with a frown. "I wish I'd kept the stupid purse. I'm starting to wonder if I made it up."

"You didn't make it up. I've smelled things and heard our conversation, Paige. You and me...even Chase."

"That can happen. Think about it. Do you remember the night swim? The one at freshman camp? I thought there were snakes in the water."

I remember Paige shuddering at the edge of the lake. We

ended up waiting out by the cabins, eating Twinkies I stole out of a vending machine.

"You were younger then," I argue. "Still afraid of the dark. This is different."

"Is it? You know what people with paranormal experiences have in common?"

"Unflattering online photographs?"

"High levels of stress. Mental health issues. These people are usually written off for a reason," she says.

"Yeah, because they're seeing something hard to believe. If this bridge isn't haunted, then what the hell is happening to me? To *us*?"

She tucks her hair behind her ear with a sigh. "I don't know. I'm not saying it isn't all completely bizarre. But strange things often have mundane explanations."

"What do you mean?"

"There's a high level of arsenic in the water. I think it's leaching out of the bridge somewhere."

"And, what, it's only making the two of us crazy? Feels like a stretch."

"How is that so much crazier than a ghost dropping pretzels in a river?"

"You think arsenic could drop pretzels in the water?"

"Of course not, but it could mess with my head. Make me think

I'm seeing things. Make you think you're hearing things. You're working on the bridge, and I'm in the water. There's a connection."

"Do you realize how unlikely this sounds?"

"What part of this isn't unlikely?" she asks.

She's wearing her stubborn face, the one she puts on when she's determined to ace a test. I tap my thumb at her ankle and watch her sigh.

"It's not some weird chemical in the water, Paige. Deep down, I think you know that."

She frowns. "I don't know what I know. That's why I need answers."

"What if we don't find one? What then?"

"I guess we'll deal with that," she says.

"Well, let's hope you get your answer before you find something even worse. And before I have to cut off the rest of those locks. Cutting off eight knocked me flat on my ass."

"Will you cut them all?"

"All but one," I say. And I can tell by the way her eyes light up that I don't have to tell her which lock will stay.

PAIGE

My search the next morning pulls fifteen solid resources with information on arsenic poisoning. Not that I can read them. All I can do is relive three minutes on a dirty couch. Three minutes with a boy I should never have kissed.

If my parents knew… I can barely even think it. There's no one I can talk to about what happened with Theo. I gaze over the top of my laptop to the other half of our dorm room. It's a mirror of my side, twin bed, small desk-shelf combo at the end. Melanie is on her laptop, poring over the industrial history of Portsville. Putting final touches on her video before we do the last hands-on research.

I don't think anything about walking out of the lab yesterday until I hear her on my way back from the restroom. Snippets of a one-sided conversation. I have no right to listen. It's eavesdropping, and it's wrong. And still I pause at the cracked door to our room, hand hesitating at the knob.

"…just disappeared. She was gone for *hours*."

Then, "I know I have to say something. But I feel weird, you know?"

I lurch back from the door, heart pounding. That was me. I'm the one who disappeared. I walked out and vanished for three hours and came back with zero explanation. How could I not think about how weird that would look?

Everyone else was getting dinner or maybe practicing sections of their presentations. But I was kissing Theo. Living my other life.

"Well, she didn't look like she'd been studying." Melanie ends it with a laugh.

My cheeks burn. I've heard enough. I retrace my steps as quietly as I can. I go all the way to the bathroom, like if I go back far enough I'll be able to unhear what she said.

I wait at the bathroom door, steadying myself with a hand on the wall. I need to breathe. And think.

What do I do? She said she needs to tell someone. And that someone has to be Dr. Lutmer or my parents, right?

So, now what? Confront her? I can't imagine a more uncomfortable conversation. We still have to finish this presentation, and no way will we get through that if we're awkward with each other.

Would it even stop her?

I think about that for a while, knowing it wouldn't. If anything, knowing I'm listening in on her private phone calls might make her that much more likely to say something. If she thinks she needs to tell, she's going to tell.

So, she needs to think there's nothing worth talking about.

I close my eyes and draw a steadying breath. Okay. This isn't rocket science. I just need to fake it, and it's not like I haven't done enough of that over the years. If I'm not disappearing or overly stressed, she'll get wrapped up in her own life again. She'll forget. Hopefully.

I clomp my way back to the room, giving her every bit of possible warning. Back in the room, I offer her one of my sodas from our tiny fridge. I comment about my new conclusion and compliment her video.

Melanie smiles and chimes in, and maybe that's all it will take. Occasionally she glances at me over the top of her laptop, when she thinks I'm not watching. I force myself to tap on the keyboard, but I feel her gaze on me, heavy enough to stall out my keystrokes.

"You seem distracted today," she says.

So much for the forgetting-all-about-it plan. I force a smile. "A little. I'm all right."

"I've been meaning to ask you. When they burst in yesterday, you kind of freaked out."

Something tells me whatever I say now will decide what she does next. I think of lying, blaming it all on that phony call.

But she knows better. The best lies contain a heavy dose of truth anyway.

I sigh. "Violence like that freaks me out. I'd been feeling really good so I didn't want to let a little drama affect that. If you have anxiety, you learn to have strategies. Rather than have a panic attack, I can take a walk. I can be in control of myself."

"That's really cool, Paige." Her expression tells me she means it. Maybe even admires me for it. The flare of heat in my chest shouldn't feel like triumph, but it does.

I click on a link, determined to change topics. "You know the plastics plant down at the river bend south of town? There was an old metal factory there that supplied several parts for the original bridge supports."

"Yeah?"

I clear my throat. "According to this historical foundation site, that factory was plagued with worker health problems and soon shut down."

"Because they were working with contaminated materials," she says.

"Exactly. I'm thinking of using that in my closing statement." I feel stronger now, more sure of the work I've done. "I'll challenge the class to consider the dangers faced by workers in the past."

"The whole presentation will be proof that we can never fully escape our own history."

My stomach drops, but she laughs.

"Right," I croak, a dull soft ache in my jaw.

"It's perfect," she says, grinning as she shuts her laptop. "That line is so perfect! Better than the stained line. Come on, let's go finish up the river work."

We need to check the supports by the bridge, and it was my idea. A good idea. But I don't want to stand by that water anymore. That weathered dock is still there with stains from my blood and bits of my broken soul. That's my history. And I don't want to believe it will always be with me.

"Earth to Paige," she says. "Are you ready?"

An electric chill coasts up the back of my neck. "Sure. But what if the water is too deep?"

"That's why we're getting the boat, remember? I think we should try to take pictures first. See if there's any obvious visible damage above the surface. The river is about four feet lower than that year, from what I researched."

"We need personal protective gear," I say.

"The biology department said we could borrow some. Longer waders and those extra-long rubber lab gloves. So, what do you think?"

What I think is that Theo is at the bridge. After what happened yesterday, would Melanie put more pieces together? Even if he's not there, will I hold it together? That bridge ratchets up all of my bad emotions. I can't have her witnessing some kind of meltdown.

But I can't think of an excuse that makes sense, so we head out. She smiles at me as we walk, but her gaze lingers when she looks at me. Can she tell I'm nervous? Is she watching me?

It's completely paranoid, and I can be better than this. She's walking like any normal person would. Still, my cheeks burn as I pull on my worn flats and force myself to smile.

The day is clear and warm, but sweat dampens my palms and back. The moment the bridge comes into view, I see him. The walking bridge is closed, and they're halfway through replacing the planking closest to our side. Almost done, then. But locks glimmer up and down the railing, so that job is still unfinished.

"Work with a view today," Melanie says, chuckling.

She's probably referring to Theo and his lack of a shirt. I've seen him shirtless plenty, but not after kissing him. I can practically feel the heat of his skin, the scrape of his stubble against my chin.

Theo shouts something at Denny, and I turn away. I think they're finishing up, because I can hear them walking around. Theo stops, and I'm pretty sure I know why. He's seen us.

Melanie looks up at the bridge, grinning. She's clearly seen him too. But the twinge in my gut isn't jealousy. It's fear.

Will she recognize him?

I glance up, wishing we'd picked a picnic table farther down the banks. Wishing he wasn't thirty feet away wearing a backward hat and a devilish grin.

I pull off my zip-up sweatshirt and throw it on one of the picnic table seats, out of plain sight. Then I put on the waders, hoping he'll ignore us.

"Hey, stranger."

I turn toward his voice. Theo's face is lost in shadow, but heat spreads through my chest all the same. I don't mean to smile, but I do.

"Hey."

"Nice outfit."

We're practically yelling to hear each other. Melanie cups her hand over her eyes. It's probably too late to hope she doesn't recognize him.

"Safety over fashion," Melanie singsongs. "Wait. You're Paige's friend, right? From the lawn the other day."

"Yeah, we're friends," he says.

My mind supplies a vivid flash of his hands on my face, his mouth soft and open and hungry. I cover my burning cheeks and realize I've forgotten my gloves.

Melanie starts to say something else, but Denny calls Theo back. Thank God. Though I'm going to be working below him. From below, he will look like that shadow I saw. Like someone who might want to jump.

I turn away, searching for the gloves. Melanie is giving me knowing looks, and I'm shaking so hard I can barely get on my boots. I can practically feel my mom eavesdropping. It's ridiculous and paranoid, but I can't shake it.

Ten minutes later, we're down the banks and thigh-deep in murky river water, trying to figure out how we can get past the first support pillars. After a quick look around, it's clear we won't be able to get close enough. And walking around the supports we can reach yields nothing.

We walk under the bridge to the boat rental kiosk attached to the ice cream shop. The boat is easier to manage than we thought, but examining the pillars is tedious work, looking at every visible inch for weakness or wear. I can almost forget that Theo is up there. I can almost forget that my teeth and heart were broken twenty feet from this place.

Footsteps and hammers and the occasional murmur of one instruction or another are our background music as we search. We check each pillar, climbing out when we can, and reaching gloved hands into the water to feel the submerged parts when we can't.

There are bird nests crammed on the top of the cement, close to the underside of the bridge. If I didn't see the nests, the streaks of gray-white down the pillar sides would tell me enough. I think of avian flu and salmonella and other diseases, and I force myself to check the filthy streaked sections anyway.

Everything is smooth and solid on the first two we check. I pull my arms out, water dripping.

"Nothing here," I shout back to Melanie.

As we're rowing to the next one, I spot a sliver of black on the cement, one that leads under the water. *Is that a crack?* I know better than to get hopeful. It's probably rust or dirt. Maybe a plant. We swing the boat around where I can see it better.

"I think I've got something," I say, pointing.

Melanie throws the anchor and scoots closer, boat bobbing in the water. She presses her fingers into the fissure, then reaches for her phone, opening the flashlight.

She nods. "Oh, yeah. This is what we're looking for."

The crack isn't much, situated on the inside facing another support beam. It'd be almost impossible to see and too small to catch any real notice or attention unless someone was obsessing like we are.

"Do you think it's big enough?" I ask.

"Wouldn't take much," Melanie says. "Think of food coloring in a bathtub. One drop would make a difference."

We spend a few minutes taking notes and pictures. We measure the width and depth and note the spaces where the cement is beginning to crumble. Tiny changes. But if this is where the arsenic is coming from, this fracture is important. And so is our presentation.

We return the boat and make our way back under the bridge on the walking path. By the time we're climbing the grassy hill back to the tables, we're both giddy.

"I can't believe we found it." Melanie says as she peels off her gloves. "I suppose it's not definitive proof."

"Hardly," I say, but my cheeks hurt from smiling.

"Yeah, but I'm going with Occam's razor," she says. "The simplest answer is usually the right one."

I grin. "I like that theory."

I strip off my gloves and shuffle up to the picnic table. The pair of sandals on top stops me dead.

They are lined up side by side, like someone just slipped them off. For half a second, I think I've interrupted a picnic. And then I look again at the gold straps. The tiny buckle. The small stain on the outside edge of the left one. Red-brown like blood.

My stomach drops like a stone.

These are my shoes from the party.

The memory blasts through me. I'm sitting on a plastic chair. I'm holding my hands over my mouth. I'm dripping blood onto my beautiful shoes.

These are the sandals I wore to the party.

I suck in a breath. My head spins. No, they have to be someone else's. The shoes I wore are gone, pushed deep in the hospital bag with hard plastic handles and letters that read *Personal Belongings*.

Bloodstained clothes don't seem like belongings, though, so I pushed them into the trash can in our garage, under our rotten food and used tissues.

I threw away these shoes, so they can't be here. Not unless someone dug them out of the trash before the truck came. *No one* would do that.

A hand falls heavily on my shoulder, and I yelp. Melanie. It's only Melanie.

"Geez, Jumpy." She looks at the shoes and scoffs. "I'm not sure they're cute enough to steal. Kind of dirty."

"They're mine." My voice sounds faraway. "I lost them."

"Oh. Maybe your friend found them and wanted to surprise you."

My body goes cold. I blink at the sandals, feeling a million miles away.

There has to be an explanation. Theo didn't have these, and Theo would never…

Would he?

"I don't know," I say.

"Ugh, I'm starving," Melanie says, struggling to fold her waders.

Her vinyl pants crinkle, reminding me to take off my gear. I move like someone else is controlling my limbs. Pull here. Bend now. Tug this part. All the while, my veins flutter with adrenaline—liquid panic. It will grow until my ribs hurt, until

I won't be able to breathe. Until I'm rocking and shivering in a full-blown anxiety attack.

My gaze is drawn to the bridge. Theo's long gone, and the so-called haunted bridge doesn't look haunted at all. Couples walk back and forth. Do I really believe there's some supernatural presence up there?

My shoes stare at me, testing me. They do not feel like ghostly business. The earring…maybe. Even the purse. But this pair of shoes isn't floating in a river of mud or sticking in my father's shoe. These sandals were *placed* here. Side by side, lined up just so.

This feels human.

And I can only think of one human who's been here to do it.

"I'm going to order subs," Melanie says, tapping at her phone, blessedly ignorant of my chattering teeth and panting. "You want one?"

I nod, not trusting myself to speak. Seeing Theo in my mind's eye, climbing down from the bridge, shirt still off and eyes on the river. I imagine him setting them up.

A rush of blood roars behind my ears. I feel dizzy.

No. Theo would not do something like this. He *wouldn't*. He cares about me. He kissed me, for God's sake.

And once upon a time he hit me too.

I gaze at the bridge where Theo and Denny were working. They're gone now. On lunch break. I try to remember hearing them leave, but I was caught up in cement pillars and impressive project scores.

Melanie's laugh makes me jump. "Well, are you going to leave them here?"

I don't know what to say or do. I feel her watching, and I remember her phone call earlier. I am forty-eight hours from this presentation, and I can't be crazy. Not with her.

"Get your shoes, already," she says.

I take the sandals.

The sun shines the whole way back. My shoes bang against my thigh with every step, but I don't look. Birds sing. Melanie talks. I don't listen, because I'm thinking of something else she said back there. Occam's razor.

The simplest answer is usually right.

THEO

Gabriel is still researching when I get to the library. He holds so still when he reads that I wonder if he's fallen asleep. But when I clear my throat, he gives me a dirty look and tells me to organize my research while he finishes up.

My research was all phone based and only loosely research based. After a few random searches, I got sucked into a bunch of cool photo galleries of bridge graffiti. And then bridge stunts. And somehow that led to card tricks. From what I can see on the table across from me, Gabriel read twenty-five books and took a thousand pages of notes.

The way I figure, there are two kinds of people in the world when it comes to studying. People like Paige and Gabriel, and then all the rest of us.

One therapist back in junior high gave me a list of careers good for high-energy individuals. That was when I got the idea of being a fireman or a paramedic. It didn't seem like a job where I'd spend much time at a desk. And I'd help people for a change.

Before all this, maybe I could have done that. Maybe I would have.

Gabriel looks up from his book, pulling my attention back to the here and now.

"Are you medicated today?" he asks me.

"What the hell kind of question is that?"

He shrugs one shoulder. "Considering the three prescription bottles in your uncle's truck, it seems like a valid one."

"You're a snoopy little shit, you know that? They could have been his."

"Not unless Denny is a nickname for Theodore. Also, you mentioned it in the library when we met. You seem really fidgety."

"Well, for the record, I *am* medicated—today, yesterday, and every day. Thanks so much for asking. Maybe you'd like to talk about my broken childhood next?"

"Not particularly." He flips his notebook closed. "So, who's going first?"

"You. Tell me what you found. Did you look into that suicide?"

"Like I said, that's not what this is about. It happened, but the guy had problems."

"But he chose to kill himself on the bridge. There could be a reason for that."

"He didn't have any history on that bridge. You're thinking of the rumors."

"Rumors usually start with some piece of truth, right?"

He pushes back from the table, looking angry. "Why are you so obsessed with that one tragedy? Things have been happening on that bridge a lot longer than the sixteen years since he died."

"Are you sure?"

"We're not looking for a tragic guy. We're looking for a tragedy *involving* the bridge and locks. Do you know what I mean?"

Suicide by jumping feels about as on-the-nose as we can get, but Gabriel's not buying it. Since he's the one with a stack of dog-eared books next to him, I slouch back into my chair.

"Okay, I give. What's your theory?"

"There was a train collision. A passenger killed on the other side of the bridge, a girl a few days from getting married."

"But it wasn't on the bridge?"

"It's still possible. The train was traveling across the bridge right before it happened. Can't be sure if they had a lock on the bridge, but since they were together in high school, it seems likely."

"Okay, what else?"

He pauses, looking like he'd been saving this one. "There was a couple who definitely had a lock on the bridge. It was, like, twenty-five years ago."

"What?"

"AT and JS. Adam Tilton and Janice Sorenson."

"All right, what about them?"

"Janice disappeared. She and Adam were both biology majors, fell in love over the microscope, you know? They broke up in early senior year, and she became obsessed with the bridge. Wrote this big article for her sorority newsletter about how all the couples with locks on the bridges were doomed."

"You found the article? Show me."

"I can't. The college confiscated the newsletter and no copies have turned up. There was a little write-up in the community paper though, because Janice was expelled."

"For being hung up on a guy?"

"Apparently for inciting campus-wide panic. She published scary stuff that had happened. Couples who had broken up, some random folks who had died. Cancer and accidents—it happens, you know?"

"Yeah, I know." I scoot forward. "That was probably when all the rumors started, right?"

"Seems like it." He shifts into motion, taking the notebook from the floor and flipping to a page. "Anyway, according to the article, Janice didn't do well after that. She moved to Rhode Island for some weird reason and wasn't heard from again."

"What happened to Adam?"

Gabriel shrugs. "Adam's still in town. He works at the DuPont factory, cutting sheets of plastic."

"Speaking of cutting." I slouch lower on the couch. Hearing voices is one thing, but there's no low-drama way to tell someone you passed out cold because you cut off some locks and heard a bunch of strange voices. Still, he's trying to help, so I tell him.

Gabriel listens in that stone-still way of his, finally sitting back, arms folded. "You know what this means?"

"That the locks are involved. I know."

"We already figured that. What's new is that this is the first time *your* actions have started one of the incidents."

I start to respond, but stop cold because he's right. Every other time, the bridge started the haunting. This time was different. I cut the lock, and the bridge made me pay.

"Okay, so we cut off the rest of the locks?"

He shakes his head slowly. "I think we need to talk to Shaun or Jerry."

I lean back, tipping my wooden library chair back on the two back legs. "Please tell me Shaun and Jerry aren't the douchebags who run the ghost tours."

"They aren't douchebags. And Shaun agreed to meet with us."

"Okay, then I'll go with the *con artists* who run the ghost tours. Worst of all, their tours skip the only haunted place in this shitty town."

"They're not con artists. Shaun has a master's degree."

"Master's in what? Witchy *woo-woo* or chain rattling?"

"I don't see why you're being so illogical about it. If you had a money problem, you'd go to a banker or an accountant. If you needed to write a paper, you'd talk to an English major, you know?"

I let my chair drop back to the floor with a thunk. "Fine. What do the ghost experts say?"

"Not much yet. I texted them. Shaun thinks you're dealing with an energy haunting."

"Like a poltergeist?"

He looks at me as if I likened the energy haunting to a bowl of macaroni and cheese. "No. *Nothing* like a poltergeist. Poltergeist comes from the German word *Polter*, which means noisy, and *Geist*, which means ghost."

"Um, isn't that pretty much exactly what this is? Playing music, making voices."

"No, a poltergeist has big physical manifestations. Doors opening and closing, glass breaking. Objects flying around the room. Poltergeists are pretty hard to ignore."

"So are ghosts that knock you out when you touch their locks, but whatever. Not a poltergeist. Paige hasn't just heard voices; she found a purse. And earrings. Both of which were from the party. So what's that about?"

He cocks his head. "She's found actual physical items."

"Yes. Items she lost are coming back to her. Do ghosts do that?"

"I've never heard of an episode like that on the bridge. Are you sure she's really finding things, not just seeing them?"

"Can you think of a reason for her to lie?"

"Guess not, but either way, none of this sounds like a ghost, if you think about it. Ghosts are usually reliving a moment from their own life, but even ghosts with some other purpose wouldn't know the details of what happened to you and Paige."

"Nothing *happened* to Paige and me. I *made* it happen."

"Regardless, something is feeding on the negativity there. Energy haunting makes sense."

"And the other voices I heard? What do they have to do with me?"

He shrugs. "From what you said, it didn't sound like they were 'happily ever after' memories either. Still negative energy. This is why I think we need Shaun."

"Why? Is he going to offer a bridge exorcism for fifty percent off?"

Gabriel closes his notepad and sits very quietly. I get the impression that I've hurt him, which means I've *definitely* hurt him. I'm not big on impressions. I'm more of a club-me-over-the-head-with-the-abundantly-obvious type.

"I heard something too, you know," he says softly.

"Yes. Some woman. And you said yourself that she was nice

to you. Which first off doesn't really line up with all the bad energy you're talking about. And it also doesn't line up since you don't have a lock on that bridge."

He stares at the table and doesn't move. The stretch of silence is sending bursts of energy dancing in my fingers and legs, but something holds me still. I wait for him to respond.

"There is a lock with my initials."

"You found a lock?"

"That's why I told you not to touch the locks. I was looking at them, and I found one. An old one. Small and blue. It had my initials. Just mine. And there was a date."

"What date?"

He looks at me, his eyes red. "My birthday."

The words send ice up my neck. I don't remember the lock he's talking about, but I can imagine it. Something you'd buy for a baby. Only one kind of person would put a true love lock on a bridge for a baby. A mother.

"You live with your grandfather, don't you?" I ask softly.

"Yes. And I lived with my uncle before that. My mom died when I was three. Heart problem."

"Is that who the voice is?"

He shrugs. "Yes. No. If it were my mother, she would still talk to me. I believe that. I have to believe that. You know what I mean?"

I nod, and Gabriel shakes his head. He looks close to tears and really pissed about it.

"I don't know what the hell it was," he says. "A memory of her, maybe. Some piece of her energy that was left behind. And I hate that it's all mixed up in this."

"Maybe it's not. Maybe part of the energy is positive."

He sniffs and pulls back his shoulders, looking a little taller. "Maybe. All I know for sure is that if there is power in those locks, it's not all bad. You can't destroy them all, because you might be taking something good too. You need to find the source of the problem."

My phone rings, and I startle at the noise. I accept the call without looking, holding up a hand in apology to Gabriel as I slip outside.

"Hello?"

"Theo?"

Paige's voice warms away the rest of the ice left by Gabriel's words.

"Hey, you. How was the river today? I'm with Gabriel again and I've got to say, this kid is—"

I cut off, abruptly aware of how weird it is that she's calling me this late. She takes a breath that shudders on the other end of the line. *Is she scared?*

"What's wrong?" I ask. "Did you find something else?"

A beat of hesitation drags on the other end of the line. "Why would you say that?"

"Because you sound upset. Are you upset?"

"No. I did find something. Just like you guessed, but how would you guess?"

She sounds weird, and I'm too tired for weird. "What did you find?"

"My shoes. The sandals I wore to the party." Her voice is small and quiet, and my fingers itch, remembering her face in my hands, her forehead against mine. Her little ballet flats tucked under her legs. Then I think of other shoes, brown sandals strapped across her pale, freckled toes. I saw blood drip onto those sandals.

"The brown ones." I close my eyes and take a deep breath that smells like rotting wood and damp grass. "Strappy and tall."

"You remember the shoes I wore to the party?"

Her tone bites a little.

I open my eyes and stare at a stack of posters advertising a tag sale at the Presbyterian church. They're dated for last weekend. We could have gotten cheap Christmas lights at that thing, I bet.

"You were drunk," she says, yanking my attention back. I didn't imagine her snippy tone. She's pissed. "How could you remember that kind of detail, Theo?"

"I wasn't drunk when I picked you up, and remember I was

in full-on obsession mode." Her harsh laugh is short and hollow, nothing like her. "What's going on, Paige? Are you all right?"

Her breath is shaky, and I wish I was there. I'm shit at this in general and hopeless as hell over the phone.

"I'm fine," she says. "Or not fine. I don't know. I have to go."

"Wait, I haven't told you what we found. I met up with Gabriel, and he has a theory about all those locks on the bridge."

"A theory."

"Yeah, he thinks we might be experiencing an energy haunting, which makes sense in a way. I mean, as much as a haunted bridge can make sense."

I hear her breathing, but she doesn't speak for a long while. Just before I ask, she adjusts the phone.

"I have to go," she says.

Her voice is flat enough to turn my stomach. She's slipping into her anxious place, where she imagines shadows around every corner. Except this time, she's right. There are shadows waiting for her. Waiting for both of us.

My free hand clenches. "Paige, wait. I promise you, I'm going to find a way to figure this out. This drama is going to end. You just have to hold on a little longer."

"Hold on for what?"

"For…I don't know. For this to *end*."

"I really need to go."

The line clicks, and I pull the phone from my ear in disbelief. There's nothing but a blank screen and dead air.

PAIGE

I don't know if it's paranoia or reality. That's the problem with anxiety disorders. My fear feels as real as any truth. So, is it true? Is Theo behind all of this?

Melanie sits down hard at the cafeteria table. My tray bumps left, and I flinch. She laughs, teeth too white and eyes too wide. She looks monstrous. Everything does.

"Sorry! I'm all elbows and knees today."

She laughs again, and I recoil from the sound. I think of cartoon witches. Then I remember her sitting across from me while I slept. Whispering about me on the phone.

Melanie scares me now. She's not only the smart, gorgeous Chicago girl with a private school background. She's the girl who's watching me. She inspects my life the way we looked at the bridge supports. Looking for cracks in the surface. Points of weakness.

And she might be reporting all that back to someone. About Theo on the bridge. About the way I hide my pill bottles. Maybe she and Dr. Lutmer have even talked about it.

I'm dreaming up all kinds of paranoid scenarios like that. Most of it's probably crazy, but the stuff I think about Theo? That feels right. He's the only one who would have known those shoes were mine.

I force down a bite of pasta salad while Melanie opens her juice.

"I've got the new bridge data layered into the presentation," she says. "Where are you on the new conclusion?"

"It's finished." Lie. "I'll import it tonight." Which means I'd better finish it.

"Or, I could—"

A scream shocks the quiet hum of conversation in the cafeteria. I whirl in my seat, searching. My heart thumps. And then races at the laughter that follows. I smell the river and taste blood. The scream is over. Everything's fine. It was Elise. I can see her laughing, slapping Noah's arm playfully.

It's flirting, but it feels dangerous to me. It feels like a cold plastic chair under my legs. Or blood on my face. My ears hum with the sawing of my own breath. My jaw aches.

Melanie touches my arm, and I jerk.

"Geez, what is going on with you? I kept calling your name."

"I'm sorry. That scream scared me." I immediately regret the admission.

Melanie's dark ponytail lies over her left shoulder. She's frowning at me. Is she worried enough to call my parents now? Has she called them already?

I take a breath and try a laugh that comes out wrong. "I didn't sleep well."

"It's okay." She stops and waves at a guy I don't know. Her smile fades when she turns back to me. "You've been acting weird since you ran off yesterday. I wish you'd talk to me. Did you go to see that boy?"

"No, I got that call from my mom." Maybe I should have said it was someone else. A boy. Melanie doesn't comment, but she doesn't believe me. I can tell by the way her lips go tight and thin. Or maybe that's how her mouth looks and I'm being ridiculous. I don't trust myself anymore.

"I'm concerned about you," she says. "You say you're fine but…"

My fork feels slippery in my sweaty hand. I put it down.

Melanie is staring expectantly, so I wipe my mouth with my napkin. I guess I have to prove that I'm fine. Which is almost funny. I'm bleeding in bathroom sinks. I'm walking across town in my sleep. I'm finding old purses and stained shoes. And I'm kissing a boy who hit me. A haunted boy who might be haunting me.

I'm a very long way from fine.

But I can't tell her that.

And I can't tell her I'm fine, when I'm not.

I take a big bite. It's like chewing pieces of garden hose, but it gives me a minute to think. I can hold up my hand and make her wait. Because whatever I say next needs to convince her that my stress is normal stress. The kind that everyone half brags about—high-pressure classes and too many extracurriculars.

"I think I'm obsessing about college apps," I say, because this is her language. Overachievement. Her eyes brighten, and I think I might convince her.

"I've been thinking maybe I love it here too much, you know? I mean, there's no reason to stay here in Portsville, right?"

She looks uncertain. "Well—"

"There are so many great science programs. It seems like a waste to come here and settle, right? I should be researching. I should have pipe-dream schools, and slight-reach schools, and a few good bets, right?"

Melanie shifts, looking uncomfortable. "Not everyone does that."

"But you did, right? I mean you're applying to some *amazing* schools. I know I can't go out east. But I haven't been considering all my options. I could look at OSU or Michigan. Or what about Purdue or Notre Dame?"

I stop myself with another shoveled bite of noodles. It's too much. I'm babbling. Melanie smiles, but I'm sure I've blown it. I don't talk like this, turning up the ends of every sentence. And I'm not considering Notre Dame.

I'm faking it, and I'm not doing it well.

I'm not anxious in the amusing, manic way everyone else is. I'm a basket case. Does it show?

I chew hard and feel the horrible hot sting of tears welling in my eyes. Melanie reaches across the table and touches me. I hate her for that, because it confirms what I thought. It *does* show. And her kindness makes it worse.

"You know," she says softly. "There's no shame in struggling with anxiety."

I glare at her. Because pity doesn't help. And neither does the soft patronizing voice she's using. My insides wind tighter with every breath.

Melanie seems to notice. She pulls her hand back and sighs. "Please don't get mad at me for suggesting this, but you know that the Student Services Department has counselors on staff."

I'm careful to keep my voice and my expression perfectly controlled. "I'm not angry, and I appreciate your concern. Still, I wish you'd respect me enough to believe that I take my issues seriously."

"I do," Melanie says. And then more softly. "I do."

"I have help. And if I need more, I'll get it."

Dr. Lutmer comes in then, gray hair mussed and creases in his slacks like he's been sitting too long. He gives us a friendly wave on his way to the coffee station. I wave back, and Melanie turns to look at him. His expression changes a bit. Like he's trying to solve a puzzle.

Is she mouthing words to him? Or gesturing at him? My heart pounds, my smile sliding off my face.

I have to stop this paranoia. It proves every one of Melanie's suspicions. I can do better than this. I can hold it together.

I scrape my way through another few bites of congealing buttered noodles. And feel her watching me.

Dr. Lutmer moves on, and my heart resettles. But the silence between us is heavy and strained. When Elise walks over, we both perk up.

"Hey, I've been looking for you," she says. She's looking at me, and she's holding out a gray sweatshirt.

My sweatshirt.

"This is yours, right?" she asks.

For a second, I'm confused. Then I remember. I took it off down by the river before we checked the pillars. I must have forgotten it when I found the sandals.

I take it and thank her, trying not to think of Theo looking down from the bridge. Trying not to imagine him placing the shoes side by side on that table.

"How did you know it was mine?" I ask her, forcing a smile a beat too late.

"Noah and I went down there for lunch."

Melanie tilts her head knowingly, and Elise laughs. "Fine, we went out there to make out. Whatever. Either way, I saw this and remembered the Blue Devil logo on the back. That's your high school, right?"

"Yes, thanks."

"No sweat! I hope you don't mind that I wore it home. It was chilly last night."

"Course not."

Melanie takes over the conversation, and I drape the sweatshirt over my arm and stand.

"You're leaving?" she asks.

"I know," I say, rolling my eyes. "I'm ridiculous. I want one more run at that conclusion."

We all laugh like it's the funniest thing. It isn't. I feel like I'm floating above my shoulders. Our laughter sounds hollow, but when I stop laughing, I choke on the silence.

My palms are slippery on the tray. My heart is banging out a strange rhythm. I have to get out of here.

I cross the lawn to the lab, feeling half sick with nerves. Nothing sounds as good as peace and quiet, but the lab isn't offering either. The Laurens are here. They're pouring new samples and arguing.

They look up at me and lower their voices. If my stomach squeezes any harder, I will throw up. I'm sure of it.

I force myself to raise my hand in greeting. The shorter Lauren—the marginally friendlier one—gives me a sheepish smile.

"We botched the first round of heavy metals testing," she admits.

The other Lauren looks like she might punch her, but my shoulders relax a little.

"We had to run extra tests too," I say.

It's a stretch on the truth. Melanie and I didn't botch our tests. We found arsenic and decided to test additional samples. Then we found more arsenic. And I've tried a hundred different ways to write a convincing conclusion about the implications, but why?

There's nothing particularly sinister in these results. There's no conspiracy. The arsenic is there because rivers are full of icky things. And because no matter how deep you bury them, they find their way back to the surface. That's the real conclusion from our research.

Back in our room, I open the almost lurid last slide of our presentation. My money shot, as Melanie called it. I slaved over it for hours, making it every bit as terrifying as I could. Now, I delete it. And I tell the truth about rivers and about filth. About Theo and me too, I guess.

For the first time, when I sit back to edit, I feel like this is a statement I believe.

It's simple and obvious; truth usually is. And that applies to haunted bridges that turn out to be damaged boys, so it probably applies to me too.

"I think it's great," Melanie says, startling me.

I find her standing behind me, reading over my shoulder. I suspect she's been here a while, quietly assessing my work. It reminds me of our conversation in the cafeteria. Tension spools around my spine like wired ribbon.

I scroll away from the conclusion to focus on earlier pieces. I force out mundane comments about data checks and scientific notation. I even show her the probability graphs I added in, thanks to last year's class in statistics. Math and science are the languages I speak best. Melanie nods along, and it's almost normal between us.

The air conditioner kicks on and I shiver, pulling the gray sweatshirt off the back of my chair. I slide my arms into the sleeves and plunge my hands into my pockets, my fingertips grazing something smooth and plastic.

My skin goes cold as I turn it over and over in my hand. I know what it is by feel alone—antibacterial gel. It was *not* in my pocket before.

At my therapist's urging, I cleaned every bottle of this stuff out of my purse and my suitcase. That was a big step in facing my fear of germs.

So, this bottle can't be here. But it is. And when I pull it out, spotting the familiar glittering berries dancing across the label, I know.

I know who bought this bottle. I know who left the sandals. I'm tired of trying to believe a complicated fabrication. This has nothing to do with the bridge, or some ghost, or my anxiety. The simplest answer is the one most likely to be true.

The simple answer is Theo.

THEO

Shaun, the ghost expert, is tall and thin with a carefully trimmed goatee and a pair of wire-rimmed glasses that I'll bet he spent a long time picking out. He's ordering a soy latte with an extra shot and light on the soy milk and a bunch of other pretentious shit that makes the barista write extra hard on her little green pad. I pretty much hate him before I've even said hello.

He sits down across from us and nods through Gabriel's awkward introductions, finally shaking my hand with a pointed frown.

"Nice to meet you," I say, but Shaun doesn't repeat the sentiment.

He wears an irritated expression like it's his natural state of being, or at the very least, his default setting. It's less meaty-fisted asshole and more intellectually pissy, like he's already sure I'll fail to properly recognize the depth of his wisdom.

Yeah, I think I'm about to *fail to recognize* all over the place.

He adjusts his prissy coffee on the white napkin. "*So*, Gabriel tells me you have an energy haunting on your hands at the pedestrian bridge on Pearl Street?"

"I don't know what kind of haunting it is."

Shaun cocks his head. "I'll *assume* that's why you called me."

Oh yeah. I hate him.

I stretch my legs out beside the table, stacking one filthy work boot on top of the other, as close as possible to his crisp jeans. "*Right.* Well, that's why we're here, isn't it? I've heard about you and your ghost tours."

Gabriel gives me an odd look, then opens his notes and passes them to Shaun.

"I thought you might be able to shed light on the details we've uncovered," Gabriel says.

Shaun flips back and forth through Gabriel's notes, silently mouthing what he reads. "So, you both have locks engraved with your initials on the bridge?"

"Right," Gabriel says.

Shaun nods. "Could be a sort of symbolism. It could channel the energy."

"Channel the energy?" I waggle my fingers, and Shaun gives me a look that could melt paint off a fender.

"You don't think it's a ghost either?" Gabriel asks him.

248

"Not with the behaviors you've listed. These are all limited to witnesses with significant attachment to the bridge. Or at least to a lock on the bridge."

"Right," Gabriel says. "The locks are definitely related."

"I'm betting the locks are the whole problem," I say.

Shaun shakes his head. "Random factory-made padlocks aren't infused with supernatural powers. The energy on that bridge is the key. Understanding how the locks connect with the energy might provide you with the tools to understand that power."

"I don't want to understand it," I say. "I want to destroy it."

Shaun blinks at me like I'm a lunatic. "You can't destroy energy. It's a universal rule."

"Like the rule about Bloody Mary showing up in a mirror if I say her name three times?"

He narrows his eyes, and Gabriel sighs. "I'm pretty sure Shaun is referring to the law of the conservation of energy. Energy is constant."

Science shit. He's probably right, but I wouldn't know. That's Paige's domain.

"Still," Shaun concedes. "There should be a way to reduce the impact of the energy from the locks—to shield yourself from it. Have you tried removing your lock?"

"The last time I cut off locks, I broke an eighty-dollar pair of bolt cutters and passed out cold on the bridge."

"Interesting." Shaun leans back and wipes his hands with his napkin again. "That almost sounds like an intelligent reaction. A protection mechanism. Did you look into the history?"

"One college student who had a lock on the bridge came up with a long list of unfortunate incidents that happened to other people with locks. It was a pretty big deal. She got kicked out of the school for inciting panic and then disappeared."

"I'm not sure that would manifest such intense negative energy. An expelled college student seems a fairly trite cause for this level of encounter."

"So, could it be a ghost then? Or is it just a haunted bridge?" I ask.

"Well, your typical residual haunting, which is what most people think of when they report ghosts or hauntings, can be loosely defined as a recording. Some people call them place memories. A spirit or location will replay or reenact some important moment in history. For example, a woman might be seen moving down the stairs over and over, carrying her husband's last soup tray to the kitchen. Or a house's windows might rattle and mist with a lashing rain from decades past. Essentially, it's a recorded memory. A moment that is trapped and replaying over and over."

"Well, there *is* a moment playing over and over," I say. "Or parts of a moment at any rate. But it's not some ghost's moment, it's *mine*."

"That's why I believe it's all about the energy," Shaun says. "Energy hauntings generally manifest as a presence or a feeling. People experience them differently. Witnesses report that they don't know how to put those encounters into words."

"I *can* put it in words. I'm smelling weird things. And hearing conversations that didn't even happen on the bridge."

"Where did it happen?" Gabriel asks. "The argument with you and Paige."

"Below the bridge. On the docks."

Shaun shrugs. "If the presence on that bridge feeds on negativity, it could easily sense intense emotion nearby. But are you sure your experiences are limited to the bridge?"

"On it or near it for me."

"But not for Paige," Gabriel says. Then he turns to me. "Right?"

Shaun perks up, putting down his cup. I'm not sure I want to answer him, but what else is the point of being here, I guess.

"No, it's different for Paige," I admit. "She's found objects from the night we argued in her room. She's had nightmares. She woke up on the bridge after sleepwalking there."

Shaun puts down his cup with another frown. "Is it possible she's possessed?"

Is he serious? I laugh, but then my face goes hard, because I think he is serious. "No, she's not *possessed*. She's freaked out because something insane is happening, and we need help."

Shaun blinks at me, unmoved. "You need to find the source of whatever terrible emotion is underneath all these manifestations."

"Do you think it's only linked to one of the locks?" Gabriel asks.

Shaun shrugs. "Maybe. If one of the locks and the bridge are somehow tangled up in an intense injustice or emotional devastation."

"Whoever had the craziest breakup?" I ask.

"I doubt it. A manifestation this strong would be bigger than simple heartbreak. This is a life lost. Utter devastation. Energy of this nature is the scar that's left behind."

"A scar?" I ask.

Shaun leans in, dropping his voice. "People who visit Auschwitz say there is evil there that transcends faith or belief in the paranormal. Even the hardest of cynics feels chilled inside those old, empty gas chambers. They stare at the claw marks on the inside of the walls and they…feel something."

We don't respond. I'm not sure there is a response to information like that. Instead, the silence stretches long. The espresso machine steams and hisses. Customers murmur orders, and a barista clangs cups and punches buttons. Shaun sits back, and I'm sure he's doing it for effect.

"You're not looking for a ghost with a chip on his shoulder," he says. "You're looking for fingernail scratches on the walls of a gas chamber."

PAIGE

I sit awake for hours in my dorm room, thinking of Theo and wondering why he'd want to scare me. My knees are pulled up, and Melanie is a softly snoring lump across the room. The room is quiet and still. My mind is neither.

The blood and the nightmares could be normal. I might have hit a capillary with my toothbrush, and a little blood seemed like buckets. Fear can do that. It messes with my perceptions. And the nightmares and sleepwalking could have easily been the sleeping pill.

It's logical.

But meds and fear don't conjure earrings or leave shoes on picnic tables. A person does that. Someone with hands and ill intent.

I still can't wrap my head around Theo with ill intent. Theo showing up late, Theo blowing his lid, racing through a red light... All of that, sure. But wanting to hurt me? Impossible.

Could he be right about the haunting?

I think of the purse in the river. It left blood on my hands. It caught on my foot. Theo couldn't have done that.

My eyes drag to the brown bag inside my closet. I dumped the sandals in there the second I got back. Folded the bag shut tight and pushed them away. A ghost doesn't leave shoes.

But could Theo?

I drop my chin onto my raised knees and close my eyes. Theo's always in my head. I can see him now, shifting back and forth on my front porch. Climbing trees. Sheepishly grinning at me in an emergency waiting room.

I love him most when I see him focus, when something manages to wholly captivate him. A flock of starlings in an oak tree. An airplane taking off. Highway traffic at night. And me, when we were kissing.

Heat floods my body as I think of it. His mouth was so impatient, so incredibly Theo. But his hands were slow and gentle, which surprised me. I felt like the only person in his world during that moment.

Could I see those same hands putting those shoes side by side?

I press my palms to my hot cheeks. It doesn't make sense that he would do this to me. You don't kiss people you want to scare.

But you hit those people?

He didn't mean to.

Does it matter what he meant?

The thoughts chase each other through my head. I think of
snakes eating their own tails. I think of all the attributes my therapist tells me about healthy relationships. Trusting, honest, open.

My insides are nonstop noise. I manage to keep my outside
quiet until four a.m. Then the noise of my own thinking drives
me out of bed.

I slide my feet into flip-flops and pull on a sweatshirt. I open
the door carefully because I don't want to wake Melanie. I don't
need her wondering where I'm creeping off to. I definitely don't
need her reporting it.

I'm not even sure she would. I could be inventing so much of
this, her talking to my parents, Dr. Lutmer. Panic has gotten the
best of me. Deep down, I know there's only one way to turn that
table. I need to confront my fear.

If the bridge is haunted, I want to see it. I want to go there
and look this in the eyes once and for all. If I don't, I'll never really
believe this is Theo. Not enough to let him go.

The dorm is quiet. The kind of quiet that plucks your nerves
like bow strings. I move down the middle of the stairs, right on
the carpet runner so my feet don't scrape against the concrete. At
the bottom floor, I pause.

The resident advisor's door is closed, but there's a stretch of
tile between me and the front entrance. I'll have to cross that

tile, tumble the lock, and push open the heavy wooden door to get out.

I did it a few nights ago, without even waking up. But now my heart pounds as I take my first step. I stare at the resident advisor's door. Will she see the shadow of my feet? Will she hear me? My fingers shake as I reach for the lock. The metal is cool under my fingers. I can hear every breath I take.

Do it. Just do it.

The lock turns with a scrape and a clunk. I clench my teeth and stare over my shoulder at the resident advisor's room. There's no sound. No fumble of a recent college grad waking from sleep and vaulting herself out of bed. No one's awake. No one's going to rush out or stop me.

I twist the brass doorknob and push. It opens with a soft whoosh, and it's done. I'm outside. The air is cool and damp, fog clinging low on the bushes flanking the buildings. The world is still asleep.

I stay to the sidewalk and move quickly. It's easy to smell the river in the morning. I can even hear it, the slow rush of water pushing through the valley. There are poisons in that water, but I can't smell them. Can't see them either. Poisons are very good at hiding.

I'm at the mouth of the bridge before I know it, but I hesitate. The bridge isn't welcoming at night. The walkway is lost in shadow. Black arms arch overhead, and fog lies heavy on the water below, a pillowy presence creeping up the banks.

I cross my arms over my chest. Maybe this can wait. I might not find anything anyway. Having a panic attack on a bridge at four in the morning doesn't sound like my best life choice.

A breeze drifts around the bridge, whispering through the grass. The hum of wind chimes. I've heard that before, chimes that brush against each other like fairies laughing.

A tiny white flower pokes up by the entrance to the walkway. Snowdrops. But snowdrops bloom in March, and it's July. I crouch down and touch the white flowers. A chill runs up my back.

This isn't right. These flowers or the chimes. Nothing is right here, and I should be afraid. Any other time, this would terrify me. But tonight, the fear is behind a thick wall of glass. I walk forward like I am not alone in the dark. I move as if there is nothing waiting for me up here. But something *is* waiting.

I can feel it.

It's the way you know when someone is standing too close behind you. Your skin prickles. Goose bumps rise on the backs of your arms. That's happening now, but I don't turn and I don't run.

My feet make soft slapping noises against the wood of the walkway. There is no comfortable rubbery thwack of my flip-flops. I am barefoot. I don't know when this happened. I can see my flip-flops back there, at the other end of the bridge, pink and strange.

Water rushes. My pulse surges. A lump of clothing twists near one of the joists. The wadded-up fabric is a flash of lime green. Theo's shirt, which he probably forgot after he took it off. If I pick it up, the front will read Froggy Daniel's Hole in the Hollow. There will be a tear just under the left armpit. I was there when he snagged it, jumping over a fence.

I take a step off the walkway, to the space where trains once ran. The tracks are broken. Thick, squared-off logs reek of creosote. Some are covered in moss. I see another snowdrop blooming in the rotten wood.

That's my sign. I'm supposed to go to that shirt. To that toolbox underneath it.

I'm careful moving closer to the frame of the bridge. My heart is slamming into my throat now. I should not do this. This is not safe. But then I look again at the snowdrop and I'm moving. I walk toward that lump of lime green and the red toolbox.

The pillar is steady, encased in the same thick concrete I found in the water yesterday. I press my hands to the cold steel beam above it and let my heart slow. My focus sharpens on each of the folds of the shirt below me.

"There's nothing here," I say aloud. My voice is rough and shockingly loud in the quiet.

I feel like I've broken a spell or maybe a rule. The steel feels cold against my back now. I don't remember turning around. I look back toward the entrance to the bridge where my flip-flops sit, forgotten.

I still don't remember leaving them. Maybe the bridge isn't haunted, and Theo isn't evil. Maybe this is me. Were my parents right to worry about me? To think I should stay home?

I slouch down, my shirt catching on the rough cement. It snags and pulls up my shirt until it scrapes my back. I sit on the rotting wood, next to Theo's shirt. I move it carefully, bunching it fold by fold.

It's just a shirt—what else did I expect? I unclasp the tool chest and flip open the lid. Wrenches and screwdrivers turned this way and that. Nothing is organized. Gum wrappers litter the bottom of the tray, every flavor you can imagine.

I finger a Juicy Fruit wrapper with a sigh. There's nothing here but Theo. Nothing scary but me on a bridge, barefoot and half insane. My fingers trace over a metal tin, and the lid pops loose. I try to push it closed, but it pops free again. Something's sticking up too high, a screw or nail. It won't latch.

Leave it.

The words are so clear that I'm sure I've heard them. And those goose bumps are back, tracking up the backs of my arms. Something is close now. I can feel it behind me, not heat or movement. No, this is a presence.

Leave it be.

I desperately want to do just that, but my fingers don't care. I watch them move like they aren't attached to my hand. Like I have no power over them at all. My fingernails catch under the unlatched lip of metal. I'm moving it up. Opening it wider.

It's not so dark that I don't recognize the hard, white kernels I find inside. I know my own teeth when I see them.

THEO

It's four twenty in the morning, and I'm still arguing with Gabriel on his grandfather's back porch. I didn't think any guardian type could beat mine in the art of throwing up your hands in an I-don't-know-what-to-do-with-him parental shrug-off, but I was wrong. Gabriel's grandfather either spends every minute he isn't at the library so stoned he can't find his ass with both hands, or he's decided fifteen is as good as adulthood.

It's not like I'm trying to hurt the kid, but damn, the guy didn't even introduce himself to the *obviously* older guy hanging out all night. The one with dirty jeans who showed up talking about a giant power saw he picked up that afternoon.

Gabriel jabs his finger at the laptop screen on the coffee table between us. "I'm telling you, you shouldn't randomly cut off the locks. Like Shaun said, we need to find which lock is the source."

"If we cut all the locks, we won't need to search!" I argue. "I'll leave yours there, okay?"

"And what about the other good ones? What about the high school sweethearts who have their kids' pictures taken with their locks?"

"Are you seriously arguing sentimentalism with me here?" I ask. "The locks have creepy-ass voodoo energy that makes me smell things and sometimes knocks me out. Plus, if you haven't forgotten, the locks have to go anyway! It's part of our contract."

"If we don't strike that energy at the right source, how are you going to cut them all? Like you keep reminding me, the last time you cut off a *handful* of locks, you passed out."

"With a power saw? Trust me, it'll work. And if it doesn't, then I'll cut off the damn railing and drop it into the river."

"Yes, I'm sure replacing the entire length of railing would be both affordable and easy."

I pick at the scratched edge of the couch arm, feeling unsettled. Gabriel has the patience and steadiness for this, but I'm champing at the bit, waiting for daylight. I want to cut the bastards off. I need to do *something*, because it feels like my life is falling into hell.

Paige hasn't called in two days and isn't responding to texts. Denny came home piss drunk and bitching about the three-day rental period on the Sawzall and warning me he can't afford another broken tool or me wasting time wandering around town or getting sick on the job.

I push my hands into my hair. "I have to take some action, Gabriel. I can't ignore this forever, because the longer I wait, the worse things are getting."

The worse I think they're getting anyway. I'm not sure about how Paige is doing, but her radio silence is scaring the shit out of me. She gets quiet like this when her anxiety is spiraling out of control.

"What if your impatience is making this worse?" he asks. "What if the answer is one book, or even one article away? Even if it is a lock, it could be one of the ones on the ballasts up high. You're not even planning on getting to those, are you?"

He's right. Denny's already said we're only taking down the locks on the railing. There are dozens of others that get to stay because they're out of the way, inconvenient to remove. And any one of those is just as likely to be the source.

"Fine," I say, my voice croaky. "What do you suggest? You still think it's the girl who got kicked out?"

"I know what Shaun said, but she seems like a good lead. She obviously had issues."

"Issues that probably had nothing to do with the bridge. You heard what Shaun said. We're not looking for some sad sorority-girl confessional; we're looking for real tragedy. Let's go back to that suicide for one second. It's the only real death we can tie to the bridge."

Gabriel sighs. "I promise the suicide is a dead end."

"How do you know?"

"I just know."

I lean forward, my calves scraping against the rough fabric of the couch. "You're totally weird about this suicide, man. Tell me why you're so sure this isn't behind it."

"Because it was my father."

I am stunned into silence.

Gabriel watches me, unblinking, and then goes on without me prodding.

"He was schizophrenic. My father." He tilts his head. "You know what schizophrenia is?"

"A little bit, yeah."

"He was a college junior, and my mom was a high school junior when she got pregnant with me. It was a four-year age difference. You know how four years means absolutely nothing for adults? Well, between high school and college, it's different."

"People weren't cool about it, I'm guessing."

"My grandfather told me it was hard. They loved each other and had planned to get married. But my father started having symptoms. Outbursts. Even hallucinations. My mom was six months pregnant when he jumped." He scuffs the ground with his foot. "Maybe it could have been different. But mental health treatment options weren't great around here back then, you know?"

"I know they're not a hell of a lot better now." I frown. "I also know that's a damn awful thing to have happen, Gabriel. That's a devastating loss."

He bursts into motion, pushing his hair back and straightening the books on the table. "He'd tried to kill himself three other times. The bridge is where it finally worked. It wasn't special or significant—it's where it ended up happening, you know?"

"Okay," I say softly.

"And in case you're wondering, there isn't a lock on the bridge with his initials on it. I checked everywhere."

"I'm sorry, man. I didn't know."

But now that I do know, it hits me—we're still no closer than we were before.

I stand up. "Look, I've got to get to work."

"I don't know why I'm holding out on the locks," Gabriel says out of nowhere. "I know cutting them off makes sense. Logically, it might work."

"But you're not convinced."

"I'm...afraid of them," he admits. "Those locks knocked you out. That was when you only cut a few. We don't understand how this energy works. Even Shaun doesn't, you know?"

"Yeah. But if the locks are the source of power, destroying them seems like a solution."

Gabriel swallows hard. "Except that's when the haunting was strongest for you before. It wasn't less powerful… It was more. Cutting them made it stronger."

I clench my jaw, memories of the voices drifting just beyond my ears. My stomach slides sideways when I think about what happened before. "I don't know what else to do."

"I know. But if I find something?"

"I'm game to try just about anything."

I smile to reassure him, but I don't think he'll find any new details. In the end, I think it comes down to sawing those locks free. And hoping to God we destroy the power instead of unleashing it.

Outside Gabriel's, I cut down the narrow steps to his townhome and head for the bridge. There are long smudges of pink across the charcoal sky by the time I get there, and I wish we'd agreed to start work a little later now that I'm not climbing around on the bridge day after day. It'd be nice to get an hour of sleep.

Denny's truck is not here, so maybe he decided he could come in later.

I consider running home for a nap, but if Denny's on his way, he'll lose it if I'm not here today. He's been a constant stream of commentary on me being a team player, so I lope up the ramp, wishing there was somewhere to get a coff—

I stop dead. Paige is on the bridge. She's dressed this time, a gray sweatshirt and a pair of ratty shorts. One look at her, and my head is full to bursting with the feel of her lips against mine. I can feel her breath coming fast and her hands on my arms and—*BAM*.

I feel myself hitting her, my fist slamming into flesh.

I have to force myself forward. This is the bridge, not us. It's feeding us every awful moment of that night. But she is so much better than that, and between the two of us, there's got to be a balance. We can be more than the sum of one shitty night.

I'm close enough to see that she's holding something in one hand and the other is by her face. She has her phone, and she's looking out over the river. My shirt is by her feet.

None of it makes sense. Is she calling me? My phone's been dead for hours. My boot scuffs on the walkway and she turns. My whole body tenses.

She's crying. Even in the shadowy predawn light, I can see the hitch of her shoulders and the shiny tear tracks down her cheeks. My heart plummets as she drops my shirt and holds up a pale fist. It's a warning. I smell lemons and brackish water. Lilacs and rot.

"Paige?"

"Stay away from me."

I hold up my hands, ice sliding up my spine, under my skin. "Okay." And again. "Okay."

"Stay back!"

"I will."

We stand there, her fist shaking and stretched out in front of her. She's holding something else; she's got her fingers curled strangely around it. Whatever she has, it isn't good.

Her teeth chatter. I hear whispers slithering down from the trusses overhead, voices circling the support beams and snaking through the railing too.

"The police are coming," Paige says, lowering her phone.

I'm not sure if the police can help us, but I have to be steady for her. "Okay."

"They're coming!"

Her voice cracks, and it breaks me. More voices push up from underneath the bridge. My ears pop and buzz, and Paige whirls with a shriek, dropping her phone. It clatters on the walkway, but it's intact. I remember another phone shattering; someone dropped one here on the night of the party.

Paige's eyes go wide—she's seeing something I can't see.

This has nothing to do with him.

She shudders, so I know she's heard it too. Heard herself. My head swims, but I push myself off the railing and inch forward.

Paige slams into the railing. For one terrifying second, I'm sure she'll break through and fall.

I reach for her and she draws back, so I pull back, hands wide.

"It's the bridge, Paige. Its bad energy messing with us."

Her laugh is sharp enough to draw blood. "The bridge." I watch the way she looks past me, sucking in a tight breath.

"There's nothing here," I say, schooling my voice to a steady rumble. "I'm not judging you, I feel it too. But we've got to be stronger than whatever's out here with us."

"*You!* You are the only one out here!"

"What?"

She shakes her head and looks down so I can't see her face. Then she makes a choked sound that I hope is a laugh. But when I touch her shoulders, I know it's a sob.

Voices—they're everywhere. I can't just hear them; I can feel them, a thin ringing behind my ears and a thickness to the air that sticks in my throat. My head fogs over.

"Talk to me," I say. "What happened tonight? What brought you here?"

Another sob. No, this time it *is* a laugh, and it's terrible.

She lifts her head, eyes glittering and smile manic. Somewhere far away I hear the whine of a siren. She holds open her fisted hand enough for me to see what she's holding—two little rocks. Pieces of plastic maybe?

"Paige?" I reach for her again, gently. "Try to take a—"

She hits me.

I don't even see it coming, or believe it, until she hits me again. Pain bursts along my left eyebrow, my whole head screaming an instant after the initial impact. There's wailing, thin and shrill in the distance. At first I think it's her and that my ears are messed up again. But it's the sirens. They're getting closer.

She hits me again. Sobs. Tires crunch up the street below the bridge. Lights, blue and red, strobe across her pale cheeks. Holy shit, she really did call the police!

My hand is at my head, covering the throb between my eyes. My smeary vision clears in time for me to see Paige rear back again.

She punches me hard, in the chest this time.

"How could you?" she screams. Car doors open and shut. I hear footsteps, and then Paige launches at me, fist flying wild from the side. My hands go up defensively as her fist pummels my shoulder. And then another—this one into the soft, fleshy part of my side. I deserve this, and I'd take it. I'd take every punch she wants to give me, but the police would see her. I try to reach for her again. "Paige, stop—"

She keeps whaling on me, panting so hard I think she'll drop. Dark blurs of police officers are moving up the far end of the bridge. We're screwed. I have to stop her.

"Paige!"

They're shouting, and Paige is still screaming. "You did this! You found my shoes! My purse! You picked up the pieces of my teeth!"

Her teeth? "I didn't—"

Something drops down from above. A shadowy, shapeless blur slithers down the iron supports, twisting along the ropes of unlit lights. Worse, I can see it rolling underneath the walkway, a thick carpet of black seeping into the cracks between each board. It hums like hornets. And smells like lilacs.

Still cocked for a punch, Paige's pale fist stills. She sees it too.

I'm done with you.

Who isn't done with me?

Her eyes lock on mine, and I know she's heard the voices as clearly as I have. This time it isn't me or her. It's haunting both of us.

Paige drops her fist and takes a tentative step back from the blackness seeping closer. The buzzing rises. Voices murmur. Officers tell us to put our hands where they can see them. Paige's lips form around my name, but she can't find her voice.

And then I hear something else—a fast, metal *click-click-click*ing. It's handcuffs. They're putting Paige in handcuffs.

PAIGE

My ears are still roaring with voices, both familiar and strange. That dark shadow is still pushing up between the boards, and there are flashes of light all around. Maybe the darkness got me.

I buck wildly, twisting and jerking. My arms are caught behind me.

Something cold has my wrists, and strange voices are talking. This isn't Chase and Theo from the party. These aren't *before* voices. They are here-and-now voices. One tells me to settle down. One tells me to take a breath, but he does it with a tug to my bound wrists.

Handcuffs. The reality sinks in fast. They are handcuffs. The police I called for Theo have come for me. A flash of what they must have seen washes over me. Me punching him over and over. He's standing across from me, hands raised and lip bleeding. He's talking fast and clearly trying to explain.

He's trying to protect me. Still. After I punched him over and over.

Because I thought I had it all figured out. I thought I could blame Theo and tie up this whole mess with a tidy, logical bow. I know better now. There is no simple explanation for that monstrosity underneath the bridge. Or the blood in my sink. Or the force that dragged me out here in my sleep. Theo didn't do it, and my crazy didn't do it. What did this defies explanation.

The wind kicks up, extra cold across my wet cheeks. I'm crying. I'm not sure when I started. I can't tell what's real and what's memory and what's the bridge.

I just know the police officers are here and they've put handcuffs on my wrists and they are leading me to a cruiser. Panic flickers to life.

"Are you settled now?" one officer asks.

"Yes." I sound choked. "I'm sorry."

"Let's get some facts here," the second officer says. "What's your name?"

Theo's eye is swelling, and his lip is bleeding. My knuckles sting and ache. I did that to him, and he wasn't the one behind this. How was I so wrong? How did I go so crazy? I'm supposed to be better now. I'm supposed to be okay.

"Your name, miss?" the first officer asks.

"I'm sorry. Paige. Paige Vinton-Young."

The second police officer moves in front of me. Between Theo and me. He looks patient but tired, with a puffy face and squinty eyes.

"All right, Paige. Why don't you tell us what's going on out here?"

"She didn't do anything."

It's Theo. He's behind the officer, skin painted pink-orange by the rising sun. The shadows are gone. The voices are silent. But I didn't dream all this up, and Theo had nothing to do with it. Maybe it happened to us because we're already crazy. Maybe it's proof that we always will be.

I start crying again, and the police officers continue to ask me questions. Theo argues, and I think of the teeth. Not the ones he broke, but the ones I found. I dropped them when I hit him. Were they really teeth or something else? Were they even there at all? I don't know where my sickness ends and this nightmare begins.

The police officers are more worried about me than Theo. One's checking my ID. He's on his radio using a low voice and codes I don't understand. The other asks me questions. Theo paces back and forth a bit apart. He pulls out his own phone and starts typing a message.

The other officer guides me to the back of the car, and I'm quiet.

"Are you cold?" he asks me. I realize my teeth are chattering, so I nod.

He turns on the heater and turns off the cruiser's lights. The world looks very ordinary without the flash of red and blue. Dawn is halfhearted. All that pretty pink from earlier has faded into milky gray.

Outside the window, the second officer is talking to Theo. Then it hits me. Theo is on *probation*. He could be in trouble, *real* trouble.

"So, are you ready to talk?" the officer in the car asks.

I take a breath. I know I need to say something, but nothing comes. How do I explain coming out here? How do I tell him I found teeth that disappeared? That I heard voices and saw shadows? He'll think I need a psychiatrist, and he'll be right.

He'll call my parents.

My head snaps up at the thought. "I'm eighteen."

He looks surprised, but takes it in stride. "You're eighteen?"

"You don't need to call my parents."

"Do you have some identification on you? A driver's license?"

"I can't reach it."

"I'll look it up. Spell your name for me please?"

I recite the information he requests, and then my address afterward. The heat is cranking now. Sweat trickles under my arms, but my teeth are still chattering. Nerves. When isn't it nerves with me?

The second officer is still talking to Theo. I'm not sure he's being as friendly as mine, and it makes me angry. Theo didn't do anything. I'm the one who hit him tonight.

"When you called 911, you said this boy was after you," the officer says, regaining my attention.

"I was confused. I panicked and exaggerated." The words fly out as fast as the decision is made. It's a lie, but I can't see another option. My cheeks burn with heat that I hope he'll read as shame.

"Are you telling me you lied to the police?"

I rub my chin on my shoulder, wishing I could calm down and stop shaking. "I didn't mean to lie. I was up too late. I think I was so tired I was imagining things."

His kind eyes narrow. "Tired or *more* than tired? Were you drinking? Were you smoking anything? Did you take anything?"

I laugh, and he turns with a new, colder expression. Dread pours through my body, but I shake my head. "I've never done drugs."

"I've heard that before."

"Not like this. I've never smoked a cigarette. Never had a sip of beer. I-I can't."

"And why's that?"

My face burns. "Because I have issues."

He looks at me blankly. He's waiting for more. My wrists ache at the strange angle of my arms, metal biting into the tender flesh of my wrists.

"I see a doctor about my anxiety. Sometimes it's intense. I'm afraid of a lot of things. That's why I wouldn't do drugs. Not ever. Too scary."

"Keep talking. Tell me about tonight," he says. Not in a therapist way. More in a get-to-the-bottom-of-this way.

I shrug. "Tonight, I kind of flipped out. I'm in a program at the college. I think the pressure might be getting to me. It was late, and I couldn't sleep. I got completely paranoid. It was an anxiety attack, and I didn't take the medicine I have for that."

I'm saying too much and nowhere near enough. He'll be able to tell. That's what cops do, isn't it? I take sharp little breaths, trying to pick and choose each word.

"Is this medication you're talking about prescribed to you?"

"Yes, but I've missed doses. I've been skipping the sleeping pill too, because it's been giving me trouble. I have bad insomnia. I should have called my doctor. I'm sorry."

"So, you didn't sleep at all tonight?"

"No."

"And a sleepless night somehow explains why you were afraid of this boy."

"I know it doesn't make sense. A lot of what I'm afraid of doesn't make sense."

He sighs and looks almost fatherly. "Paige, your history with

Theodore comes up on our system here. You've never been in any kind of trouble with the law. We're here to help you. If this boy is manipulating you…pressuring you—"

"No." I curl in on myself as best as I can with the cuffs. I feel sick that they would blame him, but of course they would. I haven't been in trouble. Theo has. "This is not him. I promise you that. This is on me."

"Are you sure? Because in truth, this boy shouldn't be near you. We'll call his parole officer—"

"Please." My voice is very soft, but it stops him. "*Please* don't." I close my eyes. Hot tears slide down my cheeks. "Theo didn't know I would be here. He works here. I knew he'd come. This is my fault, not his."

The officer waits me out, like what I said isn't quite enough to convince him. But what else is there?

Outside, the other officer is drilling Theo. And Theo is taking it, shifting back and forth on his feet. He keeps looking over the cop's shoulder toward the cruiser. I know he doesn't care about his parole. He's never been good at thinking ahead.

All he's thinking of is me. He's always been good at that. Because he's not just some boy who punched me. He's Theo. He loves me. And I love him. It's the worst, messiest version of love I can imagine.

But in this moment, it feels simple.

"Theo isn't some awful, violent guy. He has his own issues. ADHD. ODD."

The officer's expression hardens. "Hitting girls is not something you blame on mental illness."

"He wasn't aiming for me." When he frowns, I shake my head. "I know that doesn't matter. It didn't matter to me either. What he did was wrong. He knows that, and I know that."

"Yes, it was."

"Which is why he sat in jail that night. And it's why he's still on probation. He is being punished, and he would never try to get out of that."

"But he did something to make you hit him," the officer points out.

"I thought so too," I say. "But he didn't. I let myself get worked up over nothing. Just shadows."

I think of the darkness under the bridge. I remember the way it pushed up between the boards. Like it was reaching. I force out a sad laugh, because I finally believe the impossible, and I have to sell a logical lie to cover it up.

"It was just shadows," I say firmly. "I can't believe I was so ridiculous. I can't believe I called 911. I'm really embarrassed. And so sorry."

The lies are coming easier. Maybe I should have tried this before. I could have lied to my parents, maybe even my therapist.

Maybe my anxiety would be easier to deal with if I could learn to fake my way through it. If only.

Another person is walking toward the bridge now. He heads past the cruiser. He's wearing a stained green hat, and he's smoking.

That's how I recognize him. Denny. He's probably coming in to work. Worry loops my stomach into another tight knot. Theo's going to get in even more trouble.

Denny walks straight toward Theo, and he and the other officer don't look surprised. Did Theo text him? Would he really want him to come see this?

"Paige?" the officer prompts. "Did Theo call you or initiate contact?"

"I'm sorry," I say, trying to track back to his question. "No, he didn't call me or follow me. He's been very careful not to run into me. He doesn't want any more trouble. It's just… I kept finding things that reminded me of us. I blew it all out of proportion."

"What it looked like was assault, Ms. Vinton-Young."

A new fear slithers up my spine. He could arrest me. Read me my rights and take me to jail. There will be no way to hide that from my mother.

"Yes," I say simply.

The officer doesn't seem to have any more questions. He tells me to sit tight and steps out of the car. The first officer is talking to Denny now. They look friendly, shaking hands and nodding. Pointing at something across the river that I don't think has anything to do with all that's happened here tonight.

Then the officers move to the front of the car to talk. They leave me in the back and Denny with Theo. I can see Denny talking to Theo. I can't hear them of course, but I can see the cold fury on Denny's face as well as the way Theo's expression shutters.

Eventually, the officers meet with Denny and Theo again. They talk for what feels like hours but in reality is probably less than a minute. At the end, Denny pumps their hands in a hearty shake, first the tall one he seems to know. Then he greets the one who sat with me. The officers come back to the car and open my door.

At the second officer's urging, I step out and he unlocks the cuffs, all the while talking.

"We could take you down to the station, but Mr. Quinn assures us this is highly out of character for you. He says he's known you for years."

Denny won't meet my eyes, but his voice is hard and bright. "Since she was a tiny little toddler in pigtails."

Definite lie. I didn't meet Theo until I was twelve. My hair hasn't been long enough for pigtails since I was eight.

Denny gives me one last look as the police issue final warnings. I nod when they tell me to get in touch with my doctor about that medicine. Nod again when they tell me it isn't safe for a young lady to walk here before dawn. And one last time when they tell me they don't want any more trouble from me.

In the end, they drive away and Denny waves, smiling until their taillights disappear around a corner. The expression that falls over his face once they're out of sight is too cold and mean to name.

"You're fired," he says to Theo. "I'll take you home Friday after I'm done."

Theo flinches. I close my eyes. Wait to hear the shuffle of his steps as Denny leaves.

When I open them again, Theo isn't looking at Denny. He's watching me, with unlaced boots and a swollen left eye. There's still a smear of blood, dried mostly, under his nose.

The city is coming to life, but it's still quiet here, nothing but the sound of the water. Nothing but the two of us and this terrible bridge. And whatever is haunting it. I don't know what to call it. I'm not sure it has a name. I'm only sure it wants to be here. It wants to stay close. Theo doesn't want to hurt me, and I don't want to hurt him. But a feeling I can't explain tells me this darkness in the bridge wants to hurt us both. I don't think it wants anything more.

THEO

I don't know what I expect when Paige walks up to me, her little bare feet so quiet against the wood. I'm worried she'll find some glass or a splinter, so I turn like I'm going to get her shoes, but she stops me, hand on my arm and eyes filled with tears.

Her breath shakes in and out, and her touch messes with me. I can't think when she's this close. Hell, I can't think anyway, but now?

"I'm sorry," she says, choking on the words.

"Don't be."

"Let me be sorry," she says, half laughing. But then her face crumples. "I thought it was you. I thought you were doing all this. Leaving things for me to find."

"Me doing it would have made a hell of a lot more sense than whatever is actually happening."

"Stop defending me," she whispers, biting her lip.

"No."

She laughs a little, but she doesn't move her hand. Her fingers are so soft and cool, but they burn right through me. "Friday is only three days away. That's not much time."

"Maybe it'll be best. None of this happened when I was away from you."

Her fingers curl over my arms. "I don't care. I know who you are, and you are more than that night. More than everyone sees. I don't want to be away from you anymore."

My heart thuds because I'm a sucker. And an idiot. And a lot of other stupid things, but I can't think of any of them because her hand is moving up my forearm to my bicep. Her other hand is touching my chest, and I can't help myself when I'm in my right mind. I'm sure the hell not in my right mind right now.

I kiss her, and she melts into me. We both whisper apologies between kisses. I can't get her close enough and I can't stand myself for hurting her and I hate that all this badness is between us. I say all of that while I'm kissing her. I don't know what she can make out.

"I love you, Paige." That part is clear, and there isn't some melodramatic bullshit pause where she thinks about it or pulls back all contemplative. She just presses in tighter with her own choked *I love you* that I feel more than I hear.

I don't know who pulls back first, who realizes this is the

worst possible idea, given all that's gone down. Probably Paige— she is always the smart one. Either way, I know when it's over. I can feel the bruising cold of the air between us and the ache she leaves when she's not touching me anymore.

Her lips are swollen and her eyes are red, and damn it, she's crying again.

"This is so messed up," she whispers. "We are so messed up, aren't we?"

I want to argue, but I know she's right. How can I say we're anything else? Half of our last handful of encounters have ended with punches and one of us in handcuffs.

She sighs and we both turn to head off the bridge, but we're not alone. Denny's waiting at the top of the stairs, arms crossed and looking as mean as I've ever seen him. There's something about this I don't like, a lot of somethings. He said his piece before, and him being back can't be anything but trouble.

We inch our way closer, but Denny does nothing to make it easier on us. Polite to a fault, Paige mumbles a polite thank-you, which he mostly ignores. I start forward, ready to tear into him for being a dick. He cuts me off with a single look.

"Your parole officer just called. Apparently, he couldn't reach you last night on your phone."

He called yesterday? The last twenty hours rolls back through my mind, most of them spent on Gabriel's couch, chasing random search efforts and looking through old copies of history books and blueprints. "Sorry, I was at a friend's."

"I don't care where the two of you were," he snaps.

My hands roll into fists, and Paige touches my arm automatically. I ignore the warning and charge closer, growling. "Paige was on campus. I was with Gabriel."

"The creepy kid who hung around the bridge all day? Yeah, I finally figured out where I'd seen him before. That's the kid of Joe Barnum, the guy who jumped off this bridge. What kind of DNA you think that produces?"

"I'll call my PO, all right?"

"No, Theo, it's not all right. I could lose this job over your antics. I'm already three hundred dollars in the hole over those damn locks, and now you're getting tangled up with this girl, the police, and a kid with two dead parents and a guaranteed ticket to the loony bin, given his family history."

"What the hell are you talking about?"

"I'm talking about you! You need to find some friends who aren't crazy. Somebody that can level you out!"

"Go to hell, Denny!"

"Hell's better than wherever you're going to end up." The worst of it is that he doesn't yell. He simply lays the truth out, bare and terrible. He doesn't think of me as a kindred spirit. He thinks of me as a good deed. A nice favor for his sister.

Denny turns away, pulling a cigarette out of his pack as he heads down the stairs. My body slumps like someone's kicked me. I guess it's a bit like that.

I lean against the rail, staring down into the dark water. I just want this over. I want to end the awful thing on this bridge, and I don't know if I can.

Paige shoulders closer to me, and I sigh. We hold hands like it's all we have left. Not far from it, I guess. Neither one of us says much. Maybe we're afraid of what the bridge will do if we—

I stop cold and Paige looks up at me, curious.

"Wait," I say. "Can you stay for a minute?"

She nods and we stand there, hands clasped halfway across the river. The breeze is gentle and the sun is weak and I don't smell a single damn thing. I close my eyes and listen hard to the absolute peace and quiet.

And I think I understand.

"It's us," I say. "You and I together. I think it's some sort of shield."

"A shield?"

I squeeze her hand and grin. "Yeah, a shield. When we touch, I think there's some kind of magic in it. Good magic."

She arches a brow. "I think there's an eighties rock ballad trapped in your brain."

"I'm serious."

She bites her lip, her expression sobering. "You can't feel the haunting right now. And you think that's because we're touching."

"Maybe," I say. I let go of her hand and take a step back. "My friend Gabriel thinks whatever this dark energy is, it feeds on our energy. Maybe us touching, getting along—maybe that's how the good energy will win."

"Maybe." She doesn't sound like she believes it.

"Let's test the theory. Isn't that the scientific way?"

"I'm not sure what science has to do with any of this."

"You told me science is everywhere," I remind her.

"I did. I also believed that bridges were bridges and purses full of blood didn't swim through rivers."

Nothing strange is happening. A jogger passes, and then a kid on a bike. Paige moves her hands for her pockets, and I think she'd check her phone if she wasn't trying to indulge me. A great blue heron swoops low over the bridge, diving for one of the riverbanks where a piece of the river curves sluggishly around a patch of trees.

"It doesn't seem to be haunting us right now," she says.

"I've noticed."

"Maybe there's no rhyme or reason to it," she says. "Maybe it's all chaos."

I feel a pinch of frustration, or maybe it's impatience. Hard telling with me.

"I really need to get to class," she says. "Melanie's been super aware of my stress level. I'm already going to have to explain where I went, and we present tomorrow."

"I know that, but we need to figure this out too."

"Well, I might not have that luxury. I've been gone since before curfew ended. People will be looking for me. I'll probably get in trouble."

"Then go," I say. "I can stay here while you do your college thing."

"Don't say it like that?"

"Say it like what?"

Something changes. I don't know exactly what it is, but somehow the light goes cold and the shadows from the bridge beams... They aren't missing, not exactly. They're just wrong— too long and jutting off at strange angles.

Paige presses her lips together and stares at the other side of the bridge. She's not noticing any of this, so maybe it's just me. I've got plenty enough screws loose to explain some weird lighting.

"What are we even doing here?" she asks softly. "I love you. You know I do. But we have so much bad between us."

"Maybe we could be good together this time."

"Or maybe we're both too messed up."

"I don't believe that," I say. "I refuse to believe that."

"Theo, you have oppositional defiant disorder! You don't always believe red means stop or that falling from a tree will hurt."

"What the hell is that supposed to mean?"

"It means I need us to think rationally here. We can't do whatever we feel like without a single thought."

"So, what then? We go on pretending we don't feel all this? That we don't want more?"

"I'm not saying that! I just don't know—"

Something moves. There, under my feet, fast and dark beneath the boards. Paige gasps, stepping back, and I see it too, a shapeless, nameless form slipping behind the rusting beam.

It's starting again. I feel it more than I hear it, like voices so far away they're indistinguishable from background noise.

And then:

What the hell is wrong with you?

A mother is crossing the bridge with two young boys and a baby in a stroller. The first boy holds a bright-red toy hammer out in front of him as he jogs along, hair still mussed from sleep. He's pink cheeked and chattering happily, but I don't hear his voice. I hear mine.

You want the full psychiatric report?

Then the next kid comes, more serious and steady with every step. Darkness oozes up between the boards right in front of them. The little kid looks right at me, his lips opening and closing around words that belong to me.

ADD, ODD. Shit, Paige, help me out.

The darkness pushes at the boards until they groan, and the boys chatter on and on, totally unaware.

I'm done with you.

The shadow rolls under the boys and the mother, swelling until it's pushing up between all the boards now, and then when the pushing isn't enough, it slams *hard* at the underside of the planks. I jump and Paige yelps.

The darkness is everywhere, but the boys and the mother aren't looking down—they're watching us now. The mom, looking tired in a faded jogging suit and sloppy ponytail, gives me a wary frown and then takes her son's hand. His eyes are big when he looks at me, Kool-Aid-stained mouth shaping *my* words.

"Who isn't done with me?"

The mother pulls his arm and they push on, walking across boards that are oozing darkness. The black thing pushes up between those cracks, twelve inches high, then eighteen. I bite my lip so I won't scream. Paige strangles on another pained noise and starts forward, but the family is moving right past, one foot in front of the other. The back wheel of the woman's stroller bobbles sideways and forward again, pushing through the blackness. The shadow grows long and thin and sharp as though it will stab the entire family.

Paige starts forward—to stop them—but I reach for her. My fingers grazing her sleeve and then wrapping around her arm.

The shadow dissipates, and silence descends. My ears ring in the sudden quiet, the light going golden and sweet in the span of one breath. Above us, the rafters arch majestically, and the little boys jabber at the end of the bridge. They chirp about superheroes and battles in their little kid voices.

"This can't…" Paige's voice trails off, and who can blame her? What the hell is there to say? None of this is possible, and every bit of it is real.

I slide my fingers down her arm, and when we grip hands, both of our palms are tacky with sweat. My breath saws in and out, and Paige looks like she might throw up.

"All right. Theory feels pretty sound," I say. "The bridge feeds off the bad energy between us."

She's very still and quiet for a second, and then buries her head into my shoulder and then my chest. Our gripped hands are tangled at an awkward angle, and her breath hitches.

"Get me out of here," she whispers.

"What about class?"

She looks at the buildings, longing and desperation in her eyes. But her body shudders and she finally turns away. "I can't. I can't. Please, Theo."

"Okay," I say, pressing a kiss to her forehead. "Let's get you out of here."

Everything feels better in that moment, the sun and the

breeze and the grass all feel soft. Paige slips on her shoes and leans into me, and I look back at the bridge. I swear to God it wants us like this, so messed up and bound together. I pull her close to my side because I'm thinking too much. Wondering if maybe the truth is we'd be better off apart.

PAIGE

This is the dance we know best. I am shivering and sick, panic coursing through my body. Theo moves fast but steadily, talking, talking, talking.

He chatters when I panic because it helps. He winds from one subject to another while I stumble beside him, bleary-eyed and silent. We walk because he knows moving is better when I'm like this. When I'm still, my body itches and tingles. It's like I'm trying to come out of my own skin.

We walk until I stop shaking, rounding blocks and cutting through parks. Eventually, I don't think about every breath. Eventually, his words coalesce into sentences with meaning. I start to respond, clipped one-word answers turning into little comebacks and soft questions. Theo slows then, rounding us back to Denny's house. We go inside once he sees the truck is gone.

We sit on the couch, and my adrenaline ebbs. I'm left empty

and dry and terribly sad. He curls an arm around my shoulder then and lets me go quiet. We remember this part too.

I don't know what that says about us. We know how to fall apart better than anything.

After a long while, he kisses my hair, and his voice goes low and deep. Not like the chatter. That's just white noise to keep me from flipping out any worse. When he speaks now, it's what he's really thinking.

"Better?" he asks.

I feel the scrape of his unshaved jaw at my forehead. Everything smells like Denny's cigarettes, but when I kiss him, he still tastes like Theo. Like home.

I kiss him every time he tries to ask me if I'm better. Mostly, I do it because I'm allowed. It's so easy and so powerful. Kissing Theo makes me crazy in all the right ways. And it pushes out every awful, buzzing fear.

He starts to know without asking. I'm not surprised. I tug his hand toward my waist, and he scoops me closer. Kisses me deeply. We do it over and over. Dozens of kisses that make me bubble up from the inside out.

It's perfectly imperfect. Our noses bump if we move in too quickly. Sometimes Theo tries to talk right in the middle. And once, he wraps his arms around me so suddenly and tightly that our teeth clack together.

But mostly, it's magic. In kissing, Theo is not what I expected. He kisses me the way I always wanted to kiss him. He's slow and thorough and a bit desperate. Kissing him makes my stomach curl up. It heats my insides and soothes my nerves.

And nothing about it feels wrong.

We pull apart and I sigh. "We're not good together unless we're a mess. That can't be good, can it?"

"I don't know," he says. It isn't like him to leave it at that, but he does. He looks sad. "Even if we end this haunted mess on the bridge, what happens then? How could we ever explain this?"

"To your parents?" he asks.

"To *anyone*." I drop my gaze and try to steady my breathing. My heart is beating fast. The anxiety is climbing, but I know it won't be as bad. I'm too low on energy.

"What if we avoid the bridge?" he asks, taking my hand. "That would be a start, right? I'm fired anyway. You could stay on campus. What if we start over and forget all of this crazy shit ever happened?"

"It's more than the bridge, Theo," I say softly. "There's negativity between us too."

The truth of it falls heavy between us. It's inevitable and inescapable. And it makes me very tired.

My phone buzzes at 8:05. Melanie.

Where are you? Are you okay?

I show my phone to Theo. He rubs his hand over my knee. "How long has she been up?"

"Not long. Fifteen minutes maybe."

His palm is warm on my calf. His hands are warm everywhere. I want to curl so close to him that he's all I feel.

"What do you want to do?" he asks.

I turn, like it will make the question go away. Or Melanie. Maybe all of it.

"I don't want you to let go of that program," he says. "It's all you talked about for months. You drove me crazy, for God's sake. You might as well—"

"I'll say I'm sick," I say. It's not even a lie. I am sick, and I'm not sure how to get better.

I tap out a quick response.

Sorry. I'm sick.

Are you in the bathroom? I didn't see you?

No, I walked to the drugstore clinic. Long line.

What about the health clinic here? Why go off campus?

I can see her shaking her head. Or worse, maybe tightening her mouth. Second-guessing my every text. She could call my mom. God, I can't handle that right now.

My heart pounds as I think. I'm not sure how to proceed.

Finally, I type: The clinic might call Mom. She'd freak. Just want to make sure it's not strep. I'm not dying.

You sure?

Totally. Need medicine and sleep. Blah.

LOL. K. We're going to a movie after lecture. Want me to bring soup first?

I'm good, thanks. I'm going to practice for tomorrow's presentation. Have fun.

Be back by 8. Text if you need me.

The words all look convincingly benign. Who knows, though. If you look at my texts, they seem honest enough. Melanie could be lying too. She could be calling my mother right now, or she could just be a concerned roommate. I wish I were the kind of person who could tell.

My panic has burned itself out, so the thoughts chase each other into silence. I curl up, and Theo flips through the channels. My eyes grow heavy. We are messed up, but maybe it's all right this way. Maybe messed up is the only thing that fits.

I don't know I'm asleep until I'm awake.

My eyes open to see slick, muddy water sliding underneath me.

Where am I?

But I already know. This is the river. I gasp and jerk my head up. I'm outside, holding metal railing. I'm on the bridge. How? How is this happening? How am I here?

My heart beats hard, my pulse a painful throb in my neck and fingers. I can't be here. It's a dream. It *has* to be a dream.

I look around to collect whatever data I can. The sun is high and bright. My shoes are gone. The only thing I can hear over the roaring in my ears is the sibilant rush of the river.

My teeth chatter, and my knee bangs into the railing, sending locks rattling.

This is happening. I'm out here, barefoot again, standing at our lock. And I am alone.

A scream scrabbles up the back of my throat, but I swallow it down.

"You're all right." I say it to myself, out loud the way my mother might in the middle of a panic attack. The way Theo might.

Theo.

I look around wildly, pressing one hand to my face. Where is he? How did I get here? Did he let me go?

"Excuse me, miss," a woman says, bumping by. Her smile is tight. I can't blame her. I'm sure I look deranged. I'm barefoot on a bridge and obviously terrified. The woman passes by, looking once over her shoulder.

And then I'm alone again. There's no one. The air is warm, the sun already dipping slowly toward the west.

I've been gone all day. I pat my shorts, but my phone is gone. I don't know what time it is. I was with Theo, curled up on that ugly couch.

Where is Theo?

My next breath comes too short. I smell something. So strong I almost taste it. Lilacs. That can't be right. They bloomed early this year. I shouldn't be smelling that now.

I push back from the railing. *Don't think about it,* I tell myself. *Get off this bridge and figure it out later.* One step and the smell grows stronger. A soft jangling of wind chimes dances on the edge of my hearing.

Another step and I hear the voices.

She has an anxiety thing.

My heart trips. Loses its rhythm. I move faster.

Don't you, Paige?

Bang! A board in front of me jumps, and I shout. I look up, but there's no one watching. No one here but me. A choking sound erupts beneath my feet, a wheezing breath that goes in and out. It winds into a wail that sounds like my name.

Because it is my name.

And I know that voice. It's Theo crying for me. He's the dark shadow. The thing beneath the bridge, clinging to the underside of the walkway.

"No." I choke on the word.

Something drags along the wood beneath my feet, like denim on wood. A sack of laundry. Or a body.

Another board bangs, and my stomach drops. Tumbles. I

turn around, reverse my route. It doesn't matter. I'll head into the Village. I can find my way from there.

He's dragging himself after me. I see him, a shadowy mass, the dark impression of fingers between the planks. Oh, God, he's *right* there, right below me.

"Paige!"

I turn my head at the sound of my name. Theo's on the other side of the bridge. Not *Then Theo*, but *Now Theo*. And he's not crawling on the underside of the walkway. He's at the end of the bridge—for real, red-faced and obviously recovering from a run. His shoulders heave. I open my mouth to call for him.

The wail that comes next threatens to split me in two. My hands slap over my ears, and I drop low. Crouch into a ball. I think of tornado warnings in elementary school when we'd hide in the halls, hunched over our knees, pretending that would stop the bad thing from coming.

I'm still thinking of tornadoes when *Now Theo* touches my shoulders. I look up, and the world goes quiet. He looks so scared. He's holding my pink flip-flops. They look pretty and clean in his hands.

"Where were you?" I ask, crying.

"Where was I?" He gives a laugh that's closer to a sob. "Paige, I got up to use the bathroom, and when I got back, you were gone. That was over an *hour* ago."

I shake my head. My stomach cramps. My throat goes thick. "I don't remember."

"You were dead asleep, and you just—" He stops himself with a sharp breath, hands smoothing down my shoulders, my arms. "You *were* asleep, weren't you? You were sleepwalking again?"

"I don't know. It shouldn't last so long. It shouldn't..." My eyes go hot and prickly. Then I'm crying. He pulls me in to his chest.

"I should have known," he says roughly.

I shake my head. It's hard to talk. "How could you know?"

His grip tightens on me. "I should have. Shit, you could have walked into traffic."

"I shouldn't have. Sleepwalking shouldn't work like this, Theo. It never happens like this." Dread pools in my belly, liquid and cold. "Something's wrong with me."

"No," he says, his hand smoothing over my hair. "It's this damn bridge. We need to stay away from it until you're gone. Screw Denny, screw all of it."

"The bridge is *us*. It's what happened that night," I say. "How do we fight something that's coming from inside us?"

He doesn't argue. We don't bother trying to make it to the other side. The bridge doesn't hurt us when we're together. Whatever this thing is, it likes us twisted and tangled and clinging to each other.

Theo traces the heavy brass lock with our initials. "If you

want to fight it, we'll fight it. Or if you want, I'll go. Whatever you want. Just tell me what you want to do."

I touch the lock too, our fingers meeting at the first letter of my name. I remember everything about closing this lock on this rail. We were fourteen years old, and I was as desperate to have Theo as I was to hide how badly I wanted him. It was the only time I'd wanted to believe in fairy tales.

"When did you do this?" he asks, tugging the lock.

"The first time I came to visit you. You told me about the locks on the phone, about the whole tradition."

"I did? I don't remember."

"You told me it was this urban legend—locked in love for eternity. You laughed it off, but it made me hope. It was stupid. I walked to the hardware store before I came to Denny's. I was shaking so badly when I handed the clerk my money."

Theo laughs. "Did you think he'd call the police?"

"I don't know. I felt like a criminal, though. Then I had to buy a nail too, to scratch the letters. It took a while."

"What happened after you put the lock on the bridge?"

My stomach sinks. "I ran straight to Denny's to see you."

"I don't remember that either. But I remember us hanging out at the fair that night. I got into it with that kid on the football team."

"And you were kissing a girl on the couch when I got to Denny's."

His mouth parts, a mix of realization and regret shaping his features.

"Paige…"

"I was crushed," I say, shaking my head. "But how was that fair? It was ridiculous, believing this lock would be enough to *magic* us together."

I look up at him and pull his hand away from the lock like it's leaking poison into the water. Maybe it is.

"I wish I had some clue of what to say right now," he says, looking stricken.

"There isn't anything to say. It doesn't matter. It was years ago."

"And I didn't mean…"

His voice trails off, because he doesn't need to finish. That girl never appeared again. She wasn't some great love; it was just life.

I guess happily ever after has never been our story. Maybe we are meant for something else. And maybe that lie locked on this bridge is holding us from whatever that is. I hate it for being there. And for being wrong.

"Will you do something for me?" I ask him.

"You know I will."

"I want to cut off the lock," I say.

His hands tense in mine, his face furrowing. "Our lock?"

"Yes."

His shoulders sag, but he nods. "You want me to do it?"

"No. I want to cut it off together."

THEO

I don't have the tools, and Paige doesn't have time to wait for me to get them. Something about a presentation tomorrow, and since I don't want to cut it at all, I'm quick to agree. When I finally manage to sleep that night, I do it badly, tossing and turning on that half-inflated air mattress, and dreaming of kissing Paige. And hitting Paige. Paige sighing and Paige bleeding. I wake up feeling like the creepiest bastard who ever lived.

I visit Denny at the work site, hoping he'll let me help. He ignores me like it's his God-given duty, until I finally confront him with the last topic he'll want to talk about.

"What happened to you on the bridge?" I ask, and I watch the hammer he's holding go still, dropping slowly to his side. "You told me I'm not the only one who's been haunted, right?"

Denny lights a cigarette and walks toward me, looking

halfway between hateful and resigned. "You're good and obsessed with it, aren't you?"

"I've always been all or nothing," I say, scuffing my boot at the new planks. They're even and smooth. Nothing like the other half of the walkway. "It looks good."

"So do the lights," he says. "Still don't know if I'll be able to finish the locks this week."

"I'll help you with the locks," I say. "You don't have to pay me."

"It's going to be too much damn work," he says, not answering that. "I'm talking to the city about replacing the railing. It's going to be expensive as hell, but it needs to be done."

"It would take care of the lock problem."

Denny looks hard at the railing. "They've never been nothing but trouble."

"So, tell me. What happened to you?"

"The only thing you need to know is that nothing happens on this bridge if you're not already screwed up to begin with."

I step back, feeling cold. But Denny just looks at me. "It'll stop when you let her go. That's the only rhyme or reason to it, kid. You've got to let her go."

"Is that what you did?"

"Shit, it's what we all do in the end."

The sun is high and bright, a white disk burning in a pale-blue sky. It turns the water below shimmery, and the locks dance above like gold and silver. It doesn't seem so bad from up here.

"My friend Gabriel thinks you're right about those locks. They have some bad energy. He's looking for some serious tragedy to explain it. The source or whatever."

Denny laughs. "You think you need to *look* for a source. The whole damn world is the source. Life is the source."

"What do you mean?"

"Ghosts don't put these locks on the bridge," he says. "It's just us. Bastards like me and you with bad blood running in our veins. It's not a haunting... It's a warning telling you to stay the hell away."

I don't bother to tell him I can't stay away. He already knows I won't, so there's nothing left to say.

I leave with no idea what to do with my time. I text Gabriel three times about cutting off my own lock. No response. He might be spooked. Or maybe his grandfather finally decided to put down his foot about the weird older guy lurking around at all hours of the day and night.

After dinner, I sneak the Sawzall from Denny's truck and head down to the bridge at sunset to meet Paige. I'm wondering how her presentation went and if the saw will be strong enough to get the lock off. I'm not sure if I want it to be or not, but I want this to end. I want us to be free of all the bad things these locks have become.

I keep figuring a storm will come. The heat is that late-summer kind that begs for rain, leaves flipped backward on the trees and the wind whipping the river into frothy little peaks. But the sky is clear.

I stay off the bridge until I see her coming down through the campus. She's got her shoulders back and her gray Blue Devils sweatshirt on, sleeves pulled down over her hands even though it's eighty-five degrees out here.

"Hey," she says when she meets me on the walkway.

"Hey," I say, biting back every lame-ass thing I want to say about how tired she looks and how I'm worried she didn't sleep. Instead, I go with: "How'd the presentation go?"

"The Laurens went over on their time," she says with a shrug. "We go first thing tomorrow, but we practiced. I think I've got it. Are you ready to do this?"

I'm not, but she doesn't wait for an answer, just looks pointedly at the saw at my feet. Lifting it off the walkway feels like picking up my own noose, but I do it and even try to force a grin.

Her hands are cold when she reaches for mine, and I swear to God my heart drops so hard I feel it beating in my knees. I'm not ready to cut this lock, and I'm not ready to cut my losses. Being without Paige made me sick for months. I don't know how to do life without her.

"I don't want to do it," I confess, the saw heavy and awful in

309

my hands. "I know we're a shit show, and I have no damn idea how we make this work. But I want to try to make us better. To be good. I want to try."

She winces but reaches for me all the same, her cold hand on my chest, then the side of my neck. I can see the fear in the shadows under her eyes. It's been there all along, hiding behind her poise.

"What if we can't? What if there isn't better than this for us?"

"I don't believe that. Maybe we aren't great, Paige, but we don't write each other off. We see the good. That's something. That's a start. We can do something with a start."

"And what if we fail?"

"You're worth that risk to me," I say. God help my pathetic ass, I croak it out. I'm halfway to crying, and she's so calm and steady I barely recognize her. In that second, with her hands on my face and her sweatshirt sliding down off one perfect freckled shoulder, I'm sure she'll say no. I can already feel her pulling away.

"Then we risk it," she says, but her smile is brief, a flash of lightning I almost miss. Then she's grave. "But, we start by ending this. *This* was a lie, and it has to go."

She snags the lock hard and rattles it. My own fear pricks up, rows of goose bumps rising on my arms and a steady whisper slithering down from the arched metal overhead.

I swallow hard. "Then it goes."

My hands shake when I pick up the saw, my heart thumping sideways in my chest when I hit the power switch. The motor grinds to life and the saw jerks, vibrating wildly at the end of the handle. I can feel the darkness coming already. It's that feeling you get in that split second of free fall before the impact comes. You know it's going to hurt, and you know there's not a damn thing you can do to stop it.

I hesitate and Paige reaches for the saw slowly, her hands small and surprisingly steady when she takes it from me. I want to stop her, but I'm lost in the haze of what's coming, what's almost here.

She shifts the blade, and terrible images cascade through my head, the blade tumbling from her hands, slicing her belly, her thighs. Blood everywhere.

"No." My shout is hoarse, barely audible over the roar of the blade, but it's like Gabriel with the cutters. It's so real I'm sure it will happen.

"What?" she asks.

I reach for the saw, but she holds it out of my reach, so I shake my head. "I don't want you near it."

"I put the lock on this bridge," she says, and then to my horror, I see her line the blade to the metal. "I'll cut the damn thing off."

It starts before the first contact.

There isn't one second to brace myself. I take a breath with nothing but the harsh buzz of the saw in my ears. And when I let it out, I am drowning in every toxic thing that happened.

The edges of my vision go dark, and Paige's face is a blur in a sea of voices and shadows. She's shouting my name, reaching for me, but it's not her now. It's her *then*. She's wearing Chase's sweatshirt over a pretty sundress, and she's shaking her head. God, she's so angry, and so scared.

In my mind, I hit her again, the impact soft and hard and stinging me through and through. I watch her fall, and I go down on the bridge like I went down in the dirt that night. I'm reliving it all. There's a thin, awful wailing. A hurt-animal song that brought me to this bridge the first time.

It is not an animal. It is Paige on the ground, hands on her mouth and blood spilling over her fingers.

Chase is kicking me in the side, but I feel nothing there. My chest is ripped open, insides spilling out. Paige is sitting on a plastic chair, dripping blood onto her beautiful feet, and I did that, I *did* that.

But Paige is *not* on a chair, and I see that too. Here and now, she's standing strong, holding a saw, sparks flying as she cuts us both free.

I smell blood and dirt and lilacs and rot. The darkness is underneath me, pushing up around my vision and droning in my ears. Paige looks up, her face hard and determined behind the

312

sparks flying off the blade. Blood coats her lips and chin, drips in terrible splotches against the column of her neck.

She's talking to me while she cuts, that bloody mouth moving around words that belong to me. And even over the grind of metal cutting metal, those words slice right into me.

Shit, shit, shit, Paige! No!

I push myself away, toward the railing. It shudders under my impact, feeling dangerously loose. Paige looks up, no blood on her face and only worry on her features. The lock drops and then catches, the severed arm hooked over a twisting piece of railing. Determined, Paige leans in again, but the power cuts abruptly, the noise and the saw going quiet.

I can hear my own breath, coming in and out in whimpers. I'm on my hands and knees, trying to get to Paige, who's stony-eyed and glistening with sweat. Her gaze moves to the distance, to something behind me. Something on the end of the bridge.

I stagger to my feet to turn to see it. It's Gabriel. He's wiping his tear-streaked face with the sleeve of his T-shirt. And he's holding the unplugged extension cord in his hand.

PAIGE

"You can't cut them," he says.

For a second, I don't recognize him. And then I do. He's the boy from Theo's porch. The one he was talking to. I think his name is Gabriel.

I still feel the hum of the voices, but it was worse for Theo. He's bent over double, hands on his knees and coughing like he was being choked.

"What are you doing here?" Theo asks. "I texted you all day."

"It's not the locks," Gabriel says. "Cutting them won't stop this. It won't, Theo."

Theo raises his hands, his voice raspy. "I'm not cutting your lock, man. We're only cutting ours."

"It won't help because she's still here."

"It's already done," Theo says. So gentle.

"It won't matter." The kid sniffs again, shoulders hitching

with his tears. "I figured it out, you know? I figured out the source of all this."

"Okay, I'm listening."

"The locks aren't the power; they just hold it. They're not special or magical. They hold pieces of us—our energy. We put these locks on with a promise and *that's* the power. It's our promises. Do you know what I mean?"

"Maybe," Theo says softly. He drops his hands, completely serene.

I feel anything but. The lock glimmers, motionless on the rail, dangling by a broken arm. My skin prickles with the same fear I felt four years ago, when I snapped it shut. *Just let him love me forever and the rest of it will be okay.*

"It's us," Gabriel says. "People with locks—it's all our energy, good and bad."

"I believe you. My uncle doesn't think there's one source either."

Gabriel shakes his head. "No, there *is*. Someone started all this in motion. Even my mom—after so long, she's talking to me. Can you hear her too?"

My whole body is tingling now. I see something out of the corner of my eye. A flash of movement. But then there's nothing. My imagination or paranoia? Isn't it always fear for me? Fear of this bridge. Fear of the future. Fear that everyone will see how terrified I really am.

"I don't hear her," Theo answers gently. "Is she the source of this, Gabriel? Is this your mother replaying these awful memories?"

Gabriel sniffs again, shaking his head with a bitter laugh.

The air is changing, a slow building pressure against my ears. The darkness is coming to feed. It's under the bridge—*Then Theo*. The Theo from the past, from that party. He's down there, scraping at the wood. It won't stop.

"Theo," I say, trying to warn him.

"Just tell me, Gabriel," Theo says, still ignoring me. "None of this is your fault."

He chokes on a sob. "It's not my mother, Theo! How can't you see this? She's not hurting you, she wouldn't have... She'd never. But someone woke her up."

"Me," Theo says, defeated. "It was me, wasn't it? My bad energy."

But his words taste like lies in my mouth. The darkness is still coming. I can feel the swell of power now.

"My mother's promise isn't about pain!" Gabriel cries. "She suffered when my dad died, losing the person she loved—the family she wanted. But her lock was for *me*. Her promise was about love, not regret and pain. The voices, the screaming—her energy wouldn't bring this."

"But mine would. I'm sorry," Theo says.

He shouldn't be. Because he isn't the one who clamped a

lock on this bridge with a fevered wish to hide behind someone else. He isn't the one pretending that he's whole and good. I was driven by fear then, and now too.

"I did this," Theo says again.

"No."

I don't know if Gabriel says it or if I do. We both shake our heads.

"You're not the one feeding this," Gabriel says, and his eyes meet mine.

And I know.

My promise was to hold on to the boy who would hide my weakness. I wanted to cling to my safety net. The one person who'd always be crazier than me. My lock wasn't about love, it was about dread. And that dread is here, roiling black and desperate beneath us.

None of this is arsenic or ghosts or science. It's what's inside me. The fear of that row of prescription bottles. The fear of my parents being right. The fear that my crazy will swallow me, bit by bit, until there is nothing left. That's what's coming for us now, dark and hungry and wearing Theo's voice.

"What the hell?" Theo asks. He can hear it, sobbing and scraping.

"Theo, you have to go," I whisper.

Because it's coming for him. *I* am coming for him.

I am the swirling black shadow, the horror of our past, the panic of our future.

"She's right," Gabriel says, looking at me. "She's the source, Theo. It's Paige."

The boards groan and the shadow swells, pushing up on either side of the walkway, oozing through every crack. All around us, wind chimes sing and rotting lilacs cast their sickly scent in the air. Something thumps beneath the walkway, jarring the warped, rotting boards. One pops loose, and Theo stumbles.

"Stay back!" he shouts at Gabriel.

Gabriel obeys, but Theo stays. He looks right at me, still desperate to save me. To save us both.

But how can we be saved? How can we beat away the things that live in our bones?

"Theo," I cry.

Then Theo is no mere shadow now. It pants and gasps underneath my feet. Fingers scratch at the wood, and I hear it struggle. Hear *him* struggle. Gurgling for a breath. Sobbing on my name like he did on that deck. Reaching for me.

That Theo is crawling underneath my shoes, his breath whistling through the cracks between the planks.

"What is this?" Theo breathes softly, looking down in a mix of horror and wonder. "Paige, we've got to go."

He takes a step, but the entire walkway jerks. Planks ripple like an accordion, and Theo goes sideways. He slams into the rail as I drop to my knees.

He rights himself and starts for me, to help me. But he can't help me and I can't help him—we have to help ourselves.

I open my mouth to tell him. To explain. Blood rushes over my lips instead, sour and coppery, as real now as it was on the dock that night. The culmination of my darkest hour.

He calls my name again, but I hear it from below, from *Then Theo*. The boards thump like his head hitting the ground. His sobs echo off the wood and slither up through the cracks. It's that terrible night. It is *always* that terrible night. My jaw throbs and blood drips.

This is what he did to me.

Theo's face is pale across from me. He is flesh and blood and here and now, but the Theo my terror conjured snakes through the planks and around his ankles.

This is what I'm doing to him.

A glint of gold catches my eye. The lock. It's still there, caught on a bottom rung, old promises made for every wrong reason. Maybe cutting it wasn't enough.

I kick it hard, and Theo thrashes against the dark tendrils, against *Then Theo*. The bridge shudders, and Theo's knees lock together. It's got him.

I kick the lock again, and Theo—my Theo—yelps.

I haul back, my heel slamming into the lock. Metal scrapes and the arm slips free.

It clatters against the railing as it falls. *Then Theo* goes still, a voiceless shadow once more. It will fall next, and this will end. This will *end*.

"Paige?" My Theo is pale and wide-eyed across from me. I don't understand.

Then I see the remnants of the darkness, black tendrils wrapped tight around his legs. The rotten boards splinter and snap beneath his feet. Theo's body shudders violently. I lunge, but it's too late.

He's already falling.

THEO

I crack two ribs hitting a support beam underneath the walkway and land hard, wedged in a corner of metal somewhere in the bowels of the bridge. Paige is screaming and running, and Gabriel is shrieking as they rush for me.

There is no dark shadow waiting for me. No terrible smell and no voice that isn't right here and now. Nothing haunted remains, but I'm still screwed as hell.

I groan and move, but it's not good. I'm going to slip. I can feel that right away, and as a guy who's had his share of falls, I would know. I move my limbs experimentally, but my right arm is toast. No pain, just a wet, lifeless noodle dangling from my body.

Gabriel swears.

Paige screams for him to call 911.

And I almost laugh because it's all so damn ironic. But if I laugh, I'll slip more. I search with my dangling legs, bicycling wildly. There isn't a way to get them up. I'm like a letter caught halfway through a mail slot. Sooner or later, I'm going to drop.

I try desperately to even the balance, but with my ribs and my useless arm, I can't. There's no way. The water is slick and dark beneath me. Compared to the metal biting into my skin, it almost looks inviting.

Footsteps thunder closer and closer, and then Paige is there. She's sobbing out a litany of apologies and explanations, words coming so fast that my spinning head doesn't have a hope of sorting them out. God, I just wish I could see her face a little better.

"Paige," I gasp out. My arm is pinned awkwardly, and my ribs are screaming with every breath. "It's okay. I'm all right."

Which, yeah, might not exactly be true, and she doesn't buy it for a second. Her face is mostly lost in darkness, but I can hear the sharp sniff she gives.

"Gabriel is calling 911. You need to hold on."

"That…might be a bit of a problem."

"We can still fix this! You will…" She breaks off in a sob, and I struggle again, desperate to shift forward. Not to fall. Because this will haunt her too, and she's been haunted enough.

I tighten my jaw, decisions clicking into place. We can't be terrified or desperate or wrecked or any of the other shit that brought us to this place. Maybe for once, I can do better.

"Paige, I want you to look away."

"What? No! No, you are not pulling this shit with me, Theo!"

She's sobbing and it hurts, but it feels good too, because no matter what else we are, we are still us. I didn't wreck us beyond all hope, none of this did. I smile up at her, hoping I don't look like I'm going to throw up, though I feel like it.

"Paige, listen to me."

"No, I did this to you. This was my fault. I didn't mean—"

"I thought we were going to start over. A fresh new start, right?"

"Please don't fall." Her voice is small and fragile, and God, I'd give anything, anything at all to do this thing for her, to give her this. But my body slips a little more, and I grunt. Looks like I don't have anything left to give.

Denny's words ring back to me. *This won't end until you let her go.*

But it's not just me holding on—it's both of us. All wrapped up in who we were and what we did, but there's no controlling what happens next. All we control is how we deal with it.

I slip again, and I know I've got no time. I grunt, and Paige screams at Gabriel to call them again, to *get* them here!

I call her name, and my voice is fading, every ounce of my strength trained into the arm trying to hold me in place.

"Paige."

She looks down, steady and good and crying for me. It's not the worst way to face whatever the hell is about to happen.

"Paige." I say it one more time and hear her go still. She's ready to listen now, so I speak. "Let me go. This is how we do better. This is how we try. Look away and let me go."

Her sob cuts me in two, but then her head disappears and I let out a sigh. When my arm slips again, I don't fight it. I guess I'm ready to fall.

———

The impact is a blur, but the bastard pounding his fist against my diaphragm is bringing everything into high definition in the worst possible way. Rocks stab into my back, and my left hand—the one I can't move—is scraping on a patch of thornbushes. He pounds again and I heave, ribs screaming like fire as I puke up what seems like half of the river.

I push him away with my good arm, the one that doesn't actually feel good at all, and then I try to sit up, try to speak, but the world goes dark and muddy all around me.

Paige isn't there. Not before I pass out or when I wake up in the squad or when Denny bursts into the emergency room. I don't see him at first, but I'm close to the nurses' station so I hear them barking.

"Sir, you can't be in here with that!"

"My nephew's in here! Squad took him!"

"Sir, this is a nonsmoking facility!"

I hear him slamming open the doors, and then slamming them open again twenty seconds later when he comes back in apologizing gruffly. A sour-faced nurse admits him into my little partitioned area, where I'm sitting in a scratchy hospital gown, ribs wrapped in ACE bandages and arm in a sling.

I lift a hand and wince. Every damn part of me hurts like hell.

"What's the damage?" he asks me, visibly relieved.

"Two broken ribs and a shoulder situation." I look at the sling on my arm. "I'm supposed to see an orthopedic surgeon soon in Columbus. They think it's a nerve thing."

He snorts, looking wide-eyed. "What's *that* going to cost?"

"More than Mom's going to want to pay."

He waves a hand. "Figures."

He looks down again, then glances up at the TV. And hell, I'm still pissed, but he's still my uncle too. I nod at the remote. "You could turn on the TV if you want. Check the weather."

"Don't be a smart-ass," he says. Then his face softens, his voice going quiet. "I'm sorry, kid. I never... I'm just sorry."

"Me too."

Denny pulls out his phone and clears his throat, looking awkward. "Your girl's been calling. Texting too. Your phone's lost somewhere in the water, so she's been blowing up mine."

"She hasn't been here?"

"She stayed until they loaded you up. She was with you, but maybe you don't remember."

Not one bit, and I wish to hell I did. I want to know if she's all right—if *we're* all right.

"Did she say anything in the texts?"

"She wants to know if you're getting discharged. She wants you to meet her on campus tomorrow morning, which I thought was crazy. You're not going to want to walk around."

I'm already getting out of bed when his hand lands gently on my shoulder. I wouldn't call it my good shoulder at this point either. There isn't a part of my body that feels anything to close to good.

"Denny, I know how you feel and I heard your piece. But Paige isn't some girl I'm going to walk away—"

"I wasn't going to say any of that. Hold your horses, little hell-raiser."

I grin, and he drops his hand from my shoulder. I don't know what it means. Maybe I'm more to him than a good deed. And maybe he's more than the asshole who said awful things to me on the bridge.

Denny clears his throat and gestures at a duffel bag I hadn't noticed at his feet. "Figured you might want some dry pants. You should come home and make calls. Get some sleep or whatever."

I stare at the rectangle of light above my bed. "Call Mom, you mean."

"That can wait. If you want."

I roll my head to the side on the mostly flat pillow. Denny is tugging at his hat and shifting on the plastic chair. He's doing his best. I guess it's all any of us can manage.

They release me with Denny, and he takes me home, driving long blocks to avoid the bumpy roads. I follow his suggestion and sleep for six blissful hours on the couch, with the Weather Channel on and a brand-new air conditioner humming the living room into an icy cocoon. He'd installed it after work while I was stealing the SawzAll out of the back of his truck. I almost cried with joy when I opened the front door.

The shower before I head to campus is almost worse than the fall, but it's good to feel clean when I head outside. Denny wants to drive me, but I want to be on my own two feet. It's a new start, and the sun on my face feels good.

I think about taking the bridge on First Street, but Paige is right. Whatever was on that bridge is done now. History isn't eating us alive anymore. We cut it free and let it go and broke a few bones for good measure.

The guys finished the walkway while I was in the hospital, the rotten boards that dropped me through putting the whole team into high gear. Now it's a procession of smooth, even planks under my feet. The locks are still there, glittering on the fence, but they don't have anything left to say. Not to me.

I meet Paige on a bench in front of her dorm like she asked through Denny's text messages. I'm not sure what I expected, but it's definitely not this. She's in a skirt and a white blouse, hair clipped back from her face, and she looks good. Well rested.

She's also holding a paper bag with handles, like she's been shopping. So, yeah, it's different. This time last year, Paige stayed up all night researching skin infections because I cut myself on a fence and refused to get stitches. She doesn't look like she's been worrying like that.

"So, a shoulder specialist tomorrow?" she asks.

I nod. "Arm is still mostly a dead fish, so I must have ripped loose something I need."

She angles her body toward me, fingers tracing the side of my face. I smacked the bridge there too on my way down, which I didn't know until I saw my shiner in the mirror.

"You look terrible," she says softly, but before I can feel bad about it or ask if I need to brace for another we-can't-be-friends conversation, she kisses me.

It's soft and brief, and she pulls back before I'm ready.

"Did you finish your presentation?" I ask.

"Yes." She smiles. "It was good. We came in second. A couple of kids I never dreamed would be competitors had a working prototype for a new water-filtration method. Crazy."

I laugh, and then groan. "Really need to not laugh. Hey, what happened to Gabriel? Is he all right?"

She nods. "I walked him home last night after Denny went with you. He actually helped me with the presentation, let me practice the conclusion."

"He's smart like you."

She nods. "We snuck into the library. He looked up a couple of articles on other substances that have shown up in the river. All this stuff from the past keeps turning up in there."

"Could he still hear his mom? After I fell?" I ask.

She frowns and shakes her head. "I don't think so. I think he's having a hard time with it—letting go of the past, I guess."

"When are we ever ready to let go? The past feels safe."

"Sometimes you have to push past safe to get to healthy." Then she touches my face again, because she's not talking about Gabriel. "That promise I made. It wasn't good, Theo."

"I don't know. Your endless love doesn't sound so bad."

"It wasn't love at all," she says quite seriously. "It was desperation. And fear. I thought if I could keep you close enough, maybe no one would see what a mess I am. That fear is what haunted us."

"I thought it was me," I admit. "I was the one who made it so awful. I was the one who broke everything."

"We were already broken. And for once, it was my issues that boiled over, not yours."

"Paige, your issues didn't bust me through rotten wood into the river."

"Maybe not, but any power that bridge has is given to it. *We* give it the power. The lock is where it starts, but what's in us does the rest."

She turns and pulls a pair of shoes out of her bag, tall brown sandals with a silver strap. They're a little dirty. Then she pulls out a twisted-up silver earring, and I tilt my head.

"If these are get-well presents, I'm not sure they'll fit."

Another grin from Paige, but this one doesn't last. "I thought these shoes were mine. The ones I wore to the picnic."

I glance at them, and then I shake my head. "Yours had gold straps. I remember."

"I also wear an 8," she says, pointing at the faded 9 on one heel. "I also remember that the earrings I lost that night, the ones Dad brought me from Spain, had three hoops. These have two. They aren't mine. And you don't even know about the antibacterial gel I found. It was the same brand for the party and I was sure you'd left it. Convinced. But it was my friend Elise's. She'd worn my sweatshirt before returning it and left it in the pocket."

"I'm not following."

She frowns. "The things I thought I found from the party? I was wrong. They dredged up bad memories. It was all in my head."

"What happened on that bridge wasn't all in your head, Paige. That purse wasn't your head. That thing—it was crawling underneath us."

"I know it was. And somehow I know it came from my head. All this time, I've been trying to deny all my anxiety. Over you. Over my parents. Over everything. I buried it as deep as I could, but it came out. It will still come out if I don't deal with it."

"The bridge is fixed," I say. "I walked over it today, and I'm telling you that whatever happened there is finished. It's finished with us, at least."

"But I'm not," she says. "I'm not finished."

She pushes at the shoes with the tips of her fingers.

"Are you okay?" I ask.

She smiles at me, wavy hair framing her heart-shaped face. "Not yet I'm not."

My chest tightens before I speak again. "What about us? Are we okay?"

"I have no idea what we are. I guess we'll have to learn as we go."

I grin even though it hurts. "Good thing I like unpredictable."

She keeps the bag and asks me to walk with her, and despite my entire body hurting, I'm thrilled to do it. We stop at the entrance to a building labeled Student Services, and on the door, I read something about mental health.

God knows, I could always use the help, but I'm pretty sure I can't just stroll in because I'm a friend of some girl on campus. Off my look, Paige shakes her head.

"It's for me, not you. I just wanted you to walk over here with me."

"I'd walk anywhere with you," I say with a goofy grin. "I'd even fall off a bridge."

She laughs, so I see them before she does, crossing toward us with worried, tight expressions. Her mom is a taller, more freckled version of Paige, and her dad is solid and dark and scowling at me. She tenses a little when she spots them, but then forces out a breath, and to my shock, takes my hand.

A month ago—hell, maybe a day ago—I would have pulled away and headed for the hills. Today I stand straight and squeeze her fingers. I did a god-awful thing to Paige, but I've done good things too. Maybe I can learn to do more.

"A fresh new start, right?" she says as if she's reminding herself.

She lets me go and goes toward them, bag in hand and shoulders back. She looks strong on her own, and it makes me smile.

I turn my head up the sky where the sun beats down, hot and bright. Her words play through my mind.

A fresh new start.

Sounds like just the thing I need.

ACKNOWLEDGMENTS

ADHD is not a play-pretend diagnosis. Like Theo, millions of teens live with ADHD, and it affects their social, academic, and emotional lives, and many are doing so with little support and under the pain of tremendous criticism.

I'd like to thank Dr. Richard Kern, who has provided years of insight and wisdom, and Leanne Ross, who is an inspiration to teachers to look beyond labels to see the potential within.

I had an unbeatable team supporting me through Theo and Paige's journey. To Annette Pollert-Morgan, your insight and wisdom blow my mind. Thank you for helping me say what I mean. Thank you to the incredible Sourcebooks Fire team: Todd, Alex, Cassie, and my talented cover artists Nicole and Kerri. To Suzie Townsend and Sara Stricker and the team at New Leaf Literary. Being a New Leaf author is such a gift—I'm so grateful for your support.

To Romily Bernard, forever and always—nobody's breaking up this band, baby. Also, to Jody Casella, who sometimes told me to go to bed, and who often told me different is good.

To my beautiful, brilliant OHYA writers, Lisa Klein, Julia Devillers, Margaret Peterson Haddix, Edith Pattou, and Erin Richards. Edie, your gentle spirit gave me courage to go for the supernatural! Erin, thank you for understanding that professional triumph and the stomach flu can produce similar symptoms. Also, thanks to Tim for taking a panicky call on a Saturday.

To Janey and Rick, thank you for making me feel so welcome in your home and lives. And to the many other authors and friends who've been especially supportive this year: Leigh Anne Tooke, Liz Deskins, David Weaver, Robin Gianna, Sheri Adkins, Mindee Arnett, (for emails that kept my chin up), Mindy McGinnis (for working writer advice), Kurt Dinan (who encouraged me when I needed it), and Kristen Simmons (who invited me to Dayton and dinner).

Thank you to God for giving me the strength to write this book in a whirlwind year. With You, all things are possible.

And thank you to my incredible family, David, Ian, Adrienne, and Lydia. Without you there would be no Starbucks deliveries or Timbits breakfasts or much-needed documentary breaks. Ian, Adrienne, and Lydia: your love and laughter fuels every page. I love you for being exactly who you are, and I am so lucky to be your mom.

ABOUT THE AUTHOR

A lifelong Ohioan, Natalie D. Richards spent many years applying her writing skills to stunningly boring business documents.
Fortunately, she realized she's much better at making things up
and has been writing for teens ever since. A champion of aspiring
authors, Richards is a frequent speaker at schools, libraries, and
writing groups. She lives in Ohio with a Yeti and a Wookie (her
dogs) and her wonderful husband and children. *We All Fall Down*
is her fifth novel.

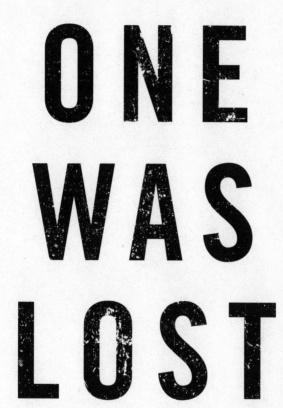

DON'T MISS
NATALIE D. RICHARDS'S

ONE WAS LOST

CHAPTER 1

No one said anything about rain in the brochures.

Not that there were brochures. There was a handwritten sign-up sheet in the cafeteria, followed by permission slips recycled from ghosts of field trips past. I'm not really sure why I was expecting a world-class production. Must be the director in me.

I stumble under the weight of my pack, sloshing through a puddle. Cold water oozes through my boots and socks. So much for Mr. Walker's plastic ponchos keeping us dry. I guess after six straight hours of rain, dry is relative anyway.

"I hope you packed your dirty clothes in the plastic bags I handed out last night," Mr. Walker booms from the front of the line. "They might stink, but they'll be dry."

The other girls cringe a little at the idea—all except Ms. Brighton, our younger, cooler teacher guide. She's very Zen about these things, nodding along in her crystal earrings and mud-dyed *Gaia Mother* T-shirt.

I'm in the last half of the group, behind Jude with his ever-present earbuds and imperious gaze. Since I'm five-two, the back of his poncho is about all I can see, but it's better than looking at Lucas.

Anything's better than looking at Lucas.

Even behind me, I can feel him. Looming. Everyone's tall measured against me, but Lucas is ridiculous. He *towers*. If there were actually a sun to be found in this Appalachian monsoon, his shoulders would cast a shadow you could hide two of me in. I have no idea what you have to eat to grow like that. Corn? Eggs? Small children?

I trudge onward, slowing to shift my backpack. The right strap is digging a painful trench into my shoulder, and I can't find a way to move it. My poncho slips with the effort, and a river of icy water slithers down my back.

"*Holy crap!*" I say, arching in a futile effort to escape.

"Keep moving, Spielberg," Lucas says behind me.

I grit my teeth and walk on. If I respond, I might have to look at him, and I've worked very hard not to do that. I've *not* looked for sixty-two days. It's a pretty good track record. I'm not going to wreck it just because he ended up on my Senior Life Experience Mission. At the last possible minute, no less.

"Is this really top speed for you?" he asks, sounding like he's on the verge of a laugh.

I stare at the line of backpacks and ponchos ahead of me, resisting the urge to snap back at him. I need to be the bigger person here. It's not like I don't know why he's picking at me.

"Still sticking with the silent treatment?" he asks. "Gotta give it to you, you're committed. Slow-moving as shit but committed."

OK, I'm bigger person-ed out.

I whirl around. I shouldn't—I know I shouldn't—but the words blurt out. "Newsflash, Lucas! I'm moving as fast as I can. Not all of us are loping around with giraffe legs like you, so if you're in such a rush, feel free to move ahead."

He steps closer, and it happens. I see him. *Really* see him.

Fricking crap.

He tilts his head until his face is visible inside his plastic hood. How does he do it? He's just as wet and miserable as the rest of us, but somehow, he's owning the hell out of a poncho that makes me look like I need a zip tie and a trip to the curb.

I should walk away, at least *look* away. Lucas is all sharp lines and hooded eyes, and I should have learned my lesson. Because standing here brings me right back to that night on the porch. My ears go buzzy with the memory of crickets singing and the backdrop of the cast party inside. My face tingles because I remember other things too—his scratchy jaw and soft mouth and my heart beating faster than it ever should.

My gaze drifts to his smirk and lead pools in my stomach.

That's what I'm really mad about. It's not his teasing or the rain or anything else. It's the fact that he turns me into the same fluttery mess I was all summer. He *still* turns me into my mother, and I hate it.

I try to move away, but he catches the edge of my poncho—keeps me facing him. "Huh."

I cross my arms. "Huh, *what*?"

"Look who suddenly remembers me," he says softly.

"Don't."

"I won't," he says, though his grin needs a parental advisory label. "I didn't then, did—"

Lightning flashes, bright enough that we both jerk.

One Mississippi.

Two Mississ—

The sound that follows is like the sky being torn in two. It ends with a bone-deep rumble that rattles the ground and bunches my spine. I close my eyes and take a breath, yoga-slow. It doesn't *cleanse* anything, so I try another.

Across from me, Lucas is searching the sky. I take the opportunity to turn and bolt ahead on the trail. Not that there's anywhere to go. Away from him is good enough.

I plow into Jude's back in my eagerness to escape. He spares me one millisecond of irritation, and then he's back to pretending we're all part of the scenery.

The trail widens here, or maybe the forest is less dense. Who knows? It gives me enough room to move past Jude until I'm next to Emily, my tent mate for the last two nights.

Emily looks back at me—a sparkle of dark eyes under her poncho—and her mouth twitches. Is she smiling at me? That's new.

"Some trip, right?" I ask.

She ducks her head. And that's as close to a conversation as we've gotten. I sigh. We have three more days of awkwardness in the woods. Three. More. Days.

"Hold up." Mr. Walker is ultra-alert. "Everybody stay right here. Don't move."

Our single file line separates, students clustering into a group. The rain is a touch lighter now, and everything's hazy and foggy. Mr. Walker clomps ahead while we wait. I roll my achy shoulders and try to ignore how damp and sticky I am under my trash bag poncho.

I can't see much, but it wouldn't matter if I could. We all look alike. I mean, Lucas is an easy spot, towering six inches over everyone here. Mr. Walker would stand out too if he hadn't walked off—he's the only one with an actual rain jacket, plus he's got that bright-yellow plastic-sleeve-protected GPS strapped to his arm. I can't see where he went though. Being short offers few advantages.

"What's going on?" Madison asks, turning to touch Lucas's arm for the fiftieth time this hour. "Can you see anything, Lucas?"

"Is something wrong with the bridge?" Hayley this time, I think. It doesn't matter. Hayley and Madison are sort of interchangeable in my head. Like bookends. In a tent.

Ms. Brighton holds up a hand high enough that even I can see it. I focus on her short, decidedly not-earthy purple nails. "Just hold tight. Mr. Walker's checking it out."

She says that like it will solve everything. It might. Back in Marietta, Mr. Walker was a math teacher with bad breath and a collection of football bobbleheads. Out here, he's Dr. Doomsday Prepper. He's got enough gear in his pack to start a new society should we get lost. I glance around the sea of drippy trees surrounding us. Scary thought.

"He's checking the bridge," Lucas says. "Something with the ballast maybe."

Plastic rustles as Madison clings harder to his arm. "Are we going to die? Oh my God, I can't die out here."

Ms. Brighton laughs. "No one's dying. Native Americans lived in these forests for generations."

Lucas snorts. "Uh, last night, you said those same Native Americans still have guru ghosts running around. Driving hunters off cliffs."

She smirks. "Guru is a Sanskrit word. That was from my first story."

"Whatever. There *were* ghosts flinging people off cliffs in the other one."

"No, the hunters found the cliff on their own," Ms. Brighton says, correcting him. "The Cherokee spirits just led them away from the sacred animals they were hunting."

"The only thing I'm hunting out here is a hot shower and cable TV," Lucas says.

Ms. Brighton's smile goes wide. "Then I'm sure you're safe. So let's all stay positive."

I'm positive I'm soaked. I'm positive I hate hiking. I'm positive this trip will go down as the worst choice of my young life, but I'm pretty sure she doesn't want to hear any of those things, so I keep my mouth shut. I squeeze my way between Jude and my tent mate, Emily, so I can see better.

"Oh, the things the forest will teach us!" Ms. Brighton seems delighted at the prospect.

I bite back a grin. Kooky or not, I like her. Granted, the Church of Brighton would be a cobbled-up mash-up of her choice—part Buddhism, part Cherokee spirituality, and a whole lot of all-organic-all-the-time. But she's nice.

She points ahead. "Oh, Mr. Walker's headed back. See? It's probably fine."

Mr. Walker stomps up the streambed, looking grim. "We've got a problem."

Or it's not fine at all.

"What problem?" I ask.

"Bridge is out." He wipes his rain-soaked face like there's nothing more to say.

I look up at the narrow metal structure. It's a little rusty and worse for the wear, but overall, it seems intact.

"It's suspended over the water," Jude says, his soft voice surprising me. "Isn't that how bridges are *supposed* to function?"

Mr. Walker turns away from Jude like he didn't say anything at all.

"Something's wrong with the supports, smart-ass," Lucas says.

Mr. Walker nods at Lucas and points out a sagging seam and some cracks in the dirt that are apparently scary dangerous signs or something. I don't care enough to make suggestions. This is somebody else's show falling apart, and I'm just going to stand here like a stagehand waiting for someone to tell me what to do.

"OK, so now what?" Ms. Brighton asks, her oh-so-positive voice dipping a little.

"We can't trust the bridge. We'll go down and cross the river on foot." Mr. Walker taps the GPS on his arm. "We got a flash flood warning a while back, so I want to get on the other side while we still can."

"But we'll get wet if we don't use the bridge!" Hayley (Madison?) gripes.

A laugh coughs out of me.

"I'm already freezing," Madison adds. Or is it Hayley? No, it's definitely Madison. I can tell because she's the one whose arm is always snaking toward Lucas.

"I want to go home," Hayley says.

We will probably lather, rinse, and repeat this twelve more times in the next hour. These two have been a torrent of complaints. I can't blame them. This place is like woodsy purgatory.

Still, Mr. Walker has a point. It's an easy descent to the stream, and it still looks shallow, but with all this rain, that might change. And then we're stuck here. We're at the halfway point of the trip now, so any kind of delay could mean another day out here. I'd cross a leech-infested river of blood if it means getting out of this forest sooner rather than later.

"Should we just camp here tonight?" Ms. Brighton asks.

"Camping by the stream is risky. We could run into a bear. Plus, we might not be able to cross tomorrow."

Ms. Brighton takes a breath like she wants to argue but goes quiet again.

"It's a bad idea," Madison says. "I don't want to cross."

"Let's stay upbeat," Ms. Brighton says. "We could talk about what purpose this might serve."

Please let's not.

Gauging from the grumbles of my fellow campers, I'm not the only one thinking it as we scrabble down the hill, mud caking thicker on my boots with every step.

"Maybe we're going to be fish in our next life."

Ms. Brighton laughs, looking pink cheeked and pretty despite the rain. "Never say never."

Madison sighs. "This whole thing is proof that I shouldn't have signed up so late."

"The homeless shelter mission had openings too," Ms. Brighton says.

"Well, this mission had certain *motivating* factors." Madison's eyes trail to Lucas. Again.

Hayley sighs. "Also, our parents didn't want us in the bad part of town."

Lucas snorts. "You do realize poor isn't contagious."

"Isn't it?" Jude asks him. They've been at it since the parking lot. It's annoying as crap.

"Everyone, quiet. We need to move." Mr. Walker's voice is tight. Something's wrong. But he's halfway across, and the water is still below his knees. It's moving quickly, but it seems OK. So why is Mr. Walker scanning the horizon like a soldier?

When he's on the other side, he relaxes. "All right, let's move. You'll get to test those waterproof boots here. Emily, you first. Then Jude and right down the line."

I stumble to the edge of the stream, rocks slipping and scattering under my boots. Jude's next to me, earbuds in and his chin tipped up like we need a reminder that he's better than us.

Emily begins to cross with Jude behind her. Then me and Lucas and the rest of the group after. I can't help but think about what we must look like, this conga line of plastic-wrapped hikers splashing its way through the river.

Jude gasps ahead of me. Before I can ask, cold water gushes over the tops of my boots, then past my ankles. I stop when it reaches my knees. It's higher. We're not even halfway across.

Lucas splashes up from behind, rising over me. "Need me to carry you?"

I don't dignify the question with a response. Behind me, Hayley and Madison shriek. I turn to see a glimpse of all three of them, Hayley on her butt in the water and Madison and Ms. Brighton rushing back for her. The girls are laughing hysterically.

"We're almost halfway," Lucas says, ignoring them. "Keep going."

"Should we help?"

"They're fine. Move."

"Stop playing around back there! Get them up, Ms. Brighton," Mr. Walker barks, then more softly to the ones climbing out, "Good job, Emily. Jude! Earbuds out!"

Mr. Walker looks downstream, and his expression hardens. "Sera, speed up now."

I look up and wish I hadn't. I don't like the urgency in his tone any more than I like the rushing sound of water I hear off to the east.

"Is that rain?" I ask because I want it to be rain. Or hail. I want it to be anything other than what I already know it is.

Mr. Walker's eyes flick upstream, his face going pale. "It's flooding," he admits.

My hope snaps like a rubber band. Fear billows out in its place, making me woozy.

"Sera, move!" Lucas says, prodding my backpack.

"I got it!" I snap, plowing ahead.

Hayley screams again behind us. They're all three shouting. Something about a shoe. Someone's stuck. Mr. Walker is yelling at Emily and Jude to *back up, back up*! And then the rain changes, the shower shifting into a driving roar with drops so hard they feel like sand spraying down. Everything is garbled. Muffled. Fear pushes the hair up on the nape of my neck.

We're not going to get across.

"Go, Sera!"

Lucas. His voice right behind me, his wide hand just under my backpack, urging me forward. I stumble, spreading my arms wide for balance.

"Lucas, help!" Madison's cry filters through the rain, but Mr. Walker shakes his head.

"No!" he bellows. "Move, Lucas! Ms. Brighton, pull Hayley and Madison back to shore!"

The water is moving quicker and higher, and my boots are sucking down into the mud at the bottom. The current pushes back at me. Steps turn into half steps. Quarter steps.

"Forget her shoes!" Mr. Walker screams. Someone's coughing back there, but I don't look, though I can hear their garbled cries. They're struggling.

"I can't get her!" Ms. Brighton's voice is suddenly young and small, nothing like the serene woman from before. This is scared little kid voice. "Help! Hel—"

Someone else screams. Hayley maybe. I turn over my shoulder to see Ms. Brighton haul Hayley up and stumble back. Water's pushing at their thighs, but they're all three up. They're OK.

Mr. Walker is screaming at them. "Get back! Faster, faster, *move*!"

I shriek as the frigid water laps up my thighs. Then—*Snap!*

Pop!—off to my right. Dread spikes through me. Something's coming downstream. I have to go. Right now.

"Come on, Sera," Mr. Walker says, sounding breathless.

I rush, feet lurching. Almost there. So close now. I stumble. Lucas grabs my pack and hauls me up, and then I'm snarling at him—"Don't touch me!"—while Mr. Walker snags one of my straps and half drags me out. Water pours down my pant legs. I'm soaked and freezing.

I take a soggy step, and my boot slips on the muddy bank. Lucas is out too, swearing and scrambling up while Mr. Walker stares across at the girls, hands in his hair, eyes wide with terror.

My knees are buckling, but I grab branches and exposed roots and, finally, Jude's smooth, dark hand. Once I'm up, I follow him past brambles that snag my poncho. My hair.

"Over here." Jude points to a vantage point near the path. No earbuds now. He's wide-eyed and utterly focused on the stream fifteen feet below us. Emily and Lucas are beside him, both shaking.

There's a tree wedged across the stream. That must have been what I heard. The water is rushing under and over it, pushing it harder and harder. And then it's loose. I hold my breath as it rolls with the mud-brown river, snapping anything in its path.

"The others," Emily says softly.

They're lined up on the other side, mud-spattered and white with fear as the log hurtles past, ripping its way through the streambed and releasing a wall of sludgy brown water in its wake. The current surges up the banks behind it, littered with smaller branches and clumps of vegetation. Madison's eyes track us across the water, finding Lucas and then me.

"They're stuck over there." I know it's obvious, but I say it anyway.

Mr. Walker barks instructions at the edge of the stream. Ms. Brighton nods along, one arm wrapped around each girl, her dark braid coiled around her pale neck like a snake.

"What's he going to do?" Jude asks.

"Nothing, rich boy," Lucas says. "There's not a damn thing he can do tonight. Can't even call for help because there's no signal anywhere with this rain."

"What will happen to them?" I ask.

"If they listen to Mr. Walker, they'll go set up camp on that ridge. We'll stay here for the night, probably farther up the path. Us here, them there. Regroup in the morning if we can."

I whirl on Lucas. "What do you mean *if*?"

"You expect us to believe he's just going to leave them?" Jude asks.

"That flood isn't going anywhere soon. And I don't give a

shit what you believe," Lucas says to him. "Since someone has to set up our tent again, I need to find a clearing."

Lucas storms away, and my eyes drag back to the stream. Three girls with arms wrapped around each other's shoulders. The river gushes along, a monstrous evolution of what I just crossed, swallowing the bridge inch by inch.

It wasn't supposed to be like this. Not like this at all.